Chasing the Moon

Books by Melanie Hooyenga

The Campfire Series
CHASING THE SUN
CHASING THE STARS

The Rules Series
THE SLOPE RULES
THE TRAIL RULES
THE EDGE RULES

The Flicker Effect Trilogy
FLICKER
FRACTURE
FADED

Anthologies
LOVE ON MAIN
THE ART OF TAKING CHANCES

Chasing the Moon

MELANIE HOOYENGA

Left-Handed Mitten
Publications

CHASING THE MOON

Published by Left-Handed Mitten Publications
ISBN-13 978-1-0880-6821-2

UPC

Book design, cover design, and ebook formatting by Left-Handed Mitten Publications.

Author website: melaniehoo.com
Email: melaniehooyenga@gmail.com
Facebook: facebook.com/MelanieHooyenga
Twitter: @melaniehoo
Instagram: @melaniehoo
Newsletter: www.melaniehoo.com/hoos-letter/

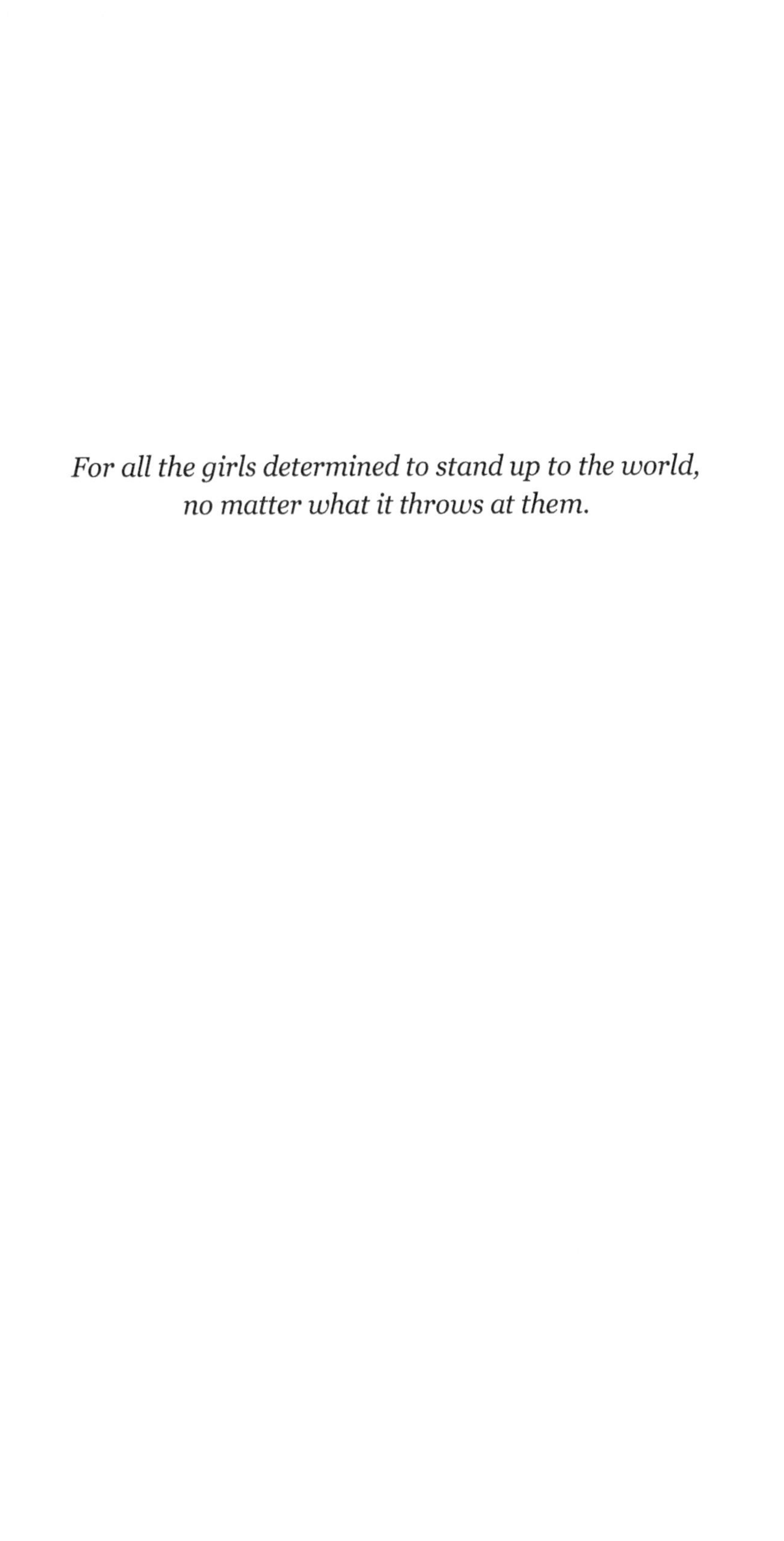

*For all the girls determined to stand up to the world,
no matter what it throws at them.*

AUTHOR'S NOTE

Writers often take liberties with the truth to serve their stories, and I am no different. The Grand Canyon has strict rules forbidding fires, but I included them in this story because you can't have a Campfire Series without a fire. If you visit the Grand Canyon, please leave the matches at home.

"I'm slipping!" Stephanie shouts. Her purple bangs swing in her eyes as she clenches her jaw in concentration.

"Grab tighter!" Jessica's dark ponytail bounces, her shoulders tense as she adjusts her grip on Steph's wrists. They're gripping each other's hands in the center of my room, spinning as fast as they can.

Laughter bubbles in my chest but I hold it back, not wanting them to stop. I walk in a slow circle around them as they spin in the opposite direction, my phone focused on their clasped hands, then zooming out to include their upper bodies.

"How does this relate to science?" Steph pants out her words, her eyes darting to me.

A ripple of longing tumbles through me but I brush it off. "You're demonstrating centrifugal force." I take another step back and my legs bump into my bed. I keep the center of my room clear because this is where I film the majority of the videos for MeltyPoint, my science-themed TikTok account, so they shouldn't trip over anything as they spin and spin and spin. It's my job as the videographer to capture it without falling over.

Jess rolls her eyes but the two of them are moving so fast it's just a flash of white.

"I really can't hold on much longer," Steph says.

"I think I have enough."

"You sure?" Jess asks. Her determined look matches Steph's. She won't stop until she's sure we've gotten the shot, even if it makes her throw up.

"Cut!" I shout, and they collapse in a heap on my rainbow striped rug. The earlier flash of longing shifts to something that feels safer:

Gratitude.

They breathe heavily. Neither speaks. Steph's curly purple hair fans around her head like a cloud and a smile spreads over her face. "That was fun."

Jess holds her stomach. "I'm regretting that last cookie."

Steph pushes to her elbows and nods at their bodies sprawled on the floor. "Did you get it?"

My two best friends put up with a lot to help me run MeltyPoint and they don't get nearly enough credit.

I drop to the rug next to them, hold my phone so they can see, and hit play. It starts with the video zoomed on their hands, Jess's pale skin contrasting against Steph's darker complexion, then pans out to their arms, then shoulders, then finally their entire upper bodies. A fast-paced tune plays in my head and I can already visualize how it'll mix with the clip. Filming is fun, but the real magic happens in editing.

Steph nudges Jess's shoulder. "You don't look like you're gonna hurl."

Jess reaches for her water bottle on my bed. "It hit me around the minute mark."

A swell of pride makes me smile. When I started MeltyPoint, Jess was excited until she realized how often she would end up as my test subject. To say she was unwilling is a stretch, but she couldn't fully envision what I saw for the account.

What I wanted to accomplish.

Three years later, I'm closing in on a million followers—who call themselves Melties—and I have two loyal assistants to help with the experiments. Together we've learned about recording and producing videos, how to compress complex scientific theories into less than three minutes, and most importantly, what types of videos might go viral.

Like when I demonstrated the theory of relative motion by walking toward the camera while lifting and lowering a ten-week old kitten.

Steph catches my eye. "I don't know how you do it, Mel, but this looks really good."

I flutter my eyes and rest my chin on my flattened hand. "How can you doubt me after all this time?" That warm gooey feeling I get whenever she looks at me comes flooding back, and my cheeks are probably as pink as theirs. I'd roll my eyes at myself but don't want her to misinterpret where my thoughts are. Because we're friends. Nothing more. Steph transferred here at the beginning of junior year and after almost two years, I've accepted that she doesn't see me that way.

Jess rolls onto her side, her dark ponytail falling over her face, and cradles her stomach.

"You okay?" I ask.

"I will be."

Steph leans forward and lightly pats Jess's belly. "You stay in there, cookies."

Jess laughs, then moans. "Mel, it looks great, but will it work for the circle challenge?"

Trends fly through TikTok faster than I can make videos. I don't jump on every one, but the current trend in SciTok, aka Science TikTok, is to incorporate circles. Sounds vague, but one-upping each other with our interpretation is what makes this fun.

"It has to. I need to post it before I go to bed."

Steph taps her phone and the screen lights up. "That's in like five hours."

My shoulders straighten. "I've made some of my most popular videos in less time than that."

"Yes," Jess says, "but you weren't also packing for a camping trip." She tilts her head at my fancy hiking backpack hanging on my desk chair. My very empty backpack that hasn't moved since Bryan, my new stepdad, presented it to me three weeks ago.

"Are you both packed?" I ask.

Steph nods. "Mamá wouldn't let me come over until she saw my bag with her own eyes. Then she threatened not to let me go 'cause she's afraid I'm gonna fall off a cliff or something."

Jess laughs. "I got that lecture, too."

They look at me expectantly. That fear has crossed my mind more than a few times, but Mom keeps saying I'm overthinking things. I flop back onto the rug and talk at the ceiling. "I swear I can pack and edit and post the video tonight." I lift my head and smile. "But if either of you wanted to throw some clothes in my backpack, I'm sure Bryan will make more cookies."

"No more cookies!" Jess cradles her belly and groans.

Mom got remarried the week before Christmas and Bryan moved in the next day. They're perfect together and I love that she's found her match after being single most of my life, but the cookies harden in my stomach thinking about the phone call I overheard last week. Bryan was in the backyard where he probably thought we couldn't hear, but my bedroom window was open and the words "move money around" and "this needs to happen ASAP" drifted up to me. At one point he glanced over his shoulder at my room like he knew I was listening, and now I can't help but worry that whatever he's hiding is going to ruin our family.

They delayed their honeymoon for three months so we could take a trip as a family over spring break, which is why we're loading into the car first thing in the morning and driving five hundred miles from Bakersfield, California, to the Grand Canyon.

There's a lunar eclipse in four days and it's on Bryan's bucket list to see eclipses from the most random places on earth. So in this case, from a giant hole in the earth.

My older brother Hunter is meeting us at the hotel tomorrow evening, which is why we have room for both Steph and Jess.

That, and Mom understands that I cannot and will not choose between my two best friends. The option of only bringing one of them is unacceptable.

The excitement for the trip and concern over whatever Bryan's hiding battle inside me. I haven't said anything to Steph or Jess, but I know I can't go the whole trip without confronting him.

Steph untangles herself from Jess and pushes to her feet. "I'd love to stay and help, really," her brows quirk and she fights a smirk. "But Mamá says she needs her Stephita time before she lets me leave for almost a week."

"Go spend time with your mom," I say. The corners of my lips tug downward, but I hide my reaction behind a yawn.

"Hey!" Steph pokes the tip of my nose. "No yawning! We leave in like twelve hours and you can sleep then."

Jess frowns at me. "Do I need to stay and help?"

"No, no." I shake my head. "You know I do my best magic when I'm zoned in on my laptop. I'll finish the video and be packed by the time you both get here in the morning."

"Your mom isn't gonna go for that," Jess says.

I bite the corner of my lip. "Then can you help me pack before you leave?"

The two of them open my drawers and throw underwear, socks, and a pile of T-shirts onto my bed. Steph grabs the backpack and peers inside its depths. "You haven't even cut off the tags." I bat my eyes at her and she rolls hers before grabbing the scissors from the mason jar on my desk. Two battery chargers sit on my laptop and she pushes them aside to hand me my computer. "If we're doing this, you need to start working."

I give her a cheesy smile and open the laptop. The video-editing app I use for my posts is always open, but that's not the screen that greets me. Instead, it's the homepage for the University of Oregon, featuring smiling undergrads walking across a tree-lined quad. They're laughing like they know something you only learn upon stepping onto campus, and every part of me wants to be there. I click to the next browser window and am greeted by a similar photo of similar kids on a slightly different quad with California State University Long Beach at the top, but the yearning to be a part of it doesn't rise within me. I toggle back and forth, my scowl deepening with each click.

"You still haven't decided?" Steph asks. I jump at her voice, and her hands rest on my shoulder. "I didn't mean to scare you."

My head rests against her arm for the briefest moment. She's the most affectionate friend I've ever had and while I've always been a hugger, she's taught me to show that I care through casual touches.

Touches that my brain insists have a deeper meaning.

Jess pulls my hiking boots—also new, but at least I've worn them a couple times—out of the closet and tosses them toward my bed. "It would be fun if you both went to Oregon." A dark look passes over her face so quickly I almost miss it, and a surge of protectiveness rushes through me. I hate when she's upset.

"It wouldn't be the same without you," I say.

"Yeah, but I didn't get into Oregon."

"You didn't apply," Steph says.

Jess sits gently on the edge of the bed, like she's afraid to disrupt things any more than she already has. We've been friends since middle school and I know what every look and reaction means. Or at least I thought I did. But ever since I was accepted to the University of Oregon and CSU Long Beach, it's like she's shut down.

And when I got a scholarship to Long Beach and she barely reacted, it hurt.

There was a brief time when I pushed her away to be friends with someone in the popular clique, and I can't shake the feeling that she thinks that's happening again.

I pick myself up and sit next to her on the bed. "You'll figure it out. It's completely normal to not know what you want to do with the rest of your life while we're still in high school." I put extra emphasis on high school, but it doesn't have the desired effect.

"You both know what you want to be," she says.

"I have a vague idea," Steph says. "Oregon has a great architecture program, but there are lots of other things that interest me and I could totally change my mind once I take a few classes."

While I haven't known Steph as long as Jess, I do know her, and I know for a fact that she wants to be an architect with an office high enough up in a building that she can look out over whichever big city she lands in. This is her dream and the University of Oregon is the first step toward getting there.

Jess shifts her focus back to me. "If I got a scholarship to a school, my parents wouldn't give me a choice. I'd have to go there."

"Mom's been quiet about it so far, but I feel like this is my first adult test and every instinct tells me to go for the less obvious choice." When I found out I got a scholarship to Long Beach, my path seemed clear. But then a thick acceptance envelope arrived from Oregon and everything's confusing again.

"You always make the right choice," Steph says.

Speaking of confusing.

My toe nudges at a stripe on my rug, and my stomach twists. The question plaguing my mind wouldn't be a big deal if we were just best friends, full stop. I take a breath and spit it out. "Is Brooklyn coming over tonight?"

Steph pauses, the scissors she'd been twirling around her finger stopping mid-air. She glances between Jess and me before moving to the desk and leaning against it. "I was gonna save this for the drive, but, um…" Her gaze drops to where my foot digs at the rug. "I have news."

"I'm breaking up with Brooklyn when I get home tonight," I say.

"What?" Jess's eyes go wide and her mouth falls open.

And Mel—I can't read the look on her face. Her hazel eyes avoid mine and she twists her dark hair over one shoulder.

"Why?" Jess asks.

I drop the scissors back in the jar and look at them both. "I'm not into her." There's a lot more to it than that, but you're kind of supposed to be attracted to the person you're dating.

"I guess that is an important detail," Jess says. "How do you think she's gonna take it?"

Mel keeps pushing her toe back and forth over the rug and I wish I could tell what she's thinking. She doesn't usually hold back her opinions, it's one of the things that makes us such good friends, but right now it's like she's trying to hide her reaction.

My breath feels heavy in my chest. "I'm not sure. It's not like we declared our love to each other, but no one likes getting dumped."

Jess grimaces. "Especially right before spring break."

"I thought this would be better. Plus we won't have cell signal and I don't want to spend the whole trip worrying if the girl I don't like is mad because she hasn't heard from me."

Mel purses her lips. "I keep hoping we'll somehow have signal."

Jess waves her hand in the air. "Hello? We're hiking into the bottom of the earth. I doubt there's cell towers down there."

Mel peeks from the side of her eyes. "Not even a booster?"

I laugh, but can't help noticing that she changed the subject from Brooklyn. "Mel, you're the relationship expert here. You've gotta have a deep thought about this."

Mel turns to the pile of clothes on her bed, her back to me. "I wouldn't call myself an expert, but I think you're doing the right thing. If you don't like her, there's no sense dragging it out." She turns to face me, her favorite purple hoodie clutched to her chest. "I think it's kind that you're telling her in person."

Heat rushes to my cheeks. "Oh, I—I didn't invite her over."

Jess's hands fall to her hips. "You can't break up over text."

"Mamá won't let me have anyone over tonight and I don't want to put this off."

Mel shakes her phone. "Video call?"

"That could work." I sigh. "I guess I should go home and get this over with."

Jess moves toward me, her arms outstretched. "Huffle."

Mel joins us, and we come together in a huffle, arms wrapped around each other, heads pressed together so tightly it's impossible to tell where I end and they begin. Huffle came from huddle and stands for Hug Ur Friends. It may or may not have been inspired by the house in a certain boy wizard's book series, but we stopped acknowledging the origins when the author revealed herself as a TERF. We inhale and exhale as one, and the tension that knotted my shoulders moments ago starts to relax.

"I'll text afterwards," I say. I imagine my words flowing through the strands of our hair, over our skin, and being inhaled on our next breath. I loosen my grip. Mel's head pops up first and our eyes connect in a way they haven't all evening. The openness in her expression and the intensity in her eyes, like she's trying to read my thoughts, catches me by surprise. I'm sure I'm imagining this, but I feel like she's trying to tell me something.

I just don't know what it is.

Jess gives us a final squeeze, and I head for the door.

"Let us know when the video's live," I say to Mel.

She smirks. "Don't I always?"

When I reach the front door, I wave goodbye to Mel's mom and stepdad, and Margo calls after me. "We'll see you bright and early!"

"Can't wait!" To anyone else my cheer might sound forced, but I really am excited for this trip. Ms. Thompson—correction, now she's Mrs. Carlson—has always treated me like part of the family and there's a warmth in their house that's been missing at home since before we moved here. My parents care for me, there's no question about that, but at some point they stopped caring for each other and it's made my life miserable.

Every light downstairs blazes when I pull into the driveway, but the upstairs is dark. If I can slip past them and get to my room, maybe I can avoid any drama.

At least until I call Brooklyn.

The door closes with a squeak and I cringe. Seconds later Mamá crosses the hallway.

"Hola, 'ama," I say.

"Stephita, oh good, you're home." She sounds happy to see me, but her usual smile is missing and her hair's come loose from its low bun. I get my curly hair from Papá, even though his is so short you'd never know it's curly. Mamá has long straight hair like Mel and Jess. "Papá and I need to talk to you."

I nod at the stairs. "Can I finish packing first?"

She plants her hands on her hips. "You said you packed before you left. I saw your bag." Her eyes narrow like she caught me lying, something not tolerated in the Ramirez household.

I move toward her until we're nose to nose, then I slide my arms through hers and snuggle my face to her neck. "Mamá, I already packed, but I have some things I gotta do and I just wanna get it over with."

"Have to," she corrects, her breath tickling my cheek. She owns a boutique downtown and is a stickler for proper grammar and enunciation. Even though she and Papá were born in LA, she's dealt with enough racial discrimination for a lifetime and swears she doesn't want that to happen to me because I sound uneducated.

"Have to," I repeat.

"What do you have to do?" My back stiffens, and she pulls away enough to look in my eyes. "Stephita, what's the matter?"

Since lying is forbidden, secrets are also on her not-approved list. "I'm breaking up with Brooklyn."

She shakes her head and sucks air through her pursed lips. "I never liked that girl."

I laugh through my nose. "Mamá, she didn't do anything. I just don't like her anymore."

Her hands press against my cheeks so she's holding my head still, her gaze locked on mine. "I just want you to be happy. You know that."

When I came out to my parents freshman year, I thought the world was gonna end. It took some time, and a lot of questions I really didn't want to answer, but their love for me never changed.

Unlike their love for each other. These quiet moments almost never happen anymore, and I try to soak in every second when they do. There's only a couple months left before graduation, and after the summer I'll be off at college, far away from their bitter comments and screamed accusations.

Mamá pats my cheek, then ushers me toward the stairs. "You be gentle with that girl. We'll talk over dinner."

As I approach my room and settle on my bed, I wish I could say I feel guilty or nervous, but like Mel, I've never been afraid of difficult conversations. People at my old school decided that made me a bitch, but I'd rather be known for being honest than talking about people behind their backs while pretending to be besties to their face.

That's not me.

I text Brooklyn, knowing she'll be waiting to hear from me. She did ask to come over tonight—Mel was right to ask—but I told her I had too much to do before the trip. Like helping with Mel's latest video. It's not lost on me that I'd rather hang out with my friends than my girlfriend, and that confirms that I need to end things.

She replies immediately.

I can talk now.

I hit the video call button and seconds later, her full lips and bright brown eyes fill the screen. Her smile softens and the guilt finally hits me. She hasn't done anything wrong. My feelings changed. And if I'm honest, I never cared for her the way she deserves.

"Hey," I say.

"Are you all packed?"

I nod and take a deep breath. "I need to say something and it's not gonna be what you wanna hear."

Her smile falls and those beautiful eyes shine with tears. "Don't do this, Steph."

My eyes close for a moment, but I force myself to look at her. I owe her that much. "I think you're a great person. I always have. But my feelings have changed and I think we should break up." Nice and easy, rip the Band-Aid off.

She blinks several times and her jaw hardens. "It didn't feel like your feelings changed when you were here last weekend."

We never slept together, but we did plenty of other things, and last weekend I may have overlooked my shifting feelings to... uhh... enjoy the perks of having a girlfriend.

"I'm sorry. I didn't want to hurt you." My voice sounds flat. Like there's no emotion left for her.

Her voice turns cold. "It sounds like you're reading from a how-to-break-up-with-your-girlfriend-for-no-reason manual."

This time I do break eye contact. "I don't expect you to be happy about this, but it's what I want."

"What about what I want?" The fire that first attracted me to her burns through the phone, but now it only exhausts me.

"I'm sorry," I say again.

"Is there someone else?"

My mind jumps to Mel and Jess. To the feeling of being accepted no matter what dumb-ass thing comes out of my mouth. "No."

Her eyes narrow. "Took you a minute to come up with that."

I sigh. "Are we really gonna drag this out?" In my mind I hear Mamá telling her to have a little respect for herself, and I have to fight a smile. Brooklyn might literally erupt if she thinks I'm laughing at her, or worse, enjoying this.

"No, I guess we're done." The screen goes black.

Relief floods through me. I flop onto my back and take a deep breath. And another. After a few minutes, I roll off the bed and brace myself for the conversation with my parents. Whatever it is, it won't change that starting tomorrow I can leave this drama behind me to spend five days with my two best friends.

Mamá and Papá are in the kitchen, silently moving around each other as she finishes dinner and he sets the table. The quiet makes the hair stand up on the back of my neck. I can't remember the last time they were in the same room without one of them nagging the other.

"What's going on?"

They both look up, matching expressions on their faces. Extra creases around their eyes, clenched jaws, and mouths that open and close but don't let out any sound. Papá drags his chair from the table with a squeak of wood on wood, and sits like he's carrying the weight of the world on his shoulders. He's the CFO—Counting Figures Officer, as I like to tease him—of a company based in LA, so he's used to carrying other peoples' weight, but this feels different.

Mamá sets a baking dish of my favorite dinner, chicken thighs in molé, next to a pan of rice, before settling into her chair with a little less dramatic flair. Papá's usually grabbing the serving spoon before she has time to lean back, but tonight he remains still, his hands gripping the edge of the table in front of him.

The scent of baked chicken and spicy chocolate sauce makes my mouth water, but no one moves. The longer they stare at the food, the faster my pulse pounds. This isn't a we-need-to-talk-to-you conversation.

This is bad.

"How did it go with Brooklyn?" Mamá asks.

Papá's head snaps to me. "What happened?"

Despite the no secrets rule, Mamá didn't share my news. This must be really bad.

"We broke up. She got pissy, but that's pretty much what I expected from her."

Mamá reaches for my hand and I can't help but notice Papá still hasn't served himself dinner. "Now you can enjoy your vacation without worrying about her."

I could let them dance around this for the next half hour while dinner gets cold, or I can force the issue. I choose the path to hotter food. "Why do I get the feeling you're about to give me something else to worry about?"

They look at each other, then face me like they're walking into a funeral. Papá clears his throat. "M'ija, this shouldn't be a surprise to you, but your Mamá and I have decided to get a divorce."

A ringing in my ears drowns out the rest of his words. The edges of my vision go dark and the cookies from earlier churn in my stomach.

I'm gonna throw up.

They can't get divorced.

We're a family.

"Are you going to say anything?" Mamá asks. She reaches for my hand again.

Holds it.

Steam rises from the móle and my stomach twists. "I'm not sure what I'm supposed to say. Congratulation? My condolences?" I pull my hand away from hers and dig my nails into the seam of my jeans. "I know you've been fighting but...."

I didn't realize it was this bad.

Papá runs a hand across his face and over his short hair. "We tried to wait until you left for college, but we can't anymore."

My empty plate taunts me. There's no way I can eat now. Their news not only exploded my entire life, it ruined my favorite meal.

I push away from the table, the chair squeaking against the wood floor, and slowly stand. "I—I can't be here."

"You need to eat," Papá says.

"We have more to talk about," Mamá says.

I shake my head, tears blurring my vision. "Save me a plate."

And I run upstairs before they can tell me anything else that will shatter everything I thought I knew.

3

MELODY

"Are you sure you're okay in the middle?" I ask Jess.

Steph leans forward so she can see me. "Should we rotate at each stop? Then no one gets screwed being in the middle?"

Jess nods while bringing her paper coffee cup to her nose and inhaling deeply. "That sounds like an excellent plan."

A backpack-style cooler sits between her feet, so she's got one foot next to mine and the other next to Steph, who's sitting behind Mom. The back of Bryan's SUV—technically it's the family's SUV now, but I'm still getting used to that—isn't as crowded as I expected, but that's because Bryan insisted we only bring what we're able to carry. Plus a small bag for the first and last day at the hotel. Our five packs sit in a neat row behind the backseat, along with a few odds and ends Mom and I insisted we bring.

"How are you feeling?" Jess asks Steph.

Steph texted last night to tell us she ended things with Brooklyn and that it quote, did not go well, but she didn't elaborate.

She seems quieter than normal, even for how early we left, but she just shrugs. "Tired. But relieved. If I'm honest with myself, and I haven't been for too long, it's been a while since I liked her the way a girlfriend should. She's a good person and deserves someone who actually wants to be with her."

Mom turns her head toward us. "That's a very mature response."

"Mom," I say, giving her a pointed look. Just because she's a therapist doesn't mean I want her analyzing my friends, and she knows that.

She holds up her hands. "Sorry, sorry. I didn't mean to intrude."

"Are you sure nothing else is bothering you?" I whisper low enough that Mom can't hear.

Steph bites the corner of her lip. "I'm just tired." She smiles but it seems forced. "Not used to waking up this early."

Jess pats Steph's knee. "You let us know if you need to talk."

Steph smiles. "I don't think I could avoid it if I wanted to."

The car falls silent and I wedge my latte between my thighs and pull up my video. True to my word, I finished packing, then edited and posted my video by midnight. I've learned to wait a few hours before checking how many views a new video has because the algorithms sometimes have a mind of their own. It can take anywhere from a few minutes to a few hours for a post to really gain traction, and staring at my phone waiting for those silly hearts will only make me crazy.

I scroll through my feed, double-tapping videos as I go, prolonging the inevitable. My brother has the patience of a monk and I never used to understand how he could put off the dopamine rush that comes with instant gratification. He actually swore off dating to focus on college—although truth be told, that didn't last very long—and I've slowly come to appreciate his mindset. Since MeltyPoint took off, I've learned to temper my expectations and put off checking my stats for as long as possible.

Jess leans against my shoulder and looks at my phone. "Have you looked yet?"

"Not yet." They both know my method, and while I suspect they secretly check my account long before I do, they always pretend to be surprised when I see for myself.

Proving my point, Steph raises her brows at me and gives me a way-too-eager smile.

I quirk a brow back at her. "You've already looked?"

"How could I not? The video turned out really cool!"

Jess nudges me. "You've stalled long enough."

Mom twists in her seat and gives me a smile.

"Not you, too."

"I will never understand where you get this ungodly patience from," Mom says. "Anytime I'm waiting on something I hit refresh so many times I'm at risk of breaking the keyboard."

Bryan chuckles. Yes, he's a chuckler. "Is that why we had such a short engagement?"

Mom rests her hand on his arm. "I didn't need anything fancy. Once I found you, I knew."

I groan while Jess and Steph say, "Awwwww."

Jess giggles. "It's sweet that you still moon over each other."

Bryan rests his hand on Mom's. "I wanted to take her on a date to the moon but I heard the atmosphere's terrible."

The others laugh, and I join them. Bryan has been good for Mom. The laser-like intensity that dominated most of my childhood has been replaced by a calmer, almost relaxed demeanor. It's a little freaky, and I'm not sure if she's just lost in newlywed bliss or if she deleted that part of her personality when she purged the house before Bryan moved in.

But the conversation I overheard changes things. I'm afraid whatever he's hiding will explode their happiness and hurt Mom worse than when Dad left.

"Mel," Steph says, and I snap my attention to her. "You're killing us here." She holds my gaze and something in my belly stirs.

"But you've already looked."

"It's still fun to watch your reaction."

"You try to play it cool," Jess says, "but we know inside you're dying to look."

I bite the corner of my lip. "Maybe a little."

Bryan taps the brakes and we all jerk forward, the seatbelts holding us in place. "Do I need to pull over and press play for you?"

Mom swats at his arm and gives him a dopey expression that makes me both happy for her and grateful that we have separate hotel rooms tonight.

I shudder at the direction my brain goes, and focus on my phone. "Okay, here goes."

I click to my profile picture and a smile plays on my lips. Jess designed the logo, a pink, purple, and blue double helix twisting around the words MeltyPoint—Melty being a play off my name, Melody Thompson—and every time I see it, I'm filled with a sense of pride that I hope never fades.

After a few quick breaths, I allow my gaze to drop to the most recent post. A tiny number that's the opposite of tiny stares at me from the lower left corner of the thumbnail. "Holy shit."

"Language," Mom says automatically.

"Holy Schmidt."

Because the views are double what they normally are eight hours after posting.

Steph bounces in her seat and pumps her fists in the air. "Ohmigod I've been dying! This was such a good idea and people love it!"

Jess bounces next to her, and soon the entire car is shouting and laughing and jumping as much as the seatbelts will allow. Steph reaches across Jess to grab my hand and I mentally count how many minutes it will be until our first stop, when we'll rotate positions and Steph will be next to me.

"You should do a response video," Steph says.

"Right now?" I ask.

"Yes!" Steph and Jess shout.

Mom and Bryan laugh in the front seats. If I can capture the joy we're feeling at this moment, that'll make what could be a boring post more exciting. I scroll through the comments, screen shot a few mean ones and one super gushy one, then text them to Steph. She hands me her phone with the screen shots displayed and I cue up the app.

I smile and hit the button to do a live post. "Hey Melties! I'm on the road and I got more hate mail 'cause I'm a girl, so what better time to do a response video? I've got my Bestie Brigade here," I angle the camera to include Jess and Steph, who wave, "and we've got some real winners for you today." I hold Steph's phone next to mine so I can read her screen, make a show of clearing my throat, then raise an eyebrow.

"You should spend more time on your makeup, then your videos would be better." I purse my lips like I'm considering that suggestion. "How 'bout no?"

I swipe to the next screen shot. "Girls only pretend to like science to get guys." I burst out laughing, and Steph tugs my arm so she can get in the frame.

"Yes, that's absolutely true," she says, holding back a laugh. Steph's never said she's gay on my account, but she's dropped enough hints that the true Melties know.

I look away from the camera to smile at her, then focus on the camera. "I guess he's never heard of Marie Curie, Jane Goodall, or Tiera Guinn."

I swipe again and roll my eyes. "Go back to your Barbies." My head shakes. "I—I don't have a comeback for that. He's right. If I spent more time with my Barbies, I could better understand female anatomy and hopefully improve the quality of women's healthcare, since so much of our current data is based on men. So thanks JiggleJohn27."

Bryan snorts from the front seat, which sets off everyone else.

"As you know, I always end on a positive note." I swipe to the last pic from a girl who's commented a lot but I've never featured. "Sammykins says thank you so much for making science easier to understand. Because of you I brought my grade from a D to a B!" I press my hand to my chest and close my eyes for a second. "And that is why I do this. Thanks everyone! I won't have signal for three days, so see you when I get back!" I blow a kiss at the camera and hit stop. "Was the kiss too much?"

Steph shakes her head. "It was perfect."

I tap a few buttons so the live video will stay on my page.

"Now you can enjoy this trip without stressing about a lack of signal," Jess says.

Yes, I hate that I won't be able to check my account, but really I wish I could spend more time comparing Oregon and Long Beach. Even though I already know where I want to go.

Mom laughs. "I don't believe that for a minute."

"This does help," I say. It'll be tough not checking my account for four whole days. The Melties always let me know if a hater leaves a snippy comment, or they put the person in their place without ever telling me. It's a level I never expected to achieve in high school, but it's proof that the research and effort I put into my posts is building credibility for my future.

We stop for a bathroom break at the edge of the Mojave Desert. The dusty air still has a cool edge from overnight, but hints of the heat to come swirl around us.

"We're pulling out in ten minutes," Bryan says.

"That's generous," Jess whispers. "My dad only gives us five."

I link my arm through hers and hurry us toward a truck stop that looks like it's been here since the main form of transportation had four legs and a tail. "He's still trying to prove he's the world's best stepdad."

Steph is oddly quiet, but she could be in shock from what greets us when we step inside. There's the usual car repair products like oil and windshield wipers, but the majority of the brightly lit space is covered with what can only be described as tourist-trap tchotchkes. Turquoise jewelry and dream catchers fill racks leading to the bathrooms, while T-shirts, hats, mugs, and pretty much anything else that can be printed on covers the walls. A bin with old DVDs sits at the end of an aisle filled with an assortment of glazed pottery.

"This will take way more than ten minutes," Jess says.

Mom appears behind us, a pair of silver earrings with turquoise stones in her hand. "This place is like something out of a dream."

Bryan wraps an arm around her waist and presses a kiss to her temple. "We're never getting out of here, are we?"

"Maybe give us twenty."

Steph leads us to the bathroom, then we lose ourselves in the rows of souvenirs.

"This is cool," Jess waves a green tank top over the aisle. We join her and she presses it against her chest. "Protect the Havasupai" splashes across the middle with a setting sun and the outline of the Grand Canyon below it.

"What do you think it means?" Steph asks.

"Let's find out." I grab Jess's hand and head to the cashier. A woman Mom's age with a long black braid and honey-brown skin like Steph's stands behind the counter. "Excuse me, can you tell us about this?"

She eyes the shirt and a smile crinkles the corners of her mouth. "The Havasupai are the last tribe to still live in the Grand Canyon." Her voice is slow and purposeful. "The money from these shirts support them."

"We'll take three," Steph says. We rush back to the rack to pick out two more—purple for me and blue for Steph. "I'd much rather own something honoring them than the touristy crap that's probably for sale at the rim of the canyon."

Jess and I nod.

Twenty minutes later we're back in the SUV, bags full of snacks at our feet and the shirts tucked in our overnight bags. We shifted to the right, which puts me in the middle and Steph on my left. She hasn't said much since we stopped, and normally I wouldn't hesitate to ask what's wrong, but it's hard to have a conversation with parents an arm's length away.

"When was the last time Hunter and Naomi saw each other?" Jess asks.

Mom's head angles toward us, clearly listening.

"I think a few years," I say. "Maybe only once since they broke up after Hunter's sophomore year."

Now Mom turns fully in her seat. "They've taken turns skipping our annual family trips to avoid seeing each other. Nancy and I have helped coordinate."

"Do you think this is gonna be weird for them?" Steph asks. She's never met Naomi in person, but since Naomi and I have stayed close, my friends have both been on video calls with her and consider Naomi a friend.

"Maybe a little, but they're both too stubborn to admit it." I clap my hands and give them a maniacal laugh, my eyes wide. "Are you ready to hear my plan?"

"Um, naturally," Steph says.

Jess rubs her hands together. "Please tell me we're getting them back together!" Jess met Naomi right after I did, back when I had fallen under the spell of a bully named Nelly and chose her over Jess. Naomi helped us repair our friendship and Jess has always admired her.

"I've named it Operation Amazing."

Jess and Mom burst out laughing, but Steph just raises a brow.

"They overused the word amazing to the point of destroying it forever, so that's the name of our secret operation to get them back together."

"Who or what is amazing in this plan?" Bryan asks.

I clasp my hands to my chest and bat my eyes at him in the review mirror. "They are. Individually and together. And them being together is amazing."

He does one of those smiles where his lips turn down like he's trying to hold back a bigger smile. "Got it."

"So what's the plan?" Jess asks.

My smile falls. "I didn't get past the name. And the fact that they need to get back together." I nudge Steph and Jess with my elbows. "That's where you two come in."

Steph strokes her chin. "It's not vacation without hijinks, and this sounds extra hijinky."

We spend the next hour plotting how to force Naomi and Hunter into situations where they'll realize they're meant to be together, all of them involving one of us faking a physical injury or pretending to be fighting when they're around. The plan isn't solid, but it's a start.

As the miles slip by, we sink lower in the seats and at some point my head ends up on Steph's shoulder. My leg and hip lean against Jess, so it's not like I'm all over Steph or anything, but I can't ignore the way my pulse accelerates when Steph adjusts and her cheek presses to my forehead. She seems to be asleep, so I can't tell if she wanted to feel my skin on hers or if she was just trying to get more comfortable.

She just broke up with Brooklyn, I remind myself. She's not thinking about me as anything other than her friend. I need to stop this way of thinking before I ruin the trip—and our friendship.

My mind flits to Brooklyn. I never told Steph, but I was friends with Brooklyn for a few months in seventh grade, and after an awkward dance in the school gym, she locked into my timeline as the first person I kissed. Now I'm glad Steph doesn't know. It's ancient history and doesn't have anything to do with our friendship.

I keep my head where it's at until the kink in my neck is so painful I can barely straighten. Steph notices me wince and her hand slides under my hair, searching for the tender spot. She squeezes the muscle, moving over my shoulder until I nod. "Yes, there."

Don't read into this.

Steph is a touchy-feely person and she's just helping her friend.

Her friend who's melting into a puddle right next to her.

"We should be at the hotel in less than twenty," Bryan announces.

"Everyone's scheduled to arrive over the next few hours," Mom says. "We'll wait to eat until Hunter gets there, but you might want a snack in the meantime."

At the hotel, the three of us wait in the lobby while Mom and Bryan check us in. The décor resembles a mix of southwest and Aztecan, with rich earth tones and geometric patterns in the carpet leading from a seating area through an open doorway into a restaurant.

I can still feel the warmth of Steph's fingers on my skin. My head rolls from side to side, loosening the tight muscles.

"Does it still hurt?" Steph asks.

I fight the urge to ask for more rubbing and instead shake my head. "Nah, I'll be okay."

A few minutes later, we're in a room on the third floor overlooking a small pool with the cover secured tightly over it.

"No pool?" Jess pouts.

"April is still a little early for pool weather," Steph says. "Especially in the desert."

"But I thought the desert was supposed to be hot?"

Steph tosses her bag on the bed closest to the bathroom and kicks off her shoes. "It's the land of extreme temperatures. Extra hot in the summer, extra cold in the winter. At least extra cold for Arizona."

I sit on the edge of the bed closest to the window. "Jess, please tell me you packed for cooler weather."

She waves her hand. "Yeah, yeah. Mom went through all my stuff and made me swap my shorts for pants. And she insisted I didn't need my bathing suit." She digs into her overnight bag and pulls out a bikini. "So you're saying I should have left this at home?"

We burst out laughing, and Steph and I pull out our bathing suits and wave them in the air.

"There's gotta be a hot tub somewhere!" Steph says.

Jess puts her bag next to Steph's and sits on the bed. They look at me expectantly, but I have no idea what they're thinking.

"What?"

"We figured since your parents—I mean, your mom and Bryan—since they drove and all that, you should get the bed to yourself."

"Oh. Yeah. That makes sense." I force a smile, hoping they don't see the disappointment coursing through me. Sharing a bed with Steph would be a bad idea. I mean, we've shared beds plenty of times when we've had sleepovers, but there's something exotic about a hotel. Maybe it's the new environment or the knowledge that Mom and Bryan can't barge in at any minute, but there's an undercurrent of excitement being in this room unsupervised.

"Should we put these on and see if we can find a hot tub?" I ask.

We change quickly, something we've done in front of each other a hundred times, but I catch myself sneaking glances at Steph as she pulls her shirt over her head, and again when she slips out of her jeans.

I need to get this under control or I'm going to completely ruin everything.

4

STEPHANIE

Bubbles tickle my chin as I sink deeper into the hot tub. "This was such a good idea." My hair is pulled up because purple hair and pool chemicals do not mix, but Mel's and Jess's ponytails dip in the water. We're the only people in the glass-enclosed room next to the outdoor pool, and the stiffness in my back from the car ride is finally loosening up. My arm started tingling about three miles after Mel fell asleep on my shoulder, but she looked so peaceful I didn't want to make her move. "How's your neck?" I ask.

She rubs the same spot I had in the car. "It's getting better." She smiles. "I guess this proves why no one wants to ride in the middle."

I return her smile, but the hot water melts my defenses and last night's conversation with my parents comes flooding back. They both notice my frown and sit up straight.

"Hey, it wasn't that bad," Mel says, moving closer in the water. She doesn't touch me, but her nearness calms me, and the emotions I've been trying to avoid rise to surface.

I bite my lip, blinking back tears.

"What's going on?" Jess moves to my other side and I'm grateful to have two friends who notice the smallest shifts in my mood and react to it. "Is this about Brooklyn?"

Okay, maybe they aren't completely dialed in to what I'm thinking. I shake my head. "I don't know the right way to say this." I take a shaky breath and look them each in the eye. "But last night my parents told me they're getting divorced."

"What?" they both say, their mouths falling open.

Mel rests her hand on my arm and Jess slides hers around my waist, resting her head on my shoulder.

"What can we do?" Jess asks. "And why did they tell you the night before you left? That seems—" She pops her head up and waves a hand in front of her, grasping for the words. "Harsh."

"I don't know why I was surprised," I say. "They fight more than they don't, but I guess I thought they'd figure it out."

I have enough friends with divorced parents to know how my future will play out. They'll promise they love me, say this is about them and not me and they still support me one hundred percent. The technical details are harder to predict, but that doesn't stop me from imagining weekend visits at Papá's apartment, having to buy duplicate toothbrushes and body wash and a new favorite mug for my morning green tea, then coming home and avoiding Mamá because she wants to know how he's doing but would never ask and I'll feel guilty for keeping secrets in her house.

My chest tightens at the memory of their words last night. "Papá said they wanted to wait until I graduated, but couldn't anymore."

"I can't even imagine," Mel says.

I tilt my head in surprise. "But your parents are divorced."

She shifts on the bench so she's cross-legged, facing me. The water bubbles against her shoulders, and the heat's made her skin pink. "Yeah, but I was little, and my dad was always traveling before that, so not much changed when he moved out. It was always me, Mom, and Hunter." She trails a finger down my nose, then seems startled by the gesture and yanks her hand back under the water. "You're at this momentous precipice in your life and they yanked the rug out from beneath you."

A smile tugs at my lips. "That seems a little dramatic."

"You don't become a famous tokker without an ear for the dramatic," Jess says.

"But it's true," Mel says. "We're already dealing with everything changing. Home is supposed to be our safe space and now that's ruined for you."

My stomach grumbles remembering the chicken molé I never ate. "They also ruined my favorite meal."

"What?!" Jess shouts, the word echoing off the tiled walls.

"I mean, not on purpose. Mamá made chicken molé as a going away thing, but they dropped their news as soon as we sat down and I lost my appetite."

Mel's eyes close. "Her chicken molé is on my top ten of favorite things."

My brain latches onto her statement and I'm filled with a sense of pride that something from my life is one of her favorite things. I already know that she loves grape candy and science and female empowerment, but it makes me curious about all the weird little things she keeps inside, the things that make her who she is. "So anyway, I don't want to be a sad panda on this trip, so you both have to keep me distracted."

Jess salutes. "On it."

Mel gets a soft smile on her face and waits to catch my eye before nodding. "We'll do whatever we can." She pauses, scrunching her lips as she thinks. "Do you want to keep this secret for now?"

"From who, your mom?"

"The whole group," Mel says. "Remember, my mom's friend Nancy is also a self-help aficionado and they'll have you sobbing on the bottom of the Grand Canyon if you let them. And they usually insist on a deep moment at the start of the trip."

"Hmm, maybe we keep this between us for now."

They both nod and pull me into a huffle.

"I'm really sorry," Jess says.

"There's no crying in the hot tub!" A male voice interrupts us and I take a deep breath, ready for a battle. But Mel scrambles out of the hot tub and runs at the guy in jeans and a dark button-down shirt standing a few feet away. His straight black hair falls in his green eyes as she flings herself into his arms.

"Theo!" she shouts.

He catches her against his chest, not seeming to care that she's soaking wet. "When did you get so grown up?"

Mel steps back and cocks her head. "I've been this height since we met five years ago."

He quirks a brow. "Yes, but you are grown up." His gaze shifts to us and while I know Mel adores him, my creeper radar flips to high alert. He smiles at Jess. "Long time, stranger!" Then he shifts his attention to me. "You must be Stephanie."

I sink lower in the water and wave my fingers near my face. "Hi. Steph is fine." My voice couldn't sound less inviting if I tried.

Mel gives me a questioning look but doesn't say anything. She grabs a towel from a nearby chair and wraps it around her body. "Did you just get here? And did you bring Dimitri?" She bats her eyes and clutches her hands to her chest.

Theo's eyes go wide. "Yes, and most definitely no. We're months away from vacation status."

My shoulders relax. Not that a gay man can't also be a creeper, but the odds are much lower.

"Is anyone else here?" Mel asks.

"Naomi and Mom are in the room getting settled." He air quotes the last words and rolls his eyes, while Mel claps. "What's there to settle? We're here for one night and I have much better things to do than spend it hanging out in my room." He drops into a chair near the hot tub like he's been traveling for days. "So what's the story?"

"Story?" Jess asks. She sits on the edge of the hot tub so only her legs are in the water, but I'm still not ready to reveal my body to a stranger. Even if I am cooking in here.

Theo leans forward with his elbows on his knees. I admit his wide smile is contagious, and he's got a relaxed aura around him that puts me at ease, despite my defenses. "You know, the gossip. That's what the kids at my school are saying."

"You're a teacher?" I ask.

His brows lower as he nods, his face serious. "Middle school."

"Oh, wow." I rest my arms on the edge closest to him so my chest is out of the water but still blocked by the hot tub. My bikini isn't that revealing, it's a basic bandeau with high-rise bottoms, but I feel better with a layer of concrete in front of me.

His bright eyes crinkle as he laughs. "I say that to myself every morning."

Mel sits in the chair next to him and catches my eye. "Not much story. Our lives are surprisingly boring right now."

I mouth "thank you" at her.

"Well, that's about to change." He nods from Mel to Jess. "You both look done, so Steph, if you're fully boiled, you all need to get dressed and come with me to find food."

"I could eat," Jess says. My stomach growls in response and Jess laughs. "And I think that's a yes."

"Give us twenty minutes?" Mel grabs another towel and hands it to me.

Theo sighs. "Mel, there is not a single person in this rustbucket of a hotel who you need to impress. You shall have ten minutes, and not a second longer." He stands and circles his hand at the door. "Let's go."

Fifteen minutes later, we're running down the stairs to the lobby. "You didn't tell me Theo's gay," I say to Mel.

She rounds the turn on the last flight of stairs. "He's actually bi, but yeah. This guy Dimitri seems great, but Theo's never had a serious relationship and I don't think he knows how to move past the fun, flirty stage."

"That's because the fun, flirty stage is so fun," I reply, a little surprised I said that because it's not how I feel about relationships. Mel glances at me over her shoulder but doesn't say anything.

"Is that what happened with Brooklyn?" Jess asks, and I miss the last step, landing hard at the door to the first floor.

"I'm sorry, what?"

Jess pauses with her hand on the door handle. "Did the flirty stage end and take the relationship with it?"

Mel watches me carefully, and I wish I could tell what she's thinking.

"Maybe," I admit.

Theo's on a low couch in the hotel's attempt at a lounge. He seems focused on his phone, but jumps to his feet when we approach. "Naomi should be down here in a couple minutes, but our friends Sage and Neb are still over an hour away." He leads us to the hotel's southwest-themed restaurant. A circular bar sits in the center of the room surrounded by wooden tables. "We should pull a couple tables together."

Nerves stir in my belly. Meeting new people isn't my favorite—I was a constant ball of stress when we moved last year—and even though it helps knowing Mel already approves of Theo and Naomi, there's always the fear that I'll say something weird and they won't like me.

"I can't wait to meet Neb," Mel says, dragging a table toward us. "And Sage, too, of course," she adds, looking at me. "Neb's like the ultimate space nerd."

"Hot space nerd," Theo says.

Jess sets chairs around the now larger table and sits. "All I know is if Sage is Naomi's best friend, she's got to be cool."

I sit next to Jess, and Mel and Theo sit across from us. A server brings waters and a pile of menus, and I try to relax.

Theo pushes his hair out of his face, and it promptly falls back over his forehead. He's a good-looking guy in a quirky, boy-band drummer way and that hair thing probably distracts more than a few of his students. "Sage is the quietest of our friends. She's super into books and reading and all that." He shudders, and Mel laughs.

"Don't you have to read books to, you know, be a teacher?" she asks.

He pats her hand. "Oh, silly, that's what the teacher's guide is for." He winks at me and Jess and leans back in his seat. "I teach social studies so I just have to know pages and pages of factoids. I leave the real reading to the kids, then let them tell me about it."

I'm pretty sure he's kidding, but his delivery makes it hard to tell.

The server returns and we order a bunch of appetizers, and my stomach growls again.

Theo notices and I inwardly cringe, but instead of making a joke of it like I expect, he smiles. "You two really captured the essence of centripetal force."

"Centripetal?" Mel's face pales.

"You watched?" Jess's eyes go wide and she beams.

"Um, yeah? What kind of friend would I be if I didn't support Mel?" He turns to her. "The science department has started sharing your videos with their classes."

Mel's mouth falls open. "Did you say centripetal? And wait, science teachers are watching my videos?"

"Who do you think your hundred thousand followers are?" he asks.

Mel's focus goes fuzzy and she looks like she's someplace else. "The Melties? Other teenagers?"

"It's not just people your age."

Her gaze bounces between me and Jess. "I obviously know people are watching. That's the whole point. But I didn't think actual science professionals would be interested."

I reach for her hand and she squeezes. "Mel, your whole thing is making science interesting. You're accessible and relatable and of course people like you."

Mel's voice goes up an octave. "Theo, why did you say centripetal?"

"Because that's what you said."

"What's wrong?" I ask her.

"Have you checked the numbers?" Jess asks. We both know she didn't while we were getting dressed, so it's been a few hours since she last looked.

Mel shakes her head, sending her dark hair over face.

"Do it," Theo whispers. "Do it now."

Her eyes connect with his and this look of adoration softens her face. She's always looked up to him and he's like a brother to her, and I get the feeling she'd do anything he asked.

Mel opens the app and after a few moments, the rest of the color drains from her face.

"Is that good or bad?" I lean toward her, trying to see her phone.

"I got duetted."

"That's good, right?" Theo asks.

"Usually," Jess says.

But Mel's reaction isn't good. It's the opposite of good.

I lean closer. "What happened?"

Her jaw clenches, her eyes close, and she inhales slowly though her nose. "Jordan Fricking Beebe happened."

"Oh noooooo," Jess says.

"What's a Jordan Fricking Beebe?" Theo asks.

"What is right," I say. "He's a science tokker who thinks he's the science police. He duets other people's videos and tries to make them look stupid." Mel doesn't talk about him often, but I know she's secretly scared he'll target her and try to trash her videos.

"What's he saying?" Jess asks.

Mel sets her phone in the middle of the table and hits play. On the right side of the screen is Mel's original centrifugal force video with me and Jess spinning until she almost puked. Mel's voiceover and expertly timed captions explain the properties, pointing out why our hair sticks out behind us and why it got harder for us to hold onto each other.

On the left side is Jordan Beebe, a guy our age who's working the geeky jock look extra hard. He seems fit, his blond hair's sort of styled, and his oversized plastic glasses manage to highlight his bright blue eyes. He crosses his arms with one hand on his chin, nodding and not-so-subtly flexing his biceps as he listens to the beginning of Mel's video.

"Here it comes," Mel says, her voice barely a whisper.

Jordan holds up a finger and side-eyes the video. "This is cute. I mean, my little sister likes to play in her room with her friends, but she at least has the good sense not to share it with the world."

He runs a hand over his hair, not through it because that would mess it up, and flexes again. A tiny smirk tugs at his mouth.

"People like this doucher?" Theo asks.

Mel shakes her head, her eyes still on the screen.

"And this would be cute," Jordan continues, "if any of it were accurate."

"He did not!" Jess shouts, drawing the attention of the server. Her outburst drowns out Jordan's voice, which I'm completely okay with. Nothing that comes out of that lizard's mouth is worth hearing.

Jordan leans closer to the screen. "What Miss Melody is demonstrating is centrifugal force, not centripetal. It's easy to mix the two up because—" He holds up a finger. "I take that back. Anyone who knows a thing about science knows the difference."

"This guy is saying a whole lot of nothing," Theo says.

"But he's right," Mel whispers.

"What?" Jess and I say.

Mel closes her eyes. Her lower lip wobbles before she sucks it between her teeth. "I said centripetal instead of centrifugal. I was so tired when I finished the video that I made a mistake. And now it's blasted to his audience."

Jordan's still talking. "Centripetal force is when an object in the center attracts another object, like magnets and gravity. Or someone with a magnetic personality." He winks at the camera and Jess makes a puking noise. "What these girls are demonstrating is centrifugal force—when the motion around an object pushes those objects away." Jordan points to his left, timing the motion to perfectly align with the moment the camera zooms and Jess's and my hands touch. "And if Miss Melody keeps screwing up like this, she's going to push her followers right out of her orbit."

Mel rubs her hands over her face. "Why can't he just say it's wrong and leave it at that? Why does he have to ridicule me?"

"Some people get off on that," Theo says.

"Theo, why didn't you tell me sooner?" Mel asks.

He looks stricken. "Science isn't my game. I would've if I'd realized."

In the video, Jess and I slow our spinning and Jordan smiles at the camera. "For more real science for real people," Jordan says, "click the follow button. And maybe leave the bedroom antics to people who know what they're doing."

The video ends and there's a moment of stunned silence. Then we all start shouting.

"This is what I hope my students don't grow up to be like," Theo says. "Can I use this as an example of how not to act?"

"We will destroy him," Jess says.

"Who are we destroying?"

We turn to see a young woman with Theo's eyes and red curls that seem to carry her through the room. "I could hear you yelling all the way in the lobby."

Mel scrambles out of her seat and buries her face in the woman's shoulder.

Theo catches my eye and hooks a thumb at them. "My sister, Naomi."

Naomi waves at us and smiles at me. "You must be Steph."

I nod, still too furious to form words.

"What'd I miss?" Naomi asks.

Jess looks from Mel, who's still tucked against Naomi's shoulder, to me, and takes charge. "Mel's video got duetted by a misogynist asshole who's using her popularity to get followers. It's disgusting and lazy and yet there's people who buy into it."

Mel sniffs. "But he's right. I got it wrong."

Naomi nods, then pushes Mel's shoulders back so she can look in her eyes. "People make mistakes. That's easy to fix. Now where are we at on the plan to destroy him?"

Mel shakes her head. "I made a vow a long time ago that I would only be positive." She glances at Jess. They share a smile that should make me happy for them because they got through that time in their lives, but instead I feel a sense of longing, like I'll never be as tight with them as they are with each other.

"If we're not destroying him," Theo says, "can we at least call out what a jerk he is?"

"Mel's right," I say. "Rising above guys like that is a part of life. We'll come up with something that puts him in his place but stays focused on your message."

Theo nods approvingly. "Back in my day, we just posted random crap to social media and stressed over how many likes we got. I don't think I ever thought about my message."

Mel moves away from Naomi and pats Theo on his head. "And that's why you're a middle school teacher and I'm a soon-to-be media mogul slash world-famous scientist." She purses her lips, but there's a gleam in her eyes that says she's already shifted from freaking out to planning her next moves.

I love that about Mel. If something knocks her down or doesn't go the way she wants, she doesn't waste weeks crying about it. She finds a way to turn things around in her favor, all without hurting anyone else in the process.

"I'll admit I made a mistake and use it to show that no one is perfect. That science is infallible, and this is how we learn. But the important thing is to own your mistakes." Mel slumps into her seat and this time Theo pats her on the head. "We just need to figure out how to do it."

"We'll never finish a new video before we head out," Jess says.

Naomi sits in the empty chair next to me. "Does it have to be today?"

"Here we go!" The server has way too much enthusiasm as she puts our apps on the table, but since we're the only people in here, maybe she has nothing better to do.

I slide plates to everyone and grab a piece of pita bread and a spoonful of spinach dip.

Mel does the same before answering Naomi. "Typically, no. But waiting almost a week to respond, especially to something as blatant as this, might make him think he got to me."

"Don't give him the satisfaction of responding," Theo says, then shovels a handful of tortilla chips in his mouth. "That's what bullies want."

"That's not all he wants," Mel says. "He wants me to go away."

"There's no way that's happening," Jess says.

Mel brings a tortilla chip loaded with dip to her mouth and smiles for real. "Not a chance."

— **5** —
MELODY

"Oh crap, oh crap, oh crap." Naomi grabs her glass of water and ducks her head.

Hunter's standing in the open doorway near the deserted host stand. He's wearing a bright blue T-shirt that I know he thinks looks good on him, and he must have gone to his room first because his dark hair looks recently styled. We're the only ones in here but he looks around like he'd rather sit anyplace than at our table.

"Hunter, my man!" Theo practically gallops to his side. They one-arm bro-hug and slap each other on the back. They don't talk as often as Naomi and I do, but I know they keep in touch and Hunter only agreed to come on this trip because Theo would be here, too.

I lean closer to Naomi. "How long has it been since you've seen each other?" My voice is casual and doesn't give away what we're plotting.

Jess and Steph widen their eyes at me and I fight back a smile.

"A couple years," Naomi says. "Damn, he looks good."

My shoulders straighten and Naomi grabs my hand.

"Don't."

"What?"

She furrows her brows at me. "Don't do whatever it is you're plotting. I can see it in your eyes."

Jess giggles and Naomi drops her head in her hand.

"Not you, too?"

Steph stops fighting her smile and a laugh bubbles out of her. She doesn't laugh like that often, and for a second it distracts me from the drama playing out in front of us.

"Do I even get a vote in this?" Naomi asks.

"A vote in what?" Theo asks.

"Nothing," the four of us say in unison.

Hunter crosses his arms to scowl at me and I swear he flexes his biceps. "I don't believe that for a minute."

I rise from my chair to give him a quick hug. "I wouldn't expect anything less."

He narrows his eyes at me before sitting at the opposite end of the table from Naomi. He nods at her and mumbles hey, she murmurs something back, and the rest of us sigh.

Theo raises his hands in front of him, palms out. "You two have until the morning to sort this out."

Naomi's head snaps toward him. "Excuse me?"

Theo points back and forth between her and Hunter. "This. My Grand Canyon experience will not become an Okay Canyon experience because I have to tiptoe around the two of you."

"It's gonna be tough to tiptoe while you're hiking," I say. My smirk turns into a full-on smile as he swivels his head toward me.

He points at me and sticks out his lower lip. "I thought you're on my side?"

"Oh, we are," Jess says.

Theo refocuses on his sister. "I mean it. I love you both and I'm sorry it didn't work out between you," he throws a look at Hunter, who nods. "But it's not fair to the rest of us, and frankly, it's exhausting." He leans back in his chair and puts his hands behind his head.

"Teacher Theo doesn't mess around," I say.

A painful expression flickers across Hunter's face, then it's back to his unreadable mask. "I can do that."

"Me too," Naomi says.

Despite their promises, an awkward silence falls over the table until the parents arrive and insist we order dinner.

"Should we wait for Sage and Neb?" Nancy asks.

Naomi holds up her phone. "She swears they're almost here. They're running late because, quote, Neb wanted to see Antelope Island in Great Salt Lake."

"Can't blame them for that," Mom says. "It's a magical place."

Naomi glances at Hunter, and his scowl softens.

"I can't believe they drove," Mom says.

Bryan leans back in his chair. "Even if they flew, they'd have to rent a car to get the rest of the way."

"No one's got the budget for that," Theo says.

"Especially not a nonprofit associate and research assistant." Naomi sighs. "I know I shouldn't romanticize things, but their lives sound so perfect."

Hunter smothers a cough. I stare at him, willing his eyes to meet mine, but the table has suddenly become the most interesting thing in his universe.

We place our orders and Sage and Neb arrive as the server brings our food. Naomi rushes to the doorway to hug Sage, and Theo's not far behind.

"Can we eat while our food's still hot?" Hunter mumbles.

Mom gives him The Look—brows raised, lips pursed—and he picks up his burger.

Jess, Steph, and I are the only ones who haven't met Neb and Sage, so once introductions are covered, Neb sits next to me.

"I hear you're into science?" he asks.

"Understatement." Steph laughs, smiling at me from across the table.

Theo wasn't kidding when he said Neb was hot. His broad shoulders turn toward me as he waits for my answer, his dark brown eyes focused only on me. He has the same sandy brown hair as Sage, but it's cut shorter than Theo's, like he doesn't have time to waste pushing hair out of his eyes.

I smile at them both and nod. "It's my mission to make science fun and interesting and show girls it can be cool."

Neb gestures at the table. "Well, you're in the right company for that."

He's not kidding. Both moms are self-help gurus, Naomi's doubled down on helping people with her new podcast, Theo's literally shaping the minds of the future—which is still mildly terrifying to think of—and from what I know about Sage, she may be quiet but she's dedicated herself to helping women reclaim their lives after men trample all over them.

"Let me know if there's anything I can help with," Neb says.

Jess leans into our conversation. "Theo said you're way into science, too?" He nods and Jess raises her brows at me. "Perhaps you can help us with Mel's next video."

He nods slowly like he's considering it. "Whatever you need."

"That's brilliant!" Theo claps his hands together. "Neb, you're too pretty to hide in a lab. Let's get you in front of thousands of teen girls."

Neb leans back in his seat, eyes wide. "What exactly did I agree to?"

I pat his arm, darting a glance at Sage to make sure she doesn't think I'm flirting with her boyfriend. But she looks as amused as Theo. "This will be painless, I promise."

His eyes grow even wider. "Theo?"

"It's not all teen girls. There's easily, what—" Theo looks at me. "A couple thousand bored housewives, too, right?"

"Theo, stop scaring him," Naomi says, but there's a twinkle in her eyes. "Neb, you were made for this. You two can geek out together about striations or whatever."

I've been wracking my brain to come up with a way to incorporate the canyon into a couple videos, and the striations in the canyon walls—the varying layers of sediment built up over the millennia that look like stripes—seem like the most obvious option. I just need to make extra certain I get the facts right.

Neb shakes his head, but a smile plays on his lips. "Let me know what you need me to do."

Jess pumps her fist over her head. "Yes! Mel, this'll be epic."

My thoughts bounce through video concepts as the conversation shifts to grad school and work and things that adults worry about. When we've finished eating, Mom gets up to go to the bathroom and motions for me to follow.

"Did you have enough to eat?" she asks.

"Um, yeah?" It's been a while since Mom has kept tabs on my eating habits.

"Are you all settled into your room okay?"

"Yes."

We enter the bathroom, but she gives me a cautious smile and tugs on my arm before going into a stall. "And how are you feeling about tomorrow? Any nerves?"

"Why all the questions?" I ask. Her smile falls and I immediately regret my tone. "Sorry, I know you're just looking out for me. I just—I have a lot on my mind."

She sighs, a long exhale that tells me she's considering her words more carefully than I did. "Is it the video or something else?" Mom asks.

"Both."

"What can you control right now?"

This is how most conversations go with my mother. Break down the problem until you're at the root issue, then work your way back up. I technically still have time to post another video tonight, but I prefer to put thought and effort into them—the same way I approach science experiments.

Which means my answer is easy, even if I don't intend to tell Mom about my feelings for Steph. "I guess the something else."

She rests a hand on my arm. "Then focus on that. You can work on videos while we're here but you can't do anything about Jordan Fricking Beebe from the canyon."

I burst out laughing. If Mom remembers my nickname for him, I need to stop letting him live rent-free in my head. "Thanks, Mom."

"Just let me know if I can help."

When everyone has finished eating, the parents leave and the rest of us shift to the lobby. The group dynamics could be weird since my friends and I are at least five years younger than the others, but they seem interested in what we have to say and don't treat us like we're children. Steph seems comfortable with Theo and Naomi, and Jess, always the glue that holds everyone together, is deep in conversation with Sage and Neb.

My phone was buzzing the whole meal, so I finally pull it out. Texts from friends and the few tokkers I've gotten to know roll in, all with one concern: Jordan Fricking Beebe. They even include the fricking as if it's part of his name.

You can't let him get away with this

We're ready to take him down. Just say the word

He's an embarrassment to SciTok

I can't disagree with that last one, but I quickly copy/paste the same message to everyone else:

Please don't do anything. He's right. I screwed up. I'm working on a response but won't have signal to post a video.

Hunter settles onto the padded bench next to me and leans against my shoulder. "You excited for tomorrow?"

"Excited, a little scared. And nervous. I've never not showered for three days."

"I'm pretty sure they've got showers down there."

"You're harshing my narrative."

He increases the pressure against my arm. "You'll be too distracted by the magnificence of the canyon to worry about anything else."

If only that were true. Choosing a school and stressing about Jordan Fricking Beebe would be enough, but I also can't stop worrying about Steph and her parents and her breakup. That's a lot to deal with all at once.

"Have you made a decision about school?"

I shake my head. "I know where I want to go, but the scholarship is to Long Beach."

"Let me be an example of how what looks good on paper isn't always the best path." His gaze slips to Naomi, who's laughing with Theo and Steph.

"Thank you for coming," I say. "I know this has to be extra weird for you."

He looks at Naomi again. This time she catches him looking, but instead of turning away, he gives her his barely smile. The one boys do that drive girls crazy. "It's not as weird as I thought it'd be."

Choirs erupt in my head. Maybe Operation Amazing won't be as hard as I thought! I try to telepathically communicate with Steph and Jess, but they just smile when they notice my eyes laser beaming at them. It'll have to wait until later.

"I'm glad." I lean my head against his shoulder, grateful to have him here. When I was little, he was my world, but the timing of him going away to college coincided with my personality hiccup in middle school, and things never really went back to the way they were, even after he transferred to a local college so he could move back home. I'll always adore my big brother, but my reliance on him to guide my every move has shifted to a reliance on my friends.

Friends who seem to be getting more tired by the minute.

"Should we head up to bed?" I ask the group.

Naomi plasters on an exaggerated smile. "Big day tomorrow!" She imitates her mom perfectly, and Theo bursts out laughing. Even Hunter manages a smile.

We gather our things, cram into the elevator to the third floor, and say our goodnights.

"Be sure to enjoy the beds," Theo says to the group. "We won't have cushy mattresses again for an eternity."

"Hanging out with middle schoolers has made your hyperbole even worse," Sage teases, and I instantly like her even more.

"Just calling it like I see it," Theo says. He gives an exaggerated bow. "Ladies, I bid you adieu."

Hunter and Naomi awkwardly shuffle past each other on their way to their rooms, and light bulbs ping-pong around in my brain. I hurry the girls into our room and lean against the closed door with a grin.

"Operation Amazing is so on!"

They watch me with wide eyes and expectant smiles.

"Hunter said it wasn't as weird to see Naomi as he expected." I rub my hands together. "He's basically plotting how to get back together with her."

Jess grabs her toothbrush and pats my arm on her way into the bathroom. "That's a bit of a leap, but still good news," she quickly adds when my brows furrow.

Steph looks inside her empty water bottle. "Think there's an ice machine nearby?"

"I can help you look." I grab the key card while she finds the ice bucket. "Jess, we'll be back in a minute."

A hush has fallen over the hallway and we walk side by side. It's barely nine o'clock, and even though the parking lot was pretty full, the other guests seem to be settled in for the night. "I guess we're not the only ones with big days tomorrow."

Steph gives me a confused look.

"There's no one around."

She tucks the ice bucket against her belly. "That's fine with me. That was a lot of people all at once."

My hand reaches for her arm but I catch myself, only allowing my fingers to graze the back of her elbow. "Are you doing okay? Did you like everyone? I hope you're not regretting coming on this trip." Jeez Mel, word vomit much?

She gives me a tired smile. "They all seem great. I can see why you like Theo and Naomi so much." We reach an open doorway and she pokes her head inside. "Jackpot."

A pair of vending machines with drinks and snacks sit next to an ice machine that looks like it came from the 1970s. She hands me her phone and approaches the machine with caution. "Do we have to pay?"

Her phone is warm from her hand, and it does goofy things to my insides. "Um, I think you just hit the button."

She does, and we both yelp as a deafening screech fills the room. "What the hell is that?" Steph yells as an avalanche of ice fills the bucket.

I burst out laughing. "The price for free ice?"

She presses it once more and ice overflows onto the floor. We jump back as cubes skitter across the tile. "I'm awake now." We kick the extra pieces under the machine, then she sets the lid on the bucket and holds her hand out for her phone. Our fingers touch and I stare at where we made contact. "Thanks."

My mouth goes dry. I'm tempted to steal an ice cube but I don't want to move. "How are you—" I pause, and she looks me in the eyes. I clear my throat. "How are you doing with everything else? Your parents, and Brooklyn?" Bringing up her ex feels like the wrong thing to do, but my mind won't let it go until I know how she's really feeling.

She leans against the doorframe and cradles the bucket to her chest. Her lips press together, like she's thinking about how to respond, and I wait her out. "My parents are..." She shakes her head. "I don't even know what to think about that. But Brooklyn—" She takes a breath. Her pulse flutters in her throat and I wish I could reach for her.

Feel the flutter beneath my lips.

I take a small step back and push those thoughts away. She just broke up with her girlfriend. She is nowhere near ready for whatever's going on in my head.

Steph clears her throat. "I'm fine. More than fine. And actually..." Her gaze drops. "I—I think it'll be good for me to be single for a while."

— 6 —

STEPHANIE

An alarm chirps from across the room way before the sun rises and a rush of adrenaline has me rolling out of bed and into the bathroom. Mel didn't push when I told her I wanted to be single, especially when I told her I'm too worried about my parents to even think about my own love life. Jess woke up long enough to throw me an "is everything okay and you know you can talk to me" look before we turned out the light. Then I dreamed my parents were mourning me separately because I fell off a cliff and plunged to my death.

Now I'm alone in the bathroom, trying not to freak out.

Because we're leaving for the Grand Canyon soon.

To hike and camp and try not to die.

"You almost done in there?" Mel's voice is scratchy through the door.

I wash my hands and open the door. "Just freaking out."

She cocks her head as she moves past me. "About today? Or something else?" Then she drops her pajama bottoms to use the toilet and I turn away to give her privacy.

"Um, yeah." My voice gets stuck in my throat. "Are we sure we're ready for this hike? I watched a video on the Discovery Channel about two grown men who attempted this and they almost died."

The water turns on as she washes her hands, and I grab my toiletry bag to get ready. We showered before bed, so getting ready means putting on moisturizer with SPF, brushing my teeth, and taming my hair with a cloth headband.

Mel turns to face me. "I told you not to watch those." She's got a hair tie in one hand and she pulls her long waves into a low messy bun. I miss being able to do that with my hair, but I wouldn't trade the purple for anything. "Bryan promised we'll have two guides with years of experience, plus we're barely hiking a fraction of the canyon, not the entire thing. Just the more popular trails."

None of this is new information. Mamá would never have let me come if there was an actual possibility of me dying of heatstroke or falling to my death off an unmarked cliff. But it's the combination of having to carry everything we'll need and putting up tents and having questionable access to running water that has me on the edge of flipping out.

"Can I get in here?" Jess stands in the doorway, rubbing sleep from her eyes.

"Enjoy the endless supply of water while you can." I leave them in the bathroom and find my bag next to the bed. The tour company gave us very clear instructions on what to bring, what not to bring, and how to best pack it. I have the recommended one pair each of shorts and pants, three shirts, underwear and socks for each day, and one microfiber hoodie to get me through. "I hope I don't hate you by the end of this trip," I whisper to the bright teal hoodie. I dress quickly, then sit on the bed and scroll through my phone.

Before I can stop myself, I'm looking up Mel's account. The views for the centrifugal force video are higher than normal, and a flutter of pride hits my chest. Mel's the imagination behind MeltyPoint, but it feels good to be part of something worthwhile. That helps other people learn. I know she's upset because she called it the wrong thing, but it's still a great video.

Then I find Jordan's post and all those fluttery feelings vanish. He doesn't have as many views as Mel, but his video trashing us has thousands more views than his other posts.

I glance at the bathroom. They're talking over the sound of running water so I should be able to peek at the comments before they're done.

I hold my breath as I tap my finger on the comment icon.

Then exhale.

The first few comments are defending Mel. Defending us. Saying that people are allowed to make mistakes and he shouldn't be such a jerk. I scroll farther down and find Jordan's usual misogynistic fans virtually high-fiving him for putting "a bunch of little girls in their place." The comments bounce back and forth between trashing and congratulating him, and I don't realize Mel's standing in front of me until she bumps my knee with hers.

"Is it bad?"

My eyes meet hers and I hand her my phone. "Not as bad as I expected. A lot of people love you and they aren't letting him trash you over one mistake."

She swipes the screen, not really reading, then hands my phone back to me. "I hate that we don't have time to make a new video before we leave."

"You always say rushed videos never do well. Patience and all that, right?" I give her a small smile and she frowns.

"That's what got me into this mess in the first place." She stares at the floor as her toe drags back and forth across the carpet. It's not like her to hold back what she's thinking.

"What?" I ask.

She looks up, her eyes shining. "Would it be weird to make a new video? Where I call it the right thing?"

I hesitate before answering. It's not like her to second-guess herself, and I hate that one mistake is making her so upset. "Is that really what you want to do?"

"No. I pinned a comment correcting my mistake to the top, but I hate that it's out there, being all wrong."

"Replicate the circumstances, then duplicate the results?"

She snorts at my Myth Busters reference. "Something like that."

"We've got the whole trip to come up with a kick-ass video that will prove how awesome you are. One mistake won't undo all your hard work."

She studies the carpet. "Thanks." Her usual confidence seems MIA and this guy made it worse. I know not all guys are bad, but Jordan Fricking Beebe is the definition of toxic masculinity: he uses his self-perceived power and dominance as a man to tear down people, especially women, he thinks are beneath him.

But I don't think that's what Mel's worrying about. "Is something else wrong?" I ask.

When she looks up, tears shine in her eyes. "I try really hard with this, you know?" She spins in a circle like she's looking for something, then leans against the dresser in front of me. "I want to create something that's good and helpful and not the crap so many accounts put out where they're bashing other people and trying to get ahead by ridiculing others."

"You're totally doing that," I say.

She swipes at a tear that runs down her cheek. "So why does Jordan Fricking Beebe feel the need to attack me?"

In seconds, I'm on my feet and pulling her into a hug. She settles against me, her head on my shoulder even though she's a couple inches taller than me, and I hope she feels as safe as I do. "Guys like that can't stand it when someone is better than them. Especially if that person's smart and funny and gorgeous. They do whatever they can to tear other people down."

"What'd I miss?" Jess asks from the bathroom door.

I wave her over and we huffle Mel between us.

"Jordan Fricking Beebe," Mel says, her breath tickling my neck.

Jess gives us both a squeeze and steps back. "Yes, he sucks to the utmost degree. But there's nothing else we can do now, right?" She watches Mel's reaction and when she finally nods, Jess pushes Mel toward her bag. "Finish getting ready. We'll come up with something by the time this trip is over."

Mel digs through her overnight bag, her smile shaky. "I don't know what I'd do without the two of you."

Twenty minutes later, our bags are loaded in the SUV and we're back in the hotel restaurant.

"Did everyone sleep well?" Margo asks us as we join them at the table. Sage and Naomi whisper to each other at one end of the table while Theo, Hunter, and Neb quietly shovel food into their mouths at the other end. Nancy and Bryan sit on either side of Margo, so the three of us sit across from them.

"Pretty good," Mel tells her mom.

"You don't look it," Hunter says, and Mel sticks her tongue out at him.

Margo sets her fork on the table. "Let's talk through our expectations of the trip before we get on the road." She and Nancy exchange nods, but the rest of them groan.

"What'd I miss?" I whisper to Jess.

"Our mothers have a bizarre preoccupation with talking about our feelings in front of everyone," Hunter says.

Alarm grips me. It was hard enough to tell Jess and Mel about my parents. I'm not ready to share with the group, especially since, as Mel said, they all love overanalyzing people's drama.

"But don't worry," Theo says with a smile. "It's like a choose your own adventure story. You get to decide how much you're willing to share."

Naomi smiles. "Which in my brother's case, is usually far beyond what the rest of the group wants to know."

He holds out his hands like an offering to the table. "I give the people what they want."

Their banter calms the panic that had started to build inside me. Telling this group of almost strangers about breaking up with Brooklyn and my parents getting divorced is not high on my list of fun activities. Even though part of me accepts that it's gonna come up at some point. You can't spend every waking minute with people without them getting inside your head.

"I'll go first," Neb says. Sage tilts her head at him, and he smiles from across the table. "At the lab, we're studying the effect of the moon's growing distance from Earth and how it impacts the tides and global ocean levels. My observations from the base of the canyon may not help my research, but I never pass up an opportunity to witness a celestial event."

Sage beams at him before clearing her throat. "I'm excited for the break from work and time to get lost in nature."

Bryan points a finger at her. "No one's getting lost on my watch."

"I think she meant figuratively," Hunter says. I haven't spent a ton of time with him, but I've learned that since he works with words all day, correcting people's grammar is like a reflex for him. Kind of like Mamá. Bryan's lips press together, and now Hunter looks like he wishes he could delete that comment. "Which you clearly already knew."

Bryan nods. "Since I have the floor, I'll share that this trip means a lot to me." His gaze moves back and forth between Hunter and Mel. "I know it's been the three of you for a long time, and I hope this gives us a chance to get to know each other better."

Margo runs her hand down her arm. "That's my goal, too."

"That's cheating," Theo says.

She shrugs and smiles at Theo. "What about you?"

Theo's smile falls, just for a second, then it's back on his face like nothing happened. "Things are pretty solid with me right now. Nothing to figure out."

"Liar," Naomi whispers.

He purses his lips at her. "Two can play that game." They raise their eyebrows at each other and if I didn't know better, I'd swear they're talking telepathically. Naomi breaks eye contact first and Theo pumps his fists in the air. "That's what I thought."

Naomi rolls her eyes and turns to Nancy. "What about you, Mom?"

Nancy plants her hands on the edge of the table. Her jaw tenses a couple times, then she takes a breath. "For those of you who aren't aware, I recently got out of a relationship."

The adults and her kids nod while my stomach twists. I don't want to talk about parents splitting up, even if they were just dating and the guy wasn't anyone's parent. Jess and I exchange an awkward look.

"I initiated the breakup, and after two years, it's enlightening to be on my own again. That said," she runs her finger around the rim of her coffee cup. "I have my moments when I'm not at my best. I hope all of you can help me navigate this new stage in my life."

Margo squeezes her hand. "You know we're here for you. Anything you need, just say it."

Naomi pushes back her chair and moves around the table to hug her mom. "What she said."

Nancy runs her hand over Naomi's hair, then clears her throat. "Okay, enough of that." She looks at Mel and smiles. "What about you, Mel? What's weighing on you right now?"

A scowl darkens Mel's face as she thinks. "I have to decide on college when we get back. I know what I should do, but I'm not sure if that's what I want to do." She doesn't hesitate saying what's on her mind.

Sweat breaks out on my lip and my heart races.

I don't want to share.

Margo leans forward. "I thought you decided on CSU Long Beach? They gave you the scholarship and..." She trails off. She's usually pretty in tune with what Mel's thinking, so maybe she figured out the problem without Mel having to say it.

Mel shakes her head. "I'm not sure what I want." Her eyes meet mine like she's trying to tell me that she does know what she wants, then she looks away and the moment passes.

"This seems to be the theme," Naomi says, "but we're here to help." They smile at each other and a rush of panic moves through me. Because Jess and I are the only ones left and I really don't want to talk.

"I'll go next," Jess says, and I'm once again grateful for her ability to find a way to help without being obvious. "I know we're supposed to be excited to graduate. To move on to the next stage in our life, blah blah." She looks at me and Mel and I get the uneasy feeling she's about to drop something that she's never told us. "It's awesome that you both know what you want to do. You've got college mostly figured out and you can see how your lives will play out. But I love my life right now and, honestly, I don't know what comes next for me. If college is even what I want."

I hook my arm through hers and rest my head on her shoulder. "Like at all?"

Her head presses against mine. "I keep thinking that something would eventually click and I'll figure out what I'm supposed to do with the rest of my life."

All I hear is that we haven't been good enough friends. She's struggling and hasn't trusted us enough to say anything.

"Jess, you don't have to know it all right now," Mel says. "I'm a weirdo who found my jam early, but you have tons of time."

"She's right," Theo says. "I had no clue what I wanted to do when I was graduating high school. I stumbled into teaching, but it could have been rodeo cowboy for as confused as I was."

Naomi snorts. "You'd fail rodeo cowboying school."

"You'd fall off in two seconds," Mel says.

"And you and large animals don't agree," Hunter says.

Theo holds up his hand. "It was a metaphor, people."

"Okay, let's give Jess some space," Margo says." She looks around the table. "Who's left."

Everyone looks at me.

My heart pounds in my chest.

My mouth goes dry.

I take a sip of juice. "Um, is it okay if I pass? I had some drama—well, a couple dramas—right before we left and I'm still processing how I feel about it." Margo and Nancy nod when I say processing, and I silently thank Mel for teaching me some of their self-help language.

"Of course, dear," Margo says. "We're here whenever you're ready. Please know that collectively, this group has been through it all, so even if you don't want to talk about it with everyone, I hope that you'll reach out to at least one of us."

"Thanks," I whisper.

Everyone gives me soft smiles, their eyes crinkled just enough to show they really mean it. Do they study that expression in the mirror? It's freaky how they all know exactly what to do.

Mel bumps her foot against mine and I look up. "You okay?" she mouths, and I nod.

At least for now.

Bryan sets down his coffee cup and rests a hand on Margo's shoulder. "We should get on the road. We've got a long day ahead of us."

Nancy drains her coffee before standing. "Bathrooms for everyone. Be in the parking lot in five minutes."

We all start talking at once, and I grab a final bite of bacon before finishing my orange juice.

"Bathrooms were by the front desk," Jess says, and the three of us follow Naomi and Sage out of the restaurant. We're at the car with seconds to spare, and this time Jess takes the middle, with Mel on her right and me behind the driver's seat and I focus on the sun rising in the distance.

It's still cool outside, not even fifty degrees, and the leather seats are cold from overnight. "Are we gonna be warm enough sleeping in tents?" I ask.

Jess elbows me. "Little late to be worrying about that now, don't you think?"

I elbow her back. "I know we've got all the gear and we wouldn't be doing this if we were gonna turn into popsicles, but it's one thing to talk about it being close to freezing outside and another to be almost there and feel it." I'm not doing a good job explaining what I mean, but now that we're almost at the Grand Canyon, it's starting to feel real. We're actually going to hike into something you can see from outer space and then we're going to sleep at the bottom. I'm not sure this is something I'd ever do if it weren't for Mel and Jess.

Mel leans forward to look at me. "It's okay to be nervous. I hate not knowing what to expect."

Margo twists in her seat. "Girls, we'll be perfectly safe. The hike down will be the most challenging part. Once we're at the bottom and have set up camp, we'll be able to relax."

"Actually, the hike back up is harder," Bryan says. "But having the three of you in one tent will keep the air nice and toasty."

My half-hearted research about this trip, meaning I searched Hiking in the Grand Canyon a couple times, did say something about having multiple bodies in one tent to help everyone keep warm.

The rest of the drive is quiet. The sun peeks over the horizon, turning the sky bright pink and orange. The stretch of highway leading to the canyon seems abandoned, and my nerves get so bad that by the time we pull into the shuttle parking lot, I feel like I'm either going to throw up or pass out.

In the distance, the jagged peaks of the canyon rise over the rooflines of the low buildings that seem part of the dusty earth at the edge of the lot. A dozen cars sit nearby, but aside from an older couple who look a little like my abuelos, there aren't any people.

"Looks like we beat the crowds," Bryan says with pride in his voice. "The shuttle to the trailhead should be here in fifteen minutes, and we need to check in at the Visitor Center. You girls want to find the lookout?"

Mel flings her door open before I've even unbuckled my seat belt. Jess rushes out after her and I expect them to run toward the signs with arrows pointing to the lookout, but when I plant my feet on the ground, they're both waiting. Mel holds out her hand. "You ready to see where we'll be staying the next few days?"

My head shakes as I take her hand. I downplayed my panic as we planned this trip. Assured them that yes, of course I'm excited to hike farther into the earth than I ever thought I'd go. That I'm not afraid of falling off the path and tumbling to my death thousands of feet below, my head cracking against every rock on my way down. That sleeping outside with nothing to protect me from wild animals but a thin piece of fabric was A-okay with me.

I still haven't moved.

A point that doesn't go unnoticed.

"Hey," Jess says, always the one to make everything okay. "We're not going to let anything happen to you. You know that, right?"

I nod, but still don't move.

Mel squeezes my hand. "One step at a time."

We walk across the parking lot, each of them holding my hand. We pass the building that the old couple entered and then it's in front of us.

The Grand Canyon.

I stop, tugging them to my side. "It's so big."

"One might say it's grand." Mel laughs under her breath, then quickly looks at me to see my reaction.

"And you're both just totally okay with hiking over the edge and sleeping down there?" Panic makes my words come out harsher than I mean to.

"It's definitely a little scary," Mel says.

"Let's go over there." Jess points at a sidewalk that leads to a lookout point. A sturdy railing surrounds the area and I slowly exhale. At least I can't fall off.

As we walk, I bounce between staring at the sidewalk and glancing at the canyon looming in front of us. "It's so big," I repeat, but this time neither of them makes a joke. Because it is big. Bigger than anything I ever imagined. The colors of the canyon walls glow in the morning sun, the reds and oranges bursting from the ground like nothing I've ever seen. The closer we get, the farther the distance to the other side stretches. The edge pulls us nearer until my hands grip the railing and I'm leaning forward to see down, down, down toward the bottom.

"I read that you can't even see the canyon floor from here," Mel says. "It's like five thousand feet down and we can only see partway."

This isn't new information. I read that, too. But reading it safe in my room in Bakersfield and seeing it with my own eyes kicks my fight or flight response into high gear. Despite my fear, I inch closer until the toes of my hiking boots hit the railing. Jess and Mel do the same and together we peer into what can only be described as an abyss.

My chest tightens, making it hard to breathe. Every now and then I feel like I might fall off the earth. That nothing's holding me here. Being at the edge of the canyon makes that feeling stronger. Like it could really happen. "I feel like it's pulling me in."

"Yeah, what is that?" Jess asks.

"It's the Grand Canyon," Theo says from behind us. "I thought that was pretty obvious."

I already know Theo well enough to know teasing is his default function, so I ignore his comment and smile at Naomi, who's joined us at the railing.

"It's really far down," she says. "This is going to be way harder than I thought." She whirls around and points at Theo. "Don't say it."

He mouths, "that's what she said" and bursts out laughing.

It's impossible not to laugh along with him. His laughter is infectious, and his smile is so open and inviting that I feel privileged to be part of whatever's bringing him such joy.

But the moment of happiness is quickly replaced by a feeling of dread that won't let go.

How are we going to hike down there without dying?

— 7 —

MELODY

Mom's assurances that this wouldn't be dangerous seem greatly downplayed. We're grouped in a haphazard circle near the visitor center, our packs—not bags as I keep calling them—at our feet. Goosebumps pebble my skin as the cold air blows over my neck, and I rub my hands together to keep them warm.

The guides, Benji and Veronica, seem to be the same age as Hunter and the rest of them, but while our group went the college route, Benji and Veronica—or Ronny as he keeps calling her—look like they were raised for outdoor living. They've got what I think of as a surfer look—long lean muscles, skin that's permanently tan, and hair that does whatever it wants—but instead of being one with the ocean, they're one with the earth.

And right now they're demonstrating how to pull someone to safety if they fall off the trail.

Not fall on the trail.

Fall *off* the trail.

But only if they fall a little, because taking the fall line, which Benji explains is the most direct route down the canyon, would require air rescue. He didn't linger on that thought, but my brain has leapt to what it would take for a helicopter to pull a broken body from the bottom of the canyon.

Benji mentions something about veggie belay and my brain snaps to attention.

"I'm sorry, what?"

He points at a small bush near the trail. "Veggie. And belay's when you secure yourself with a rope."

"Sometimes you have to use whatever you can to survive," Ronny says. "But it's our job to make sure you all stay safe."

Naomi nudges a bush with her boot. "I never thought a bush could save my life."

"As we explained during prep," Ronny continues, "food's provided at the campsite, so the bulk of your weight should be water." She holds up a steel bottle with a screw top. "This is one liter. You need to camel up with four of these before we go."

"Camel up?" Jess whispers, and we giggle.

"If you don't—" Ronny puts the bottle back in her bag and searches each of our eyes. Her face grows serious and I prepare myself for warnings of dying of dehydration on the trail, then she smirks. "They sell bottles in the lodge. I strongly recommend you make sure you have what we need before we leave."

"We're all set there," Bryan says.

Fortunately for us, Bryan was thorough and I received four reinforced steel water bottles for Christmas. I actually opened that gift before the envelope that explained the trip—hello, who wants to open a boring envelope first?—so I thought he was super worried about my water intake.

He notices me watching him and smiles, and I can't shake the concern about what he's hiding.

Naomi and Theo exchange worried looks. "Umm, I might need to make a quick stop before we go," Naomi says.

Ronny smiles at her. "That's why I bring it up before we head out."

Naomi gives Ronny a grateful smile. I'm glad our guide was nice and didn't make Naomi feel stupid. It'd be easy to belittle someone for not being prepared, but that's probably not the best way to start off a four-day trip with people you've just met.

Benji holds up a couple energy bars. "Make sure you've got food for the hike. We'll get to the campsite in time for dinner, but the Kaibab's no joke."

They run through the rest of the required supplies, all of which Bryan's taken care of. We skipped the maps since we'll have guides, but we all have flashlights, sunscreen, phone chargers, and a multi-tool pocket knife thing, plus small walkie-talkies since phones won't work at the bottom of the canyon.

We're sent to the lodge for one last bathroom break, and as we gather near a covered shelter, nervous energy ripples through us. By the time the bus rumbles into the lot, I'm ready to jump out of my skin. That energy fills the bus on the short drive and spills out with us as we unload near a sign that says South Kaibab Trailhead.

I pull out my phone to check my messages one last time. The response video has the usual heart and smiley face emojis, and in one side thread a group of die-hard Melties speculate if there's something going on with me and Steph. I glance at her, even though I'm pretty sure she hasn't read the comments. My finger twitches over the shrug emoji, but I like their comments instead.

I switch to the private messages for my video account. The regular notifications are turned off but I like to know when the messages come through because that's where I really connect with people. Sure, lots of strange men proposition me there, but a lot of girls reach out thanking me for explaining a concept they were having trouble with or requesting that I cover certain topics.

Today all the messages are about Jordan. Fricking. Beebe.

What are you waiting for???

You gotta take him down!!

He isn't worthy enough to lick your boots.

I glance at my hiking boots and have to admit, the visual of Jordan licking the Grand Canyon dust from the bottom of my shoes is appealing.

Other messages are more involved, including an analysis of his most recent videos that outlines how I can humiliate him by calling out his surface-level explanations and reliance on his pretty-boy looks.

"I wouldn't call him a pretty boy," I murmur.

This is intense, thanks, I write back. *You've given me lots to think about.*

What I don't say is that I'm not going to use any of it. Would flaming him in front of hundreds of thousands of viewers be epic? Naturally. But I've built my reputation on not getting hung up on the drama that comes with the platform. My videos focus on what I want to tell my followers, not reacting to some no-talent wannabe who thinks slamming his competition is how to get famous.

Even if in this case, he's right.

Nothing he can come up with will top the footage I'll get in the canyon. I'm not sure how it'll all come together, but I can get weeks' worth of material from this trip.

And there's nothing Jordan Fricking Beebe can do about it.

I answer the rest of the messages with a flaming turd emoji or a heart, depending on what they said, then we're strapping on our packs and walking toward the edge of the canyon.

"Did you put on sunscreen?" Mom asks.

"Mom, it's barely fifty degrees out. I'm fine."

She pulls out her bottle and hands it to me. "This trail has very little shade. The last thing you need on top of sore legs and feet is a sunburn."

"Okay, fine." I slather a dollop on my cheeks and glance at Steph and Jess. They both hold out their hands, so I squirt some in their palms before giving the bottle back to Mom. "Thanks."

Steph's been quiet since her minor freak-out since we got out of the car. When we first talked about this trip she seemed excited, but guilt gnaws at me. I claim to be a wonderful friend, so how did I miss how nervous she is?

"Are you sure you're okay with this?" I ask her, my voice low. "I don't want to force you to do anything you're not comfortable with."

Her purple hair practically glows in the early morning light, but it doesn't distract from the tension on her face. "It'll be okay. I'm semi freaking out, but it's 'cause I don't know what to expect." She glances at me. "It's the anticipation, you know?"

Ronny leads us to the end of the sidewalk onto a dirt path, and my stomach flips.

Despite the quickly steepening trail and the fact that I'm very aware of how far away the bottom of the canyon is, a flurry of butterflies let loose in my belly. "I do."

Jess grabs Steph's and my arms. "We've started!"

We jump in a circle, which is more of a bounce considering how much crap we have strapped to our backs, then continue forward with the group.

Sage and Neb lead the way behind Ronny, who's our point—the person who keeps us headed in the right direction—followed by Naomi, Theo, and Hunter. From what I can tell, Hunter and Naomi haven't actually spoken, but their proximity bodes well for Operation Amazing. The parents are behind the three of us, followed by Benji, who's the sweep—the person who makes sure no one gets hurt or left behind. We seemed to naturally fall in line this way, but I'm betting the guides will always be at the front and rear of the group.

A sign warns us that the trail ahead is treacherous and those with physical limitations should proceed with caution. Neb fist bumps it and gives it a nod as we pass, like he's acknowledging the risk and giving the trail respect.

Steph does the same and gives me a sheepish smile. "I'll take all the good karma I can get."

I turn to tap my knuckles against the metal sign, then hurry back to my spot between Steph and Jess. Then stop in my tracks.

The sun's risen high enough to shine on the canyon wall in front of us, and it's like a palette of watercolors exploded across the jagged rock. Every shade of orange and purple in the canyon walls blends with the pinks in the sky and my breath catches in my throat. "How is this real?" I whisper to myself and stumble over a loose rock.

"Careful, Mel," Mom says behind me, and a pulse of frustration shoots through me. I know she's just being my mom, but I hate being treated like a baby.

"Eyes on the road!" Bryan calls from behind her.

Jess sighs. "Are they going to be like this the whole time?"

"I really hope not," I say.

"I'm kind of okay with them keeping us from falling over the edge," Steph says.

The ground begins to steepen, and I'm forced to pay attention to the path. Cacti and small shrubs cover the ground, and everything else is a muted shade of brown. The trail hugs the side of the canyon with a sharp drop-off, the hard-packed dirt a far cry from the sidewalks back home. Then we round a bend and the length of the Grand Canyon stretches out in front of us and none of that matters. My video-brain, as Steph calls it, kicks on and I grab my phone from the pocket on my right thigh.

Because yeah, despite my protests that I wouldn't be caught dead in something this hideous, we're wearing cargo pants. And I've got another pair in my bag.

I swipe to the video app and record the horizon of the opposite edge as far as I can see. Most of my videos have a voice-over laid on top later, so I don't worry about narrating. And I don't know what I'd say anyway. You can only repeat, "This is unbelievable," so many times. As soon as my phone is tucked safely back in my pocket, anxiety about the mistake and being targeted by Jordan Fricking Beebe comes rushing back.

Everything I've worked so hard for could fall apart while we're having the vacation of a lifetime, but I push those thoughts away. I can't do anything else to correct the mistake and I refuse to let him ruin this trip.

The dirt trail is wide enough for two people to walk side by side, but we've fallen into a single file line. Wooden railroad ties cut across the trail every couple feet to break the trail into steps, and my mind flashes to the ramps and elevator lifts everywhere back home. There's no way someone with physical limitations could ever experience this. My privilege makes me feel guilty, then immediately shifts to how I can use that privilege to help others. Maybe I can do a separate video of this hike to show people who can't come here themselves.

"I have an idea for a video," I say.

"Of course you do," Jess says with a laugh.

"I'm just thinking. There probably aren't many people in the world who could ever do this hike. What if I produced something that highlights this trip?"

"How would you get all that into a couple minutes?" Steph asks. The platform allows longer videos but my views drop off after the 90-second mark and plummet at 150 seconds, so I edit them as tight as I can.

"Maybe I'd post it someplace else."

"Ooh, you could do a teaser," Jess says. "Then put the longer video on your website."

"I don't have a website."

"I've been meaning to talk to you about that," Jess says.

Steph looks over her shoulder at me. "It's a good idea."

Mom doesn't say anything, but I imagine her reprimanding me to focus on the scenery in front of us. But I can't turn off my brain. Once it latches onto a new idea, that's all I can think about until it's finished. A website would take some work, but I've tackled harder things before. And I could sell merchandise like Naomi does for her podcast.

But none of that can happen until I respond to the duet, and I still have no idea what that will look like.

Instead I focus on the trail ahead and the expansive views that stretch across the width of the canyon. The trail switches back and forth as we descend, getting steeper with every turn. I try not to think about how long we'll be hiking, but the fact that we left at sunrise to make sure we get to the campsite before dark is more than a little intimidating.

We take another turn, but instead of following the trail, Ronny steps onto a rocky bluff and points at a hand-carved sign the size of a license plate that says *Ooh Ahh Point*. "This is the first stop," she says, her clear voice carrying over the group.

"Five minutes to take pictures, then we're back at it."

"It's actually called Ooh Ahh Point?" Naomi's brow quirks as she studies the small sign.

"Seems appropriate," Hunter says. He taps his knuckles to the sign—apparently that's going to be a thing—and moves past Naomi closer to the drop-off.

"Careful!" Mom says.

Hunter throws her a look that says "really?" before turning back to the view. I join him at the edge, careful not to get too close. "This is amazing," he says, and I hold back a laugh. He bumps his arm against mine. "Go ahead and say it."

"I thought that word was off limits."

He's quiet for a moment, then the others move closer and I don't think he'll answer, but he finally whispers. "I thought so, too."

I loop my arm through his. "I'll spare you right now, but this is not the end of this conversation."

He nods once. "Understood."

We've already been here a couple minutes and in the short time I've known Ronny, she doesn't seem like the type to dawdle. I record another panoramic video, then tuck my phone away and try my best to live in the moment.

Steph moves to my side. "This makes it worth it."

This? My heart wishes she means being so close to me, but she made it clear that she doesn't want a relationship. My heart thuds and my palms sweat despite the cool air. "The pictures online didn't do this justice. It's so... majestic." I shift slightly closer until our shoulders touch. "Are you doing okay?"

She lets out a sigh that tells me she's not, but she's trying. It's the same as when she's studied all night for a test and despite being totally prepared, thinks she's going to fail. "Stops like this help. It breaks it up so I'm not thinking about how far we're actually going to hike today. And it keeps my mind off my parents. "

Benji whistles before I can respond. "Thirty seconds and we're back on the trail." Apparently he's not going to let us linger either.

My hand brushes against Steph's before I can stop it. "Just focus on the path in front of us. We'll be there before you know it."

She gives me a lopsided smile. "You're very wise this morning." Then her smile falls. "Not that you aren't every day. I mean—you know what I mean."

We smile awkwardly as the group files back to the trail. A hawk or eagle—basically a very large bird with a pointy beak and sharp talons—swoops much too close to where we're standing, and we both jump back. We manage to get behind the parents this time, and my shoulders relax despite the heavy pack weighing them down. Mom means well, but sometimes I feel like I can't make a single move without her watching, and I have too much on my mind to add worrying about her to the list.

The trail continues to switch back and forth against the side of the canyon, and a calm quiet falls over the group. Anyone who's ever heard of the Grand Canyon knows that the layers of sedimentary rock are what make it so spectacular, but seeing the layers in person, being able to touch them as you walk by, is like touching history. Thousands, probably millions, of years live in these walls. This canyon was here long before us and will continue standing long after we're gone. It's a sobering thought and makes me more aware of my mortality than anything else I've ever experienced.

And that's not just because one wrong step could send me hurtling to my death.

Okay, maybe not hurtling, but screaming and falling and breaking.

And the canyon will be here tomorrow, like nothing happened.

The trail flattens for a moment and I pull out my phone to take more pictures, careful not to get too close to the edge. The peaks and valleys below us look like another planet, the red dusty rocks and scraggly plants uninhabitable, and I still can't believe we're going to be here for three days.

"The next lookout will have awesome views," Benji says

behind me. He must have stopped when I did, because we're the last two in the group. Steph and Jess must be zoned out because normally they would wait with me.

Benji has a slight vibe like the jocks at my school who think the world exists for them and they're free to take whatever they please, but his gaze stays on my eyes and his hands stay wrapped around the straps of his pack. Maybe he's learned to control that urge that pushes certain classmates to call me lesbo as they pass in the hall. It's a childish, ignorant word that isn't even accurate since I'm bi, but it still hurts.

Or maybe I'm not giving him enough credit and he's actually a nice guy.

"Is there anyplace here that doesn't have awesome views?" I turn away from him and continue walking.

He laughs softly. "You can't see as much closer to the bottom. But the first half is like this. A lot of groups, we have to keep reminding them to pay attention to where they're walking."

I look over my shoulder, my eyes wide. "Has anyone ever fallen?"

He points at the trail. "Here, yes. There," he hooks a thumb at the massive canyon. "No. Not with me anyway."

"I guess that's reassuring?"

He pats my pack but it's so full, all I feel is a slight pressure on my back. "Y'all will be fine. You're better prepared than half the people we see out here."

Despite the compliment, I'm curious how he would even know that based on two seconds of conversation. But I don't dwell on it. Instead I hurry to catch up with the group, pushing Benji and Jordan and any other boys out of my head.

Because this trip is about my family and the two girls in front of me.

Steph turns, waving at me to catch up.

Okay, maybe one girl more than anyone else.

— **8** —

STEPHANIE

"What do we do if we have to pee?" Jess's eyes open extra wide and she scrunches her face in a 'this is semi-urgent' expression.

"The next stop has bathrooms," Benji says from behind us. "Nothing fancy. But it's private."

"Private is good," Jess says, and Mel and I nod along with her.

I've camped exactly one time in my life—in my backyard under a blue tarp that Mamá pretended was a tent. When I dragged my bedding through the grass I swore I wouldn't go inside until morning, but when I snuck inside to use the bathroom, the pokey bushes along the edge of the yard were sharp against my bare skin and once I was sure my parents were asleep, I fell asleep on my unmade bed.

Thinking of my parents is like a punch to the gut. How long does a divorce take? Will they split up before I graduate, or will the next couple months be more of the same, them pretending not to fight when I enter the room, until one day one of them just isn't there anymore? And who will keep the house? Suddenly my visits home from college look very different than I imagined. Instead of baking with Mamá with the latest trashy reality show on in the background, Papá complaining about how it's rotting our brains, one of them will be in a new place, alone.

"How long until that stop?" Jess asks, snapping me out of my mental spiral.

"At least an hour," Benji says.

"We'll shield you if you need to go now," I say. Mel warned us that there might be some al fresco peeing, as she called it, and I really hope I don't have to pop a squat in the middle of a trail.

Jess looks from the high rock walls at the edge of the trail to Benji, who's doing his best to pretend not to listen. "I can hold it."

Up ahead, Theo breaks from our single file row and climbs over a low rock. By the time we reach him, his back is to the trail and his pants are unzipped.

"Show off!" Mel says as we walk by.

"I use my man perks proudly," Theo calls over his shoulder.

A moment later, he falls in step between me and Mel. "How's the view back here?"

"Quite grand," Mel says.

Sometimes I envy her ability to throw out a one-liner without overthinking it, while I always feel like I'm stumbling over my words. I can't even blame English being my second language because my parents taught me English and Spanish at the same time.

Jess laughs, and my envy grows. Even though I know they consider me part of the Bestie Brigade, every once in a while I'm reminded how many years they were friends before I came along. I'll never be able to compete with their history.

The line in front of us stops abruptly. I bump into Nancy, but before I can apologize, she slips an arm around my back. "Do you see it?" She points farther ahead and my breath catches. The largest animal I've ever seen snorts and paws at the trail. Its dark brown fur blends with the reds and browns of the canyon wall and its antlers stretch as wide as the path.

"Is that a deer?" My wild animal experience is limited to the squirrels and raccoons that piss off Papá by knocking over our garbage can the night before trash pickup. This creature looks like it could toss each of us off the cliff without breaking a sweat.

"Elk," Theo says.

"Have you been studying the enemy?" Mel asks, and Theo laughs before tapping the side of his head.

"Teachers know everything."

"I don't know about that," Jess says.

Theo's shoulders slump. "Okay, I looked up what large animals we might encounter so we could be fully prepared." He nudges Mel and she smiles. "No bison out here."

"Thank god," she says, and I'm yanked right back into my emotional turmoil of feeling left out while standing in the middle of the group.

"He shouldn't bother us," Benji says. "But Ronny won't let him get too close."

We watch as the elk eats grass at the edge of the trail, then without warning, he lifts his head and stares directly above us. A moment later, he turns and runs farther down the trail.

Mel, Jess, and I follow where he looked. "What spooked him?" Jess asks.

"We're clear to keep moving," Benji says.

"Should we be worried?" Theo asks. "I feel like we should be worried."

The group starts walking and I fight the urge to rush to the front. "Wild animals have instincts for a reason," I say. "If he's running, I want to run, too."

A moment later, a shower of tiny rocks and dust fall where we'd been standing.

"Rockslide!" Theo shouts, and Benji rushes to his side.

He rests his hand on Theo's arm and leans close. "Hey, hey, hey. You can't yell that out here."

Theo's eyes are as wide as I've ever seen a pair of eyes. He points at where the elk had looked, shaking off Benji's hand. "Did. You. Not. Just. See. Those. Rocks. Fall?" His words come out fast and low, and there's a slight tremor in his voice.

"Theo, rocks fall all the time out here. The canyon is a constantly changing place." Benji spreads his arms wide and faces the edge of the trail. "We're merely passing through."

Mel raises her hand like we're in class. "So, how do we avoid getting caught in one of the changing moments?"

Benji nods, apparently approving of her question. "Keep your wits about you. There's usually a subtle noise when a rock breaks loose. Like stones rolling over concrete."

Theo laughs, a single short bark. "Or keep your eyes on the wild animals and run when they do."

Jess wraps her arms over her chest. "I don't feel reassured."

"Come on," Benji says. "We need to stay with the group."

The group, who's already made it to the next switchback below us. Mel and Jess speed up, stepping over the railroad ties with a new energy, but Theo hangs back next to me.

"I dig your hair," he says.

My fingers immediately tug at the longest strands. It's not completely even thanks to a Tuesday night not too long ago when I decided I wanted a choppy fringe. Mom hates it almost more than the purple. "Thanks."

"Not everyone can pull off that color."

"I had rainbow stripes sophomore year when I came out, but it was too much upkeep." Why am I telling him this? Until yesterday, he was a stranger. Maybe it's because Mel loves him and her opinion means everything to me.

He taps his chest. "Sophomore year for me, too." I look at him quickly, careful not to trip. "Is the purple just for fun, or does it represent?"

I twist a strand around my fingers. "Just for fun."

"I tried purple and blue but my hair's too dark and bleaching first seemed like a lot of work."

Everyone knows the rainbow represents all LGBTQ people, but not everyone knows there's different color combinations for bi, pan, trans, enby, asexual, and at least half a dozen others. Blue, purple, and pink represent bisexuality, so I'm guessing this is Theo's way of telling me he's bi.

"My natural color is dark brown, so yeah, I've spent some quality time with hair bleach. It's not so bad once you get used to it."

He shakes his head and smiles. "I've seen every color with my students. I'd pay you to teach them how to make it look this good."

Heat flushes my cheeks. So far all I'd seen of Theo's personality is that he likes to make everyone laugh. This softer side is unexpected.

"Mel said you got into the University of Oregon," he says. "I transferred there after two years at a community college near home. And now I teach in Bend."

"I'm pretty sure you and Naomi are why she's obsessed with Oregon. Especially you."

"It's nice to have someone you know nearby." His brow quirks. "That'd be cool if you and Mel were both Ducks."

"Yeah, it would be. If she goes." My voice sounds too high-pitched. Having one of my best friends there will make being away from home a lot easier, but I haven't said that to Mel because I want it to be her decision.

He glances at me from the corner of his eye. "It sounds like that's what she wants."

I give him my steadiest smile. "I hope so." Then I turn my attention back to the trail. Theo picks up on my unspoken message and we walk in a comfortable silence. Benji's still right behind us, and I wonder how many secrets he's heard out here. He doesn't react when I catch his eye, he just smiles and keeps his focus on where we're headed.

Someone shouts up ahead and Benji laughs.

"Every time," he whispers.

Mel and I exchange confused looks.

There's another whoop, this one echoing off the canyon walls, repeating over and over until it fades to nothing.

"What's going on?" Mel asks.

"We're almost to Cedar Point. And bathrooms."

"Oh, hells yes!" Jess shouts, adding her voice to the cheers.

The pace speeds up, and soon we're at the next stop. The moms rush to the pair of wooden outhouses tucked against the canyon wall, Jess right behind them. The rest of us drop our packs and crowd near the edge of the trail to look out over the gaping hole in the earth. No one talks, and a sense of calm sweeps through me.

We only stay long enough for everyone to pee, then we're back at it. The trail switches back and forth so much I forget what it's like to walk in a straight line, and each step over the rough wooden railroad ties feels like I'm inching toward something unknown. Getting away from real life is exactly what I needed, but I'm worried about what's waiting for me at home.

After what seems like fifteen thousand switchbacks, there's another shout from the front of the line. We look back at Benji, who juts his chin ahead of us. "Skeleton Point. And our first view of the Colorado River."

Bags drop to the ground and we gather at the lookout. The words to describe how incredible this place is don't exist in my head. Mountain-like plateaus sit in a row like squat buildings that get narrower at the top and they seem to go on forever. "They're like nature's pyramids."

Naomi nods. "It's incredible that anything this big exists." She quickly points a finger at Theo in warning, and he presses a hand to his chest.

"I'm offended you think I would make a joke about your incredulity at something being so large," he says. "I'm as amazed as you are."

Hunter's head snaps toward Theo, and I swear a faint blush colors his cheeks.

Naomi's cheeks redden, too, but that could be from the hike.

Ronny points past the sign that reads Skeleton Point. "If you go around the corner you can see the Colorado River."

The others move like a herd of wild animals, but the three of us hang back.

"Did you see that?" Mel whispers to me and Jess.

"Did we see what?" Jess waves at the peaks and valleys in front of us. "Everything here is mind-blowing."

It's like another world exists below the surface. The hoodoos—small peaks that almost look like statues—and plateaus follow an empty space that must be the Colorado River, like nature built its own city here at the bottom of the earth.

"Naomi and Hunter!" Mel whisper-shouts. "Theo said their magic word and they both blushed."

Theo's moved closer to the edge and is chatting with Neb and Sage. He seems super laid back, like nothing bothers him, and yet it's like he knows exactly what to say to each person to push them toward what they want.

Mel's excitement is hard to ignore, even if I still don't really get the whole amazing thing. "They're going to make this easy," she says.

"Tell me again why you're so determined to get them back together?" I ask. Hunter and Naomi are standing close enough to talk, but stare quietly at the landscape. I can see how they'd make a cute couple, but that's not enough reason to push two people together. Brooklyn and I are a perfect example of that.

Mel sighs and holds her clasped hands over her heart. "Because I've never seen my brother as happy as he was when they were together. He fought it at first. Had this whole thing about how relationships had to wait until he was done with school, blah blah, but Naomi..." She sighs again. "Naomi was impossible for him to ignore."

Something in my chest stirs at her words. Even though I said I want to be single, I still hope my perfect person is out there.

"So why did they break up?" I ask.

"It wasn't their time," Mel says.

My head jerks toward her. I figured it was the distance, or one of them found someone else, or another storybook reason two people can't make it work. "But now it is?"

She shrugs. "I don't know. I hope so." Her eyes water as she watches her brother. "He's done so much for me. I want to give that back, you know?"

A lump catches in my throat. Not because I want to help Hunter be happy, but because Mel's so genuine and caring and compassionate and I don't know what I did to deserve her as a friend. "He's lucky to have you." My voice is scratchy, and she quirks a brow at me.

"Are you feeling the love, Stephita?" A smile plays on her lips and the stirring in my heart grows. I love that our friendship is so strong that we can tease and still know we care for each other.

"You make it hard not to."

"It'd be really cool if we were both Ducks," she whispers.

I loop our arms together and rest my head against hers. "That would make me really happy." It's the closest I've come to telling her I really hope she chooses Oregon, but saying the words out loud feels like I'm asking her to choose me over Jess.

She angles her face to look at me.

My gaze jumps from the flecks of gold in her hazel eyes to the tiny scar on her nose from some unknown injury. My finger brushes the scar. "How'd you get this?"

Mel blinks when I touch her. Her breath is warm on my face and she looks down at me with an expression I've never seen before. At least not from her. Brooklyn used to look at me like this right before she leaned in for a kiss, but that's not what Mel's thinking. We're friends. Close friends. The kind of friends who hug and touch and aren't afraid to be affectionate with each other.

She smiles. "Video accident."

I tilt my head in confusion.

Mel looks past me. "Remember when I dropped those wooden blocks on my face?"

Jess laughs from behind me, and I quickly step back. If Jess thinks anything's weird about how close we were standing, she doesn't show it. "I still can't believe you thought you could balance all of those on your head."

Mel touches the spot on her nose where my finger was. "I was trying to demonstrate balance and counterbalance with wooden blocks, and it went very, very bad."

This sounds familiar. "I've seen that video. You showed how you could balance a stack of blocks in each hand. But you were holding them." I don't recall a cut on Mel's face in that video.

"Holy backlist, Batman," Mel says. Her voice is teasing, but her brows rise in appreciation. "We recorded that the summer before high school."

I shrug off the comment. "What can I say. The drive to my abuela's is really long."

Mel touches her scar again. "I didn't use the part where I hurt myself. Back then I was still nervous about seeming less than perfect."

"Five minutes!" Ronny shouts.

Mel gives me a lingering look before she and Jess run to the toilets, leaving me wondering what just happened.

9

MELODY

My breathing finally returns to normal once we're back on the trail and Steph is safely behind me. Something shifted at Skeleton Point—there's a phrase you don't say every day—and for a second I thought we might kiss.

I wanted her to kiss me.

But there's no way. She just broke up with her girlfriend and she's worried about her parents. Her emotions are on edge. That's all I saw.

Besides, my propensity to always think in video clips and my not-so-mild obsession with the old show Myth Busters has driven away everyone I've dated. People say that if you're friends before you date, the relationship can be even stronger, but what if it doesn't work out? If something did happen with Steph and then I drove her away, I'll not only be brokenhearted, I won't have my friend to run to for comfort.

I pull out my phone to record the rock formations jutting up all around us, even though I'm not sure yet how I'll use it. As they say on the show, if it's worth doing, it's worth overdoing. When I'm coming up with ideas for content, they start out blurry and I have to focus on the parts that will be good. Kind of like with real cameras. The ones that don't have phones and games and all that. My photojournalism teacher complains that smart phones have made photographers lazy, but I don't feel guilty for using the tools people way smarter than me have invented.

With real cameras, you have to manually turn the dials to get the aperture to capture what you're looking at, and sometimes you miss things that are moving too fast, although I don't think that'll be a problem out here. These rocks haven't moved in thousands of years.

Most of them, anyway.

The trail shifts into a series of switchbacks that lead us closer and closer to the Colorado River and the bottom of the Grand Canyon. The views, which have been breathtaking and spectacular and every other flowery adjective I can think of, open even more and it's unlike anything I imagined. As far as we can see, plateaus jut into the air, the layered rock beneath them telling stories of the thousands of years it took for them to get to this place right here, right now.

"How many people do you think have done this?" Steph asks.

My brain jumps back to thoughts of us kissing, and Benji speaks as I fumble for a response.

"Only one percent of the people who visit the canyon actually go to the bottom. Roughly fifty thousand a year."

"And the Havasupai tribe still live here, so they do for sure," Jess says.

Benji points across the canyon. "A number of tribes had settlements in and around the canyon. The Navajo learned to herd sheep and weave blankets from the Spanish, and they still sell the blankets."

"That would be a cool thing to bring home," Jess says.

"The tribes rely on tourism," Benji says. "Most of the land surrounding the canyon is reservations."

We fall silent after that. At some point Hunter works his way toward the back of the row and walks next to me. "This is incredible."

I appreciate that he's making time to hang out with me. We used to be closer, and even though I know I'm the one who pulled away, I miss the connection we used to have. "It's so much better than I imagined."

"Kind of makes everything else feel less important, right?" he asks.

An eagle circles lazily in the distance. A weird sense of vertigo hits me and my vision blurs. The eagle's flying thousands of feet in the air, but he's at the same height as us. One wrong step and we could be his next meal. I move closer to the rough canyon wall and take a deep breath until everything comes back into focus.

The layers of Hunter's words weigh on me like the rock surrounding us. All the things on my mind.

Bryan's secret.

My decision about school.

The video mistake.

And Steph, but Hunter doesn't need to know about that.

I answer him indirectly. "My thighs are burning, but it's totally worth it."

We make our way around another switchback and my gaze travels along the horizon. Living in California, I'm used to it being dry and barren, but this is how I imagine Mars—all dust and rocks and a completely uninhabitable landscape.

"What's going on?" Hunter asks.

Steph and Jess give me a sympathetic smile as they step around us. Now we're at the back of the line and Benji's about to learn another secret.

"Talk to me, Mel."

It'd be easy to unload my concerns about Bryan. To get Hunter's opinion on what he might be hiding and not carry that alone. But I don't want to accuse my stepdad of something until I know for sure what it is. "I don't know what to do about college."

"I thought you'd already made up your mind about Long Beach?"

I silence the voice in my head insisting that I should be a good girl, take the scholarship, and move on with my mediocre life. "Hunt, I know the logical choice is to stay in California. It won't put me in debt for the next thirty years and will basically give me the same education." And I'm sure I'll make friends and be happy.

"But that's not what you want."

I shake my head.

Hunter knows better than anyone that just because something seems logical, that doesn't mean it's the right decision. He went to his dream school and ended up leaving because the dream eventually got bigger than his reality. "Is there a way to make Oregon work?"

"I don't know." The unspoken fear hangs in the air between us: What makes me so special that I can turn down a scholarship simply because I want something different?

"Have you talked to Mom?" My eyebrows rise so high he laughs. "Okay, fair. But give her a chance. I was terrified to tell her I wanted to leave Berkeley, but she was surprisingly supportive."

The trail levels out and everyone slows. The same scrubby bushes that were on the trail dot the open space and rocks border the edge of the trail.

"This is Tip Off, where our trail intersects with the Tonto Trail," Benji says. "We're on the Tonto Plateau."

"That's why it's so flat," Hunter says.

My eyes roll on their own. "Yes, thank you. I passed Geography in eighth grade."

Hunter scowls, and I reach for his arm.

"Sorry. Snark is a reflex and it's especially bad when I'm on edge."

Theo comes out of nowhere and points at where the trail drops off into nothing. "You're definitely on edge here."

Bryan holds up a sheet of paper. "Is this the last stop before we reach the Colorado?"

Ronny nods. "Now's a good time to grab a snack and rest your legs. The hike is steep from here on out."

"So what was that?" Theo points up the trail from where we came.

"A warm-up." Benji says under his breath with a smirk, then quickly grows serious. "Y'all are doing great and we'll get to the campsite with plenty of daylight. But let's try to keep up the pace." His gaze sweeps over all of us but I swear it lingers on me.

"Just because we're in the back of the line doesn't mean we're the slowest," I say to no one.

"Want to be at the front after this?" Steph asks.

"Yeah!" Jess shouts. "Let's show this canyon who's boss!"

We inhale jerky and dried fruit while resting on large rocks near the trail. Three hikers with walking sticks and packs like ours pass by, then two guys Hunter's age jog by with light packs and looks of pure determination on their faces.

"Aren't their packs too light?" Naomi asks.

"They're day trippers," Ronny says between sips of water. We all watch her, waiting for an explanation. "They're hiking down and back in one day."

"My legs would fall off," Theo says. "We've already surpassed my comfort zone for physical activity."

As the guys disappear down the trail, my gaze follows the trail toward the top of the canyon. We're so far down that the surface is no longer visible, and a spike of panic thrums through me. It's not normal to be inside the earth, even if we can still see the sky. And we're supposed to sleep down here? A low buzzing drowns out the others' conversation, and I rock gently back and forth.

Steph grabs my hand and squeezes. Her skin is warm against mine and I instinctively lean toward her. "I thought I was the one freaking out?"

I look up, confused.

She runs her other hand over my arm before squeezing my hand again. "It's okay to admit you're scared."

"Oh, god, was I groaning out loud?"

Jess presses closer on my other side. "I don't think anyone else noticed. But what's going on?"

I struggle for a breath, focusing on a row of prickly bushes lining the edge of the trail. "I guess I've had so much on my mind that I didn't give much thought to what it'd be like once we got here. Now it's too late to turn around and we're about to spend three days at the bottom of the earth. It feels like a lot, you know?"

Their eyes never leave my face as I talk, and the pressure in my chest loosens.

Steph leans against my arm. "Kind of makes you wonder how we all convinced each other this would be fun."

"It will be fun," Jess stands, looking beyond our group to the small white rocks that mark where the trails cross. "It's already fun. I mean, it's exhausting, but it's really cool that we get to experience this together, you know?"

I smile up at her. "I do know."

"We'll figure out a video that will make the internet forget all about Jordan Fricking Beebe," she adds.

"Challenge accepted," Steph says, standing next to Jess.

They each hold out a hand and pull me to my feet.

"Let's show this canyon who's boss," I repeat Jess's earlier statement. Maybe if I say it enough, it'll sink into my bones and I'll believe it.

A few minutes later, we're back on the trail, and the guides weren't exaggerating. This trail is steep. Mom and Nancy pull out collapsible walking sticks from the sides of their packs and I wish I hadn't rolled my eyes at Mom when she offered to buy me a set as well. Walking downhill sounds simple enough, but after hours of nothing but decline, the pressure on my knees and the front of my thighs has my entire body trembling.

The mid-afternoon sun warms the air and brightens the shades of brown and red that surround us. Ronny peeks over her shoulder at us, a smile playing on her lips.

"Why do I feel like you're plotting something?" I ask.

She laughs. "The next turn is my favorite part. I love watching newbies' reactions."

"This isn't gonna turn into a Cliffhanger situation, is it?" Jess asks. We came downstairs when Mom was watching the '90s movie right after they booked this trip and were properly traumatized by the scene with the woman dangling off a bridge thousands of feet in the air. Mom swore that wouldn't happen to us, but you can never be too sure.

Ronny full-on snorts, and I decide I like her. "There is a bridge up ahead."

My eyes widen. Mom was wrong.

"There really is a bridge?" Steph asks.

Jess swats at us. "It's not gonna be like in the movie."

"Does that mean we're almost to the river?" I ask.

Naomi rushes up behind me, making me jump. "Did I hear we're almost to the bridge?"

Ronny gestures where the trail curves sharply. "Almost there."

"You know," Naomi says. "That would be a pretty cool place to get a group selfie."

"I volunteer Neb!" Theo shouts.

Neb cocks his head from farther down the trail.

"You've got the longest arms," Theo says.

He shrugs, and I shake off my Cliffhanger fears. Based on how many barriers were at the top of the canyon, there's no way the park people would have a bridge that we could fall off.

We round the corner and the canyon opens up, revealing the brownish-green river responsible for everything around us. It's definitely got a current, but it's not raging or thrashing like I imagined, it's just working its way past us like it has every day for thousands of years. The water goes right to the edge of the rock wall and it feels like we're in the bottom of a quarry, except this isn't manmade. Far from it.

"This is unreal," Naomi says.

Neb moves past us down the trail and is already on the bridge when it comes into view. Metal fencing rises as high as my shoulders and is topped with black steel that looks strong enough to survive a rock slide. Wooden slats connect the two sides. Neb's standing in the middle, staring up toward the surface with what can only be described as wonderment.

The rest of the group clomps onto the bridge, and for a moment my stomach flutters. After so many hours of hiking, the bottom of the Grand Canyon is right here.

But it's still far enough below us that falling, while not necessarily killing us, could definitely cause severe bodily harm.

"Everyone get behind Neb." Naomi hands him her phone.

He turns so he's facing the direction we came from and stretches out his arm with the camera pointing at us. We spread out along the length of the bridge, everyone jostling to make sure they're in the frame. Steph links her arms through mine and Jess's, and excitement pushes away my nerves. We squeeze and giggle and smile for the camera, and there's nowhere else I'd rather be.

"We did it!" Jess says.

"Almost," Steph replies, voicing my thoughts.

"When did you two become so pessimistic?" Jess asks.

My lips press together and I search for the words to explain how I'm feeling. "This hike is huge. Like bucket-list huge. I still can't believe we're here, and that we're almost to the bottom."

"But there's still that tiny bit of nerves that something bad could happen," Steph says, and I nod.

"Why is that?" I ask.

Naomi slides closer and boops the tip of my nose. "You need to focus on the good that can happen. Tell me three good things." For as long as I've known her, Naomi has sworn that you can find three good things in any situation. Her first podcast was founded on that idea and it's what led to her success today.

"We've made it this far," I say.

"The obvious beauty of the canyon," Jess says.

Steph raises a finger. "When we get to the campsite, we won't have to move for two days if we don't want to."

"That sounds like heaven," Theo says. "I've already obliterated my weekly step goal."

Naomi tousles his hair, then jumps away, closer to Sage and Neb. "Don't listen to him. He works out at the gym but will never admit it because he has an image to preserve." She air quotes the last part, and once again I'm reminded how similar

I am to Theo. There are things I want that I'm too afraid to admit because I don't know how others will react. That's surely not the healthiest way to go through life, but I never claimed to be perfect.

Steph loosens her grip on my arm, and her fingers gently squeeze mine before she leans against the barricade. "Cliffhanger could totally happen here."

"You girls stop it," Mom says. "No one's falling off this bridge."

Ronny bangs her hand against the metal fencing to get our attention and the three of us squeal. "We need to keep moving."

I pull out my phone and record more footage, then we're back on the trail.

As we take the final steps to the bottom, I know I should be amazed by the majesty surrounding us, but I just want this to be over. The rock walls seem to lean in closer, making it impossible to see the surface.

"The bottom is seriously lacking majestic awe," says Theo, pouting at the sky.

"I can't believe we hiked all of this," Steph says.

The sense of accomplishment is unlike anything I've ever felt. Going viral with my videos and building a reputation as a scientist is wonderful, but this is totally different. Hiking six and a half miles to the bottom of the canyon seemed impossible when Mom and Bryan first brought up the trip, but here we are.

As if she can read my thoughts, Mom moves next to me. "Pretty amazing that we did this, right?" She slaps her hand over her mouth and lowers her voice. "Are we allowed to use that word?"

Jess and Steph giggle as I nod. "We're plotting to get them back together."

"Lord help them," Mom says.

"But, yes," I say. "Thank you for making this trip happen. I know I wasn't always the most enthusiastic, but this is incredible."

She wraps her arm around my shoulder and hugs me to her side. "I want to thank you for welcoming Bryan into the family.

Adding a new person is never perfect, but I appreciate the effort you've made to make him feel at home."

"Of course, Mom." I should tell her about the phone call. Maybe she knows about it and he's not keeping secrets that could destroy our new family before he fully settles in.

Before she can say more, the trail widens and a clearing stretches in front of us. "This is Phantom Ranch," Ronny says. "Bathroom, meals, pay phones, and med center are all here. The Bright Angel Campground is farther down this path."

We walk past tidy rows of brown wooden cabins no bigger than a school bus and other stone structures that look like they've endured years of harsh weather. Benches sit in welcoming groups beneath scraggly trees and the dusty trail winds past the lodge. The ever-present canyon walls make a striking backdrop, sheltering us from the outside world.

"I think that's where we get food," Jess says.

"Just a bit farther," Ronny says.

"I don't believe you," Theo whines from behind us, and Ronny smirks over her shoulder.

A few minutes later, she stops and turns to face us. "This is where the campground begins. Be sure to put all your food in the metal boxes. All of it." Her eyes travel over each of us and when we nod, a smile breaks over her face. "See you in the morning!"

She and Benji wave as they head farther down the trail, then we're on our own.

"Cheers to our home for the next couple nights." Bryan holds up his water bottle. Most of us are dragging our feet, too exhausted to care, but he seems energized.

Mom taps her bottle against his, then hugs him and stands on her toes to kiss his cheek. "Happy wedding."

My heart suddenly feels too big for my chest. What if he's hiding something huge, like a secret family or astronomical debt that could bankrupt us? The heartbreak would crush Mom. If I can protect her from that, the way she's protected me my entire life, I need to try.

Steph taps her finger to my forehead. "Why the scowl?"

I blink away my thoughts and sigh. "Just feeling like I don't appreciate my mom enough. Like I've been ungrateful for all this."

"You're not ungrateful. In fact—" Her gaze drops to the ground between us. "One of the things I like most about you is how much you do appreciate everything." I tilt my head and she continues. "You don't take things for granted like lots of kids our age. And you always say what you're thinking."

I'm suddenly aware of how close we're standing. Her breath tickles my chin and when her eyes flick to my lips, my breath stops. "Th-thank you for saying that." Even though I can't say what I'm thinking right now.

Is it possible she can tell just by looking at me?

"Am I interrupting?" Jess has a weird look on her face, and her tone is snarkier than usual. She can switch from cheerleader to sus-leader pretty quickly, but this is different. She seems suspicious.

Steph and I step apart, and my breath returns in a rush.

"Mel's worried about her mom," Steph says.

Jess watches the moms and Bryan turn in slow circles in the center of the campsite. From the smile on his face you'd never know we hiked all day. Or maybe he's really good at hiding his true feelings.

"She seems fine," Jess says.

"It's not a big deal," I say. I don't know why she's suddenly acting so distant. "I just need to get over myself."

Bryan waves us to a clearing tucked between trees and grasses and ringed with large rocks similar to what lined the trail on the hike down. Each site has a ten-foot pole, a metal picnic table, and a pair of metal boxes the size of coolers. With the river gurgling nearby, you wouldn't know we were standing at the bottom of a canyon. It seems like any other place I've camped.

"We've got to fit five tents in two sites," Bryan says. "Margo, Nancy, and I will take one end so you kids can all be together."

Naomi sighs next to me. "Which means I'm in the old folks section." Because she's sharing a tent with her mom.

I elbow her arm. "You could always swap with Theo."

Her eyes go wide, and a moment later she bites her lower lip and points at me.

My shoulders lift. "I'm just saying, Hunter could be fun to share a tent with." My nose wrinkles. "Ew, no. I can't believe I said that."

Naomi bursts out laughing, drawing the attention of my dear brother. I raise my brows and purse my lips, gesturing toward Naomi, but he shakes his head and picks a spot for his tent.

Neb and Sage pick a spot closest to the water, which leaves me, Jess, and Steph closest to the trail. Jess pulls the tent from her pack—she offered to carry it so Steph and I put some of her things in our bags—and we get to work setting it up.

Half an hour later, we're sitting inside on our mats with our things spread out around us, and I finally relax. Steph's sprawled on her back with her eyes closed, and I have to stop myself from staring at how vulnerable she looks with her eyes closed. We've had plenty of sleepovers, but we don't actually go to sleep until long after the lights are out and I don't think I've ever noticed how peaceful she looks.

Or how inviting.

Jess makes a noise in her throat.

"You okay?" I ask.

She shoves on her campsite shoes—the ones meant for walking around so we can give our hiking boots a break—and scowls at me. Jess, who hasn't scowled at me since we were in middle school and I chose Nelly over her. Her gaze flicks between me and Steph and her scowl deepens. "Yeah, just great."

Before I can say another word, she unzips the tent flap and stomps outside.

10
STEPHANIE

"What was that about?" I ask without opening my eyes. I want to open my eyes, I do, but I'm so tired. My legs feel like they weigh two hundred pounds and my lower back aches from carrying my pack almost seven miles to the bottom of the Grand Fricking Canyon.

But I did it.

We all did.

And no one died.

My lips curve into a smile and I open my eyes to find Mel watching me.

"I'm not really sure," she says. "I was zoned out and she got all pissy and stormed off." Something flickers in her eyes and she looks away for a second.

"That's not like her."

Mel shakes her head, making her ponytail brush against her cheek. I push onto my elbows and she rolls onto her side, closer to me.

"I'll go talk to her." The urge to stay here in this bubble with Mel surprises me. But we've got days to hang out. Right now the most important thing is making sure Jess is okay. Because if she's mad, this whole trip will suck.

"That's probably a good idea." Her voice is almost sad, like she doesn't want me to leave either.

My back protests as I sit up so I stretch forward to reach my toes. "My legs feel like I hiked a canyon." Mel snorts, which makes me smile. Then I roll to my feet and head outside to find Jess.

It doesn't take long. She's sitting on top of the picnic table near the edge of the campsite. The other tents are mostly put together, but everyone must be inside them because we're the only ones out here. She looks up when I approach and rolls her eyes before she turns away. I sit on the bench next to her feet and lean against the table.

The trees form a canopy over and around the campsite, shielding our five tents from the rest of the world. If someone dropped you here blindfolded, you'd never know where you were.

"Do you know where Benji and Ronny are staying?" I ask.

Jess nods through the trees. "They set up their tents on another campsite. Mr. Carlson said he hired them for our whole trip so they can guide us on other hikes while we're down here."

That sounds familiar, but honestly, I was so nervous about the hike I didn't pay much attention to the rest of the details. "I didn't realize there'd be so many trees," I say. When she doesn't respond, I keep rambling. "I figured it would be like we were on another planet. All rocks and dust and maybe some cactuses."

"Cacti," Jess says, and I fight back a smile.

I lean my shoulder against her leg and rest my head on her knee. "What's going on?"

"Something's changed between you two."

My head pops up. Has it? I feel like we've gotten closer recently, but friendships do that, right?

She shakes her head. "Don't deny it. Maybe you're not sure or you're scared or I don't know what, but I know you both better than anyone and I'm telling you, something is different."

Yeah, there've been a couple times when I thought Mel looked at me differently. Okay, more than a few times. Earlier, when I wanted to stay in the tent with her, our connection felt stronger than normal, but that's all part of friendship. "I—I don't know what to say."

Jess meets my eyes for a moment before looking to the sky. "I'm not mad. I don't want you to think that. But we've always been the Bestie Brigade and all of a sudden I feel like a third wheel."

I twist around on the bench so I'm facing her. "No! You and Mel have been friends forever. If anything, I'm the third wheel." My fingers trace the smooth edge of the metal table. "I'm always secretly afraid you're gonna decide you've had enough of the Bestie Brigade, disprove the myth that I'm an essential part of the group, and declare me busted."

She smirks. "She got you to watch Myth Busters?"

"Maybe a couple episodes," I admit. "But you're not and will never be a third wheel."

"But you two are traipsing off to Oregon together while I'm stuck in Bakersfield trying to figure out what to do with the rest of my life."

"Mel hasn't decided where she's going yet."

She purses her lips, then her gaze drops to her lap.

"Hey," I say. "It's okay to not have your future figured out. We're still in high school." I avoid the part about Mel and me being at the same school and leaving her alone.

"For two more months."

I grab her hands and look in her eyes. "You've got time to figure it out. And we'll help you. Because the Bestie Brigade is not a myth, it's one hundred percent confirmed."

This time she laughs, and the sparkle is back in her eyes. "Enough with the Myth Busters!" She looks over my shoulder as Mel approaches. Mel sits next to Jess on the tabletop and wraps an arm around her waist.

"Are we good?" Mel asks.

Jess nods against her head. "Yeah."

Soon the others emerge from their tents and Margo claps her hands together to get everyone's attention. It used to scare the crap out of me, but Mel does it too, and now it's just part of the fun of the Thompson family. Well, Thompson-Carlson.

Margo points through the trees toward the stone and wooden building not far from our campsite. "As you all know, we're getting our meals from Phantom Ranch. They're ready at 6:30 sharp and I need a few people to help."

Sage and Naomi raise their hands, and Neb and Hunter quickly join them. A smile brightens Mel's face and I realize Operation Amazing has the added perk of keeping her distracted from the video and her decision about school, and if that makes her happy, I'll do whatever I can to help.

A firepit with rocks bigger than my head sits in the center of the clearing. Bryan sends Theo to collect sticks, and Jess follows. Nancy, Naomi and Hunter's mom, smiles at me and Mel. "How'd you two get the lucky straw?"

I cock my head, but Mel laughs. "I swear we'll offer to help next time," she says. "But I don't think I can walk another step until I eat."

Bryan gives her a steady look. "Be sure to stretch your legs—'specially your hammies. Otherwise you really won't be able to walk tomorrow." He shifts his gaze to me. "Or the next day."

My laugh comes out strangled. "Good thing we don't have to go anywhere for a couple days." I know he's trying hard to fit into the family, but he can be so awkward.

"Oh girls," Nancy says. "You won't want to miss the hiking around here. It won't have the same vertical as today, but it's supposed to be breathtaking."

"And we might have a couple surprises in store," Bryan says as Theo and Jess return with their arms full of sticks. They drop the pile next to Bryan and Theo waves Jess to the edge of the clearing, where they whisper to each other.

"What do you think that's about?" I ask.

Mel watches them for a moment before answering. "Hard to say. But Theo's got a magical ability to make people feel better without them realizing he's doing it, so hopefully he's helping."

Jess glances our way and smiles, but it's the smile she gives teachers when they catch us talking in class. Like she's doing something wrong.

I don't have time to worry about it because the group arrives with stacks of cardboard boxes that they set on the picnic table in the old folks' section.

"Dinner's served!" Margo says as we hurry over. "There's beef and veggie stew, salads and cornbread, and brownie bars for dessert."

"Thanks," Sage says, grabbing two vegetarian boxes and handing one to Neb.

I tear into my box, not caring what's inside. The snacks on the trail kept us going, but it feels like it's been a week since breakfast. The stew is missing the kick of chipotle powder Mamá usually adds to our meals, but right now, this is the best stew I've ever had.

There aren't chairs since there's no way we were carrying those on the hike, so we're stuck with one lonely picnic table on each campsite. But no one seems to care. Except for the scrape of spoons on bowls, it's completely silent.

Even after people finish eating, no one moves. The sun has already lowered past the horizon high above us, and the moon peeks through the trees ringing the campsite, hinting at what's to come with the eclipse the day after tomorrow.

I lean close to Mel. "Do we tell scary stories now?"

She rolls her eyes. "I wish." When I tilt my head, she laughs. "Just wait."

A few minutes later, Nancy and Naomi get up to collect everyone's trash and Margo claps. "I know we're all tired and need to go to bed soon, but I'd really love it if we could all chat a little first."

Theo and Mel groan, but the rest of us exchange nervous looks. Why does this need an announcement? Doesn't chatting before bed happen naturally?

Nancy moves to Margo's side and Theo groans again. "I thought we were off the hook when there wasn't homework this time," he says.

Nancy shoots him a look that shuts him up. "We thought a group email with this many people might get out of hand."

"That's your only reason?" he asks.

Naomi throws a twig at him and it bounces off his arm.

"As I was saying," Margo says. "Our families should have expected this, so I'm a little surprised you didn't see this coming, Theo."

Sage and Neb shoot nervous looks to Naomi while Bryan crosses his arms over his chest and watches his wife with a smile. I try to catch Mel's eye, but she's focused on Margo, and Jess seems to have completely aligned herself with Theo.

She won't even look our way.

"In the past," Margo says, "we've asked everyone to share their thoughts and feelings about the trip, as well as any personal struggles you may be working through."

Nancy continues. "Because we're all tired and there are ten of us, we'll skip the thoughts about the trip and jump right into the good stuff."

"Didn't we already do this?" I whisper to Mel.

"Confessional two point oh," she whispers back. "Now with more depth and emotion."

Margo smiles at the group, her eyes a little wider than necessary. "I know we touched on this at breakfast, but we're hoping we can dig a little deeper."

Mel quirks her brow at me and I hold back a laugh.

"We're already as deep as we can go," Theo says, waving an arm at the canyon walls.

Margo ignores Theo, moving next to Bryan and resting her hand on the back of his neck. "I have to admit, my life is pretty close to perfect right now." Bryan turns to smile at her and she drops a kiss on his lips.

Mel stiffens next to me.

"But every relationship needs work, no matter how good it is," Margo says. "I'm hoping this time away from our regular lives will reinforce what we've committed to each other, while also bringing the four of us closer together as a family."

"Oh, so we're jumping right in," I say.

Mel blinks a few times before nodding. "You have to say something, but you don't have to say everything." Her hand finds mine beneath the table and she squeezes. "Just talk more about the end of high school or college or whatever. You don't need to share about your parents."

"Thanks." Her thumb's tracing the back of my hand, over and over, and I don't know if she even realizes she's doing it.

Bryan kisses Margo's cheek and I try not to squirm. It's wonderful to see adults in a happy relationship. So much better than what I have at home. And what's coming in the next months.

"I think you all know how excited I am to bring the moon to honeymoon," Bryan says. Everyone groans and he smiles like he told the best joke in the world. "I've seen lunar eclipses from the ocean and from the top of Mount Rainier. That was a guided tour and I almost didn't make it to top, but that feeling when I did…" He presses a hand to his chest and closes his eyes for a moment. "I've been on a mission to see celestial events in unique places ever since. Being at what feels like the center of the earth for the extraterrestrial experience in two days is—" He looks to the sky and does a chef's kiss with his fingers to his mouth. "It's like I'm completing a lifelong dream."

I glance around the campsite. Everyone's watching Bryan, but Neb seems transfixed.

Bryan reaches for Margo's hand and kisses her knuckles. "Margo covered everything else for me. I agree that family is important and I hope this time together will help us get to know each other better."

Hunter gives him a warm smile and when Bryan turns his gaze to Mel, she tightens her grip on my hand. This time it's my turn to squeeze, and when I do, she inhales sharply. She must also smile, because Bryan looks away with a content look on his face.

Nancy leans forward with her elbow on her knees. "While these two are sinking deeper into wedded bliss, I'm doing a bit of the opposite." Naomi and Margo both move like they're about to get up, but she waves them off. "It's fine. I'm fine."

Naomi ignores her mom's pointed look and crosses the open space to sit next to her. She wraps an arm around her mom's waist and they press their heads close. Their red curls mingle together, and Nancy straightens like she's pulling energy from her daughter.

"This trip, this week away, will help me reach the clarity I've been unable to find at home in my everyday life."

Is that what I need? Clarity?

Nancy searches each of our faces and my skin flushes when she smiles at me. It's like she can read my thoughts. Can see well enough in the fading light to know I'm not gonna tell the group I'm barely hanging on. "I've been on my own for a long time. I need to look inside myself to remember how strong I am."

Margo rushes to Nancy and grabs her in a hug. Their whispers are too low for us to hear, but when they pull away, they're both wiping tears from their eyes.

"I don't have a ton to add," Sage says. Her hands fold tightly in her lap and she looks at Naomi, who nods. "There was a time when my life was falling apart all around me. But now I'm in a really good place, and there honestly isn't much else that I need."

Neb reaches for her hand and my heart melts. It actually melts.

"Life goals," Mel whispers.

"I hate to be cliché," Neb says. "But I'm with Sage in that good place." They share a smile that makes me both jealous and a little uncomfortable, like we shouldn't be watching this.

Theo cups his hands around his mouth and shouts, "Get a room!"

Sage looks down like she's embarrassed, but Neb doesn't flinch.

"My research is focused on things up there," Neb points at the stars above us before touching his fingers to his breastbone. "Even though this is a vacation, I'd never miss the opportunity to see an eclipse. Having other space geeks here makes it even better."

Bryan holds up his hand like he's giving Neb a high five from across the campsite, and Neb air high fives him back.

Neb reaches for Sage's hand. "There isn't much that can make this trip more perfect."

All the women say, "Awwwww." Even Jess, who still seems determined not to look at me or Mel.

Theo clears his throat loudly and stands at the center of the group. Mel bounces in her seat next to me and smiles like she did when Theo first arrived, like something good's about to happen and she's thrilled she gets to witness it. He spreads out his arms and spins in a slow circle. "This may come as a surprise to some of you, but my life has sorted itself out quite nicely. I have no great dilemma to solve in this deep canyon split into the earth." He winks at Mel and she giggles. "As I am not a selfish creature, I'm offering my ear to anyone who needs it." His gaze lands on Jess and she gives him a small smile.

"I call bullshit," Naomi says. "We'll pick the secrets out of you, dear brother."

Theo bows deeply in her direction. "The gauntlet is thrown by my lovely sister. Alas, I believe her attentions will be best served elsewhere." He continues moving in a circle until he's looking at Hunter, who's eyes widen.

"What?"

Theo points at him and winks again.

"Does this mean it's my turn?" Hunter asks.

Theo shrugs. "Sure. But my offer is for anyone who needs it."

"Teaching has changed you," Naomi says.

"But not in a bad way," Sage says while nodding. "I like helpful Theo."

Theo sits, and everyone's attention turns to Hunter.

He clasps his hands in front of him and looks quickly around the group before staring at the campfire in the center of the clearing. Flames sway back and forth, making it hard to look away. "I've missed a few of these trips, so I'm out of practice with the campfire confessionals." He glances at Naomi and you'd have to be dead to miss the smile they share. "For a long time, I thought things in my life had to happen in a certain order. That to be successful, I had to stay focused." Another side glance at Naomi. "But now that I've achieved what I set out to do and I'm actually editing books at a publishing house, my life isn't as fulfilled as I'd hoped."

"They are totally getting back together," Mel whispers.

"Do you know who it is you want to fill?" Theo asks. Naomi's lightning fast with a stick and a dirty look. It bounces off his leg and he pushes out his lower lip. "What? I'm trying to help."

Hunter shakes his head, but a small smile lifts the corner of his mouth. It's weirdly similar to the adorable half-smile Mel does that always gets comments from the fan-girls on her account. "I have a few ideas." He looks at Naomi again and no one speaks.

When ten seconds stretches to a minute, my skin starts to twitch. I hate uncomfortable silences almost as much as I hate sharing details of my life with people I don't know.

Several pairs of eyes fall on me.

"M-my turn?"

Everyone's attentive and caring and the voice inside me yells to shut up. They might be the most understanding people in the world, but the more I say that my parents are getting divorced, the more real it becomes.

If Mel wasn't holding my hand so tightly, I might drift away with the smoke from the fire.

"Is it okay if I pass?"

"That's an option?" Theo says.

"Of course, sweetie," Margo says.

"Thanks." My head dips so pieces of hair hang in my face. "I don't want to make this a big thing, but I'm not ready to talk yet."

"You'll share when you're ready," Theo says. "It's the campfire. Gets ya every time."

"Yeah," Naomi says. "And a few of us are quite skilled at doling out the advice. If that's what you want."

"I'll go," Jess says, diverting the attention away from me. I shoot her a grateful look but she barely looks at me or Mel.

Instead her focus is on Theo, who gives her a small nod. "Mine's pretty basic 'woe is me, what am I going to do with the rest of my life' kind of stuff."

"That's not basic," Sage says. "It's a big decision."

Jess blinks at Sage before flicking her gaze at us again. "Everyone I know is excited for college, but that's never felt like the right thing for me."

And we talk about college in front of Jess all the time without considering her feelings. Mel gives me an 'oh crap' look, like she's thinking the same thing.

Jess looks at Hunter. "And I'm definitely not joining the military."

Hunter's mouth falls open and he crosses an arm over his chest. "Theo, you're still holding that over me?"

"What am I missing?" I whisper to Mel.

"On our first family trip, Hunter suggested Theo join the military instead of college."

My head shakes. "Oh, he definitely missed the mark there."

"Anyway," Jess says. "Theo pointed out that spending this time with all of you might help me figure out what I want to do." She smiles, and the guilt in my chest grows stronger.

Why hasn't she talked to us about this?

Mel gives Jess her look that means she wants to talk more about this later, then clears her throat. "I don't think it's any shock what's on my mind. The video, obviously, but for the purpose of the fire, I'll say it's deciding where to go to school." She loosens her grip on my hand and loops her arm through mine.

"When do you have to decide?" Neb asks.

"I've got a few weeks, but I really want to make it official." Mel squeezes my hand but I'm not sure what she's trying to tell me.

"I hate having unknown things hanging over me," Mel says.

"Don't we all," Naomi says.

"Perfect transition, as usual," Theo says.

"How did I end up last?" Naomi asks.

"Because you're used to listening to people on your show," Hunter says. "You let them get it all out before you share what you're thinking."

Her gaze drops to her hands and her hair falls in her face. "You still listen?"

He shrugs and gives her that adorable half smile.

"You give me too much credit." A smile curls Naomi's lips. "But I do have a few opinions that I'm happy to share with all of you. Privately of course."

"You're deflecting," Theo sings out the words.

Naomi shrugs. "For once, I'm not really sure what I'm working on. The show is great, the master's program I'm in is exciting and challenging, but I still feel like something's missing, you know?" She looks each of us in the eye.

I nod when she looks at me. The soft ache in my heart grows stronger. Because even though my brain says I need to forget about love for a while, I don't think it's gonna be that easy.

11

MELODY

I'm about to lose my fricking mind. Steph and Jess have both been quiet since the campfire confessional and I want to shake their thoughts out of them. No one spoke while we brushed our teeth in the lodge—thank goodness it has running water!—and now we're almost back to our tent. My legs are about to collapse beneath me, but I refuse to go to sleep until we resolve whatever weirdness has taken over.

I stop in the path, and they both bump into me.

"Is it a snake?" Jess whisper-shouts. "Did you see a snake?"

"No, there's no snake." I shine my flashlight around the path. "Although I guess there could be a snake. But that's not why I stopped. I don't know what happened between this morning and right now, but no one's going to bed angry."

Both their heads snap up.

"I'm not angry," Steph says, looking between us both. "Did you think I'm angry?"

We both look at Jess, who quickly turns away.

"Jess, what's going on?" I ask.

"I'm tired," she says. "I want nothing more than to crawl into my sleeping bag and go to sleep." She finally meets my eyes.

She really does look tired, and even though I don't believe her, I let it go. "I guess I read into something that wasn't there?"

Jess exhales. "I'm not mad, I'm just…" She tilts her head back and studies the stars. "Can we do this tomorrow?"

"Of course." I pull her into a hug and even though she stiffens against me, she doesn't pull away.

She says good night and hurries down the path and now it's just me and Steph standing beneath the almost full moon. There are a thousand things I want to say, each one more dramatic than the next, but the tiny voice in my head warns me to calm myself.

Steph shifts from one foot to the other.

"Do you know what's bothering her?" I ask.

Her gaze bounces everywhere but my face, and my heart twists. It's not like them to keep secrets from me and it hurts.

"Did I do something?" I ask.

Her eyes widen and she quickly shakes her head. "No! No. It's not you. Well, not only you." Her lips press together and she pushes her hair out of her eyes.

My fingers itch to follow hers through the purple strands and I don't stop my hand as it lifts near her throat. Touches the hair that brushes her shoulder. Grazes the skin at the collar of her shirt.

She inhales sharply and for a moment, a split second barely longer than a heartbeat, I swear she leans toward me. But then I blink and she blinks and we're two friends at the bottom of the Grand Canyon, both so tired we're about to fall asleep standing.

"We—we should probably go to bed?" It comes out a question, a soft lilt at the end of my sentence that I hope says no, I don't want to go to bed. I want to stay here with you beneath the stars and the moon and find out if my feelings are bigger than my imagination.

She touches the spot on her neck where my fingers were. Her eyes close as her lips part, just for a second, then her mouth closes and she nods. "Probably."

We walk side by side to the tent, and I hold the flap open so she can climb in. A Jess-shaped lump fills the sleeping bag farthest from the opening. "I need to plug in my phone," I whisper before shoving my hand into the depths of my pack.

But the battery chargers aren't there. I unzip every pocket, dumping deodorant and sunscreen and rolled-up socks onto my sleeping bag, but still no chargers.

"Do you remember packing my chargers?" I ask Steph in a low voice.

She shakes her head, then her eyes go wide. "I think I pushed them aside when I gave you your laptop to work on the video." Her nose scrunches and she squeezes her lips together. "I'm really sorry."

I rest my hand on her arm. "It's not your fault. I checked my bags and totally missed them. My mom probably has one I can use tomorrow."

"Are you sure?"

"I couldn't be mad at you," I say.

We crawl into our beds—giggling as we bump elbows and knock hips trying to slide into our sleeping bags—but Jess doesn't move. She's either asleep or avoiding talking to us.

I whisper "good night" into the air but only Steph replies. She shifts next to me, rolling in her bedding until her knee presses against my leg. Within minutes her soft breathing is the only sound in the tent, and I'm left staring at the faint outline of the moon in the canvas ceiling.

I must fall asleep at some point, because the next time I look up, it's bright outside. My leg muscles threaten to cramp as I roll over. Jess's empty sleeping bag is a reminder of the tension last night, but Steph is still here, lying on her side, watching me.

"Good morning," she whispers. It feels like a secret just for me, or maybe I spent too much time fantasizing about what it would be like if she thought about me the way I think about her.

"Morning," I whisper back. The door flap is zipped shut, making it feel more private in here than it really is.

"It sounds like people are awake," she says.

"Did you see Jess before she got up?"

Steph shakes her head.

"Did she actually tell you what's wrong? Or were you just guessing?"

She watches me for what feels like an eternity, her gaze bouncing between my eyes and lips, and why is she looking at my lips? She drags in a breath, and not until she exhales does she reply. "She feels like a third wheel."

I push into a sitting position. "What? How? I mean, yeah, there are three of us, but we're the Bestie Brigade. There are no wheels in the Bestie Brigade."

A smile tugs at Steph's lips and in a flash I understand exactly why Jess is upset. Because the smile Steph's giving me isn't the smile of a best friend. It's something more, and I can guarantee the smile it prompts from me matches hers.

Steph tucks her feet under her legs and runs her hands over her shins. "No wheels, but any time there's an odd number of people, someone's gonna feel left out." It feels like she has more to say, but I don't want to push her.

"And that's all she said?"

"More or less." The corner of her mouth sucks between her teeth, her tell when she's lying.

"I'll try to talk to her." I unzip my sleeping bag and slip on my shoes. Even though my legs have no interest in moving, my bladder has other ideas. "Do you need to go to the bathroom?"

She's quick to her feet and suddenly we're standing chest to chest. We've hugged more times than I could possibly count, but this is different than a huffle.

My heart acts like this is the first time we've stood this close.

Her gaze flicks to my throat.

Can she see how fast my pulse is?

Her fingers brush my arm. We both look to where she made contact, then she takes a tiny step back. "Let me know if I can help with Jess."

All moisture has left my throat so I simply nod.

When we step outside, the parents and the guys hover near boxes of scrambled eggs, bacon, pancakes, and fruit salad spread out on the picnic table. A carton of orange juice calls to me, but I pass the table and lead Steph to the bathrooms.

Sage and Naomi leave the bathroom as we approach, with Jess trailing behind them. They laugh at something Jess says and Sage smiles when they reach us. "Melody, did you really make a video where you attempted to do silly body tricks?" While she sounds amused, her eyes are kind.

But Jess's smile falls as soon as I look at her, and she avoids my eyes.

It's like Jordan Fricking Beebe all over again. His goal was to make me look and feel stupid, and while I know in the bottom of my soul that Jess isn't trying to hurt me, that's how I feel.

The video in question isn't something I wanted to share, but Jess convinced me it showed my authentic self and isn't that the whole point of my account? To show girls that it's cool to be interested in things like physics and biology and chemistry, and so what if I look silly while doing it? That's what makes it real.

I can still hear her convincing me, and even though I didn't like the final cut, she was right. It's one of my most shared videos. Some people duet it to laugh at me, but the majority are nice. It was a great example of how to learn through experimentation while still being human. That video pushed me over the threshold to be able to monetize my account, so it was more than worth a little embarrassment.

Or at least that's what I tell myself.

"Yeah." I force a laugh. "I'm kind of obsessed with the show Myth Busters—"

"Kind of," Jess interrupts. Her smile seems genuine but my brain leaps to questioning her intentions.

I roll my eyes. "I showed that you can't lick your own elbow or sneeze with your eyes open. That was a tricky one to record. Then I tried to do things that some people are able to, like do the Vulcan salute."

I demonstrate how to form a V with my index and middle finger pointing one way, and my pinkie and ring finger pointing the other.

"Doubling crossing your fingers."

"Oh, like this?" Sage hooks her middle finger over her index finger, then her ring over her pinkie finger.

"Show off," Steph says with a laugh.

"Yes, exactly," I say. "And finally, curling your tongue." I stick out my tongue, which absolutely refuses to curl, before pointing at Steph, whose tongue curls like a pasta noodle. My heart flutters for a moment, but then I catch Jess looking away and the uneasiness returns.

"How fun!" Sage says.

"Anything for clicks, right?" My voice comes out flat.

Naomi's head tilts. She knows me well enough to know that's absolutely not my goal, not by a long shot, but she also knows me well enough to know I have a reason for lying.

Sage's smile fades. "I'm hardly ever on social media, but l have to check out your account. Neb keeps telling me how cool it is."

"Wait, Neb's watched my videos?" Excitement replaces my angst from two seconds ago. Neb's a real scientist, or at least as close to a real one that I know outside of my teachers at school.

Sage nods. "He loves them. Half his department follows you." My jaw drops and she pokes my arm. "He's excited to chat with you."

Naomi throws me a smile while she tugs Sage's arm and leads her toward the campsite. Jess follows them without another word.

Steph pushes the bathroom door open and beelines for one of the stalls.

"I figured he was just being nice when he said he'd be in a video."

"I can't believe his research people follow you," Steph says.

I assumed some adults followed MeltyPoint, but I never imagined that real-life scientists would be interested in my ramblings. Suddenly the video Sage mentioned seems even more idiotic. "Should I take down the silly video?"

"What? No!"

"But if I want to be taken seriously, I need to be serious."

The toilet flushes and Steph waits for me to join her at the sink before responding. "Mel, your charm is that you don't care what other people think of you. Even if those of us who love you know that you do care, to the Melties, you're this cool-ass chick teaching them about science and letting the haters die of jealousy."

Of course my brain locks in on the fact that she just said she loves me, not the part about her calling me a cool-ass chick. "I know you're right. But why would Jess bring that up? She knows how it makes me feel."

"You're gonna have to ask her. Get this cleared up before it gets worse."

I know she's right, but I hate conflict almost as much as I hate not being taken seriously.

The food's cold by the time we get to the campsite, but my stomach growls anyways. A small jar of strawberry jelly sits unopened next to the fruit. "Thanks, Mom."

She takes a sip of coffee before smiling. "Don't thank me. Thank your brother."

I grab it and hold it to my chest. "Hunt! You carried a jar of jelly for me?"

A full smile stretches across his face, not his usual smirk. "Anything for my little sister. But I'm sorry there's nothing to put it on. I thought there'd be bagels or toast."

It's impossible to miss the way Naomi watches Hunter. Her smile grows until he looks her way, then she quickly takes another bite of food.

"Everything's better with jelly," I say.

Mom laughs. "There will be bagels in our sack lunches."

Steph and I finally sit down to eat when Mom claps her hands to get everyone's attention. "I know we promised a quiet day at the campsite, but we have another option if you're interested."

The thought of climbing over rocks makes me want to cry. Even though we're in this incredible place that's unlike anything I've experienced, all I want to do is relax by the river with my friends and brainstorm video ideas.

I must not be the only one, because several groans sound around us.

"Don't tell me you're tired!" Nancy jumps to her feet and dances around to perhaps demonstrate how not-tired she is. "The fun's about to start!"

"Mom, if you say anything that hints at a hike, I'm disowning you," Theo says.

Naomi raises her hand. "I won't disown you, but I might not talk to you for the rest of the trip."

Hunter rubs his hands together. "It'll be fun, I promise."

"Hey!" My head snaps up. "How come you know?"

He rolls his eyes. "If everyone knew, it wouldn't be a surprise."

"It was his idea," Mom says.

"Dear canyon gods, help us." Theo clutches one hand to his chest and presses the other to his forehead.

"I'd like to know what the surprise is," Sage says. Her earnestness tempers Theo's dramatics and makes Mom smile.

"Hunter, would you like to share?" Mom says.

He jumps to his feet and punches a fist in the air.

He actually punches the air.

"We're going river rafting!"

Steph's eyes go wide and for a second I'm worried she won't want to go, but she gives me a huge smile. "A boat ride sounds fun."

"Totally." I try to catch Jess's eye but she's turned so far away she's literally giving me the cold shoulder.

That's it, I'm talking to her as soon as we're done with breakfast. We aren't ruining this trip because she's mad about something she won't even talk about.

"If everyone is game," Mom says. "We'll take two boats."

Nancy points at Theo and Naomi, then smiles sweetly at Neb and Sage. "That's how many we reserved, so we'd really appreciate not losing our deposit on the second one."

Theo claps his hands together and pastes on a cheesy grin. "I could not be more excited."

"Yeah, it sounds great," Jess says. Her voice sounds beyond unenthused. She finally looks at me, but I can't read the expression on her face. It's not anger or frustration, it's almost like she's lonely.

Tears burn my eyes. I don't understand what has her so upset. She hasn't acted this way since middle school. I promised I'd never again make her feel like she isn't important to me, but it's obvious I've hurt her.

"We leave in an hour," Nancy says. "So have more breakfast or coffee if you'd like, or relax and enjoy the scenery."

Neb shifts in his chair and props his chin in his hand so he's staring at Sage. Her cheeks turn bright red and she swats at him, but he doesn't look away.

"Oh, to have someone look at me that way," Steph says under her breath. Her eyes slide to me, and I swear she gives me the same look that was just on Neb's face.

Words.

I have no words.

At least not for Steph. That will have to wait.

The conversation shifts to what we'll need on the boats, so I grab our trash and walk up to Jess. My heart pounds in my ears, but I force myself to speak. "Can we go for a walk?"

She looks at her feet before giving me a pouty expression. One I know is not a normal reaction for her. "I'd rather not. My feet are killing me."

"Jess, please. We don't have to go far." I lower my voice. "But I need to know why you're upset."

She glances across the campsite, but I keep my eyes trained on her. I can't hear anything over my racing heart. Finally, after several breaths, she nods.

I toss my trash in the bin and hope she's following. Once we pass the bathrooms, I sit on the nearest bench and stare at the ground until she joins me. "Steph said you feel like a third wheel and I'm so sorry if I've done something to make you feel that way. You know you're my best friend. You mean everything to me and I hate that I've upset you." She quirks a brow and the corner of my mouth lifts. "Sorry, that was a lot. But it's all true. I just wish you'd tell me what's wrong."

She's quiet for a moment and I want to shake a response out of her. "Yes, the third wheel thing is getting annoying, but—"

"How are you a third wheel? We're the Bestie Brigade. It has no wheels!"

Jess doesn't laugh like Steph did earlier. She doesn't even crack a smile. "Can I finish?"

I twist my lips with my fingers and nod.

She studies the ground for several minutes, and when she looks up, tears fill her eyes. "Since we were in middle school, you've always known what you want to do with your life."

"Not always," I protest, and she gives me a pointed look. "Sorry."

"You love science and you know you want to teach it to kids. That's awesome. It really is. I love helping you with the videos, and not just because it's helped my grades." A smile finally brushes her lips, but it doesn't last. "But I have no idea what I want to do. Everyone talks about college likes it's a forgone conclusion, but every time it comes up, I get all twitchy and anxious."

"I'm sorry that I've been oblivious to your feelings."

"I like the idea of going away and living in a dorm and hanging out with friends, but I could get a job and an apartment and do that." She picks at her fingernail. "Being here with all these hyper-educated people is making me feel like a complete loser."

I reach for her hand. A group of hikers walk by and watch us for a beat, but I ignore them. "You are not a loser. There isn't one perfect path to becoming an adult, and there are options besides college. We can help you figure out what makes sense for you."

She bristles at the 'we.'

"This isn't all that's bothering you." It's not a question. When you hang out with someone almost every day, including spending hours editing videos of them, you learn what each tick and twitch means. The way her jaw clenches and her nostrils flare means she's not necessarily pissed, but she's definitely upset.

Her head shakes, and tears fill her eyes. Another group passes us and she wipes a tear from her cheek.

"Jess, please talk to me. I hate seeing you upset. You know I wouldn't do anything to jeopardize our friendship."

She takes a deep breath. "We always tell each other everything, but lately you've been keeping a secret and I hate it." The hurt in her eyes makes me feel sick. "We tell each other when we have a crush, and I can tell you like someone." I tilt my head and she smiles. "You walk around with this dopey expression on your face when you think no one's watching, and you're even more cheerful than usual."

I can't stop the blush that creeps up my cheeks.

"I knew you were interested in someone, but you didn't say anything. Then you and Steph both started acting weird, and even though it doesn't seem like you've told each other how you feel, it's obvious. At least to me. And now everything is awkward and I'm a third wheel."

Her words are like a punch to the gut. Here I thought she was keeping a secret from me, but it's my secret that's causing problems. I've been keeping my feelings for Steph to myself because I didn't want to screw up the Bestie Brigade, but I've screwed us up anyway. "You will never be a third wheel. You're the greasy chain that keeps us all together."

"I'm a greasy chain?"

"It was a poor attempt at a metaphor." My shoulders relax and I lean back against the bench. Then something else she said catches on my brain. "Steph likes me?"

She rolls her eyes and a smile tugs at the corner of her mouth. "I'm shocked you can't tell."

"I mean, I thought maybe. But I was afraid it was all in my head and I don't want to ruin our friendship and wow, do you really think she likes me?"

"I think this is a conversation you two need to have." She nudges me with her shoulder. "Or, you could skip the talking part and just kiss her."

My eyes nearly pop out of my head. "I can't kiss her."

"I thought you were going to after I went to bed last night."

A thought strikes me. "Is that why you went to bed early?"

Her smile slides into a frown. "I'd like to say I'm that good of a friend, but no. I was too delirious to deal with anything. But now that my head's clear, I'm telling you that I'm ninety-eight percent certain Steph likes you."

"But she and Brooklyn just broke up." And she told me she wants to be single. But the way she's been acting says she feels differently. "Wow, am I always this thick?"

This time she smiles for real. "Not always."

More hikers pass by, but we make no move to get up. "Are we okay?" I ask.

"Yeah. I'm scared about not having my life figured out, but I know it's not fair to be mad at you for that. Just do me a favor?"

"Anything."

"Please don't hook up while I'm in the tent."

"Omigod, Jess!" I smack her arm and a woman Mom's age frowns at me. "My head's nowhere near there."

Jess gives me her I-don't-believe-you look—brows raised, lips pursed to one side—and makes a noise in her throat. "Right."

"I mean, yeah, I've thought about kissing her, but nothing more. And not in the tent!" Although now that she's put the idea in my head, there are benefits to same-sex sleeping arrangements. Something that surely won't be allowed if we actually start dating.

"That's all I ask," Jess says. "Now, can we go get ready for this boating adventure?"

We link our arms together and walk toward the campsite. "Let's go ride the Colorado."

And hopefully come up with a video that will not only confirm my status as an up-and-coming queen of SciTok, but make everyone forget about my mistake and knock Jordan Fricking Beebe so far down that he never returns.

12
STEPHANIE

Everyone's moving around the campsite like they know exactly what to expect from this boat ride, and I'm freaked that my hat and sunscreen aren't enough.

Jess and Mel come back from their talk smiling, but their smiles fade as I rush over to them, eyes wide. "I thought this was just a boat ride. Why are they prepping like we're going on another hike?"

Mel watches the parents shove snacks and bottles of water into a pack with as much enthusiasm as I feel. "I don't know," she says, touching my arm. "I'll find out."

As she heads over, I turn to Jess. "You okay?" She shrugs, and I pull her into a hug. "You're allowed to not be okay. But you have to tell us."

She tucks her head against my shoulder and sniffs. "There's a lot in my head and too much time down here to think."

I laugh into her hair. "Don't I know it." I pull back and look in her eyes. "Anything I can do to help?"

"Not unless you know what I should do with the rest of my life."

I tap the side of my head. "I'll come up with something." She doesn't smile like I expect. "Did you two talk about the third wheel thing?"

She nods. Then breaks eye contact and bites her lip.

My heart stutters. "What did you do?"

Her lips pull back in a grimace. "We were sharing and I was feeling emotional. And I may have told her I was pretty sure you like her."

I inhale sharply. "Why would you say that?" Several heads turn our way and I angle my back toward them.

"Don't you?"

"No!"

She raises a brow. "I don't believe you"

Do I like Mel? Yeah, I like hanging out with her. She's one of my favorite people, but that doesn't mean I like her. Or does it? Memories of all the times we've held hands or hugged warm me from the inside.

Maybe the reason I never felt a connection with Brooklyn is because Mel is the one my heart wants. The one I want to be with. "What did she say?"

"She likes you."

"Oh." It comes out breathy and now my heart's hammering in my chest.

"Apparently this is more intense than we thought," Mel says from behind me.

It takes me a second to put together what she's talking about. My brain is locked on the fact that my best friend told my other best friend that I like her. But the look on Mel's face makes me think this might be a good thing.

Mel points at the river at the edge of the campsite. "The boats? They're more like white water rafting boats, but Mom insists there won't be any big rapids."

"Define big." My heart pounds, but now it's from straight-up fear. "Can we like, fall out?" I only signed up for possible death by falling off a cliff, not drowning in the river.

"We shouldn't," Mel says.

Jess gives me a side hug. "They won't make us do anything that could get us injured."

I point at the cliffs surrounding us. "Did you not do the same hike as me yesterday?"

"Okay," Jess says. "Maybe a little danger. But it sounds fun."

Yeah, fun if you know how to swim. Which I don't. "Will there at least be life jackets?"

Half an hour later, we've hiked a short distance to a sandy beach at a bend in the river. A pile of life jackets rests next to a pile of plastic oars, and my terror eases a little. Neb and Sage stand with Hunter, Naomi, and Theo near two of the gray rubber boats—two of at least a dozen lined up ready for other people—while the parents listen to a pair of guides in matching khaki shorts and blue T-shirts. They look about the same age as Benji and Ronny, who are nowhere to be seen.

"Aren't our guides supposed to be here?" I ask.

"Maybe they aren't licensed for the river," Jess says.

Mel chews on her fingernail, her alert eyes taking in the scene around us. "Does this seem really commercial? Like, surprisingly so considering the fact that what makes this place so incredible is the natural beauty of it all."

Groups of four to six people arrive at the beach from the same path we took. They're greeted by guides dressed like ours, then settle into boats like ours.

"I pictured us being the only ones on the river," Mel says. "Kind of a woman versus nature thing. But this is like a fricking amusement park."

"Maybe they stagger us," Jess says.

"Like a roller coaster." I laugh, but it's from nerves. The water's calm, and seeing this many tourists climbing into boats, including a number of people who don't look like they'd survive rapids, lessens my anxiety a bit more.

We wander closer to the boats.

"How are we splitting up?" Naomi asks.

"Please don't say big kids in one and little kids with the parents," Mel says. There's a whiny edge to her voice that isn't normally there and I reach for her arm without thinking.

"I wouldn't mind being with Bryan or Neb," I say. "They seem the most capable of pulling me out of the river if I fall in." As much as it kills me to admit it, they're the two biggest guys, and even though I know life jackets will prevent me from drowning, the less time I spend splashing around in the river, the better.

The parents wave us over and introduce the guides, two dark-skinned women with short afros who could be sisters, as Tonya and Tamara. "You all can choose how we split up," Nancy says. "But each boat gets a guide and a parent."

Margo gives Mel a pleading look and Mel sighs dramatically. "Yes, we'll ride with you."

"I know you're practically an adult," Margo says. "But you're still my baby and I don't want anything to happen to you."

Bryan puts an arm around Margo. "I won't let anything happen to any of you."

I move closer to them. "I'm, uh, gonna hold you to that."

"Deal." Bryan pulls me against his other side and I hate to admit how safe I feel. My parents raised me to take care of myself and not rely on others for anything, and especially to be careful of toxic men who do whatever it takes to get their way, but with the threat of drowning in the near future, this doesn't feel so bad.

Theo leaves the others and joins our group. "Can I ride with you all?"

"Um, yes please!" Mel holds up her hand for a high five, and they slap hands.

"You don't want to ride with them?" Jess gestures at the big kids.

Theo makes a show of counting the five of us. "More people means less work from me."

"The more the merrier," Bryan says, offering up a high five. Theirs is more awkward, but it's obvious Bryan wants everyone to like him.

Or maybe he genuinely likes everyone and there's no pretense. I don't mean to be so jaded when it comes to guys, but it's a learned response from the jerks at school.

"I'll ride with the big kids," Nancy says. She and Margo do a weird thing where they seem to communicate without talking, and Nancy nods. "It's fine. We need to keep the boats balanced."

Margo gives her a quick hug. "As long as that's all it is."

Nancy nods again and joins the others in front of their boat.

During our paddling instructions, we discover I'm the only person who's never done anything like this. Then we climb in the boats and Tamara pushes us into the river like a warrior ready to take battle. She jumps on the back in one swift movement, and I instantly feel safer with her in charge.

It's unreal being in the actual middle of the canyon. Unlike being on a road or sidewalk, which were designed by a human for a specific purpose, the river follows the path it chose without giving mankind an opinion. It's about the width of a city block and the other boat floats too far away to talk without shouting. I imitate everyone else and dip my paddle in the water, but like Theo, I'm relying on the others to carry my weight. At least until I get more comfortable.

Jess and I are in the middle of the boat, with Mel in front of me next to Theo, and the parents and Tamara behind us.

Mel twists around to look at us. "Are we all good?" She's really asking Jess, but I nod.

"Very."

"Very?" Mel repeats.

I run a hand over the edge of the boat. "Okay, very might be strong. Pretty much."

Jess laughs, and that seems to be enough of an answer for Mel because she turns back around.

"Up ahead is a section of the canyon that's impossible to navigate without climbing gear." Tamara points a paddle at a wall of rock that stretches straight to the sky. It reminds me of how cities used to position the backside of buildings and factories toward the river, their windowless walls blocking the view from shore, before they appreciated the beauty flowing through their cities.

"Back in the day," Tamara says, "people claimed there were Egyptian tombs and whole cities hidden deep inside the canyon."

Jess and I exchange wide-eyed looks before gazing at the canyon walls.

"They never found the alleged city," Tamara continues. "Odds are whatever artifacts they saw were Native American but were mistaken for Egyptian. Those explorers couldn't imagine that people from these lands could build something civilized."

Mel straightens, and I can almost see her wheels turning at the idea of a myth to bust. "There's probably no way to find that cave, huh?"

"I'm thinking no," I say.

"Do you have any ideas yet?" Jess asks.

Mel shakes her head, sending her ponytail bouncing over her shoulders. Her grip tightens on her paddle. "My brain is totally stuck. We're surrounded by real life science in action and I can't think of a single way to make that relatable."

"Not a single way?" I ask.

"Okay, I've had lots of ideas, but they're all terrible."

"Hit us up," Theo says.

I can tell Mel rolls her eyes even without seeing her face, and I smile. She's constantly second-guessing herself, but once we get her talking, she and Jess usually pick out a winning idea.

I stretch my leg under her bench and nudge her calf with my toes. "Let's hear them."

Mel dips her paddle in the water and watches the ripples in the current. "There's the obvious thing with the layers in the rock walls. How the deeper we've gone into the canyon, the farther back we go into history." She points her paddle at the sheer cliff wall. "They're a physical example that everything we know now is built upon the learnings of the past."

"That's heavy," Theo says.

"Too heavy for my audience?" she asks.

"No!" we all shout.

Mel tilts her head back to look at the sky above us. "Then there's the stars, and tomorrow's lunar eclipse. I'll record that for a later video, but not the response to Jordan Fricking Beebe."

I hold in a laugh. It cracks me up how she uses his full name, plus the Fricking with a capital F, every time she mentions him.

"This place makes you feel your connection to the earth as a planet," Jess says. "I know earth sciences aren't your focus, but being so deep inside the earth while still seeing into the galaxies is pretty cool."

"Jess, you are a gift," Margo says, and Jess blushes. "Don't ever lose that perspective on the world."

Jess responds by paddling harder.

"Maybe this should be more of a thinky feely post," Mel says. "I'm always talking about what sets me apart from the other tokkers, and this could do it."

Excitement builds inside me. I don't consider myself a super creative person when it comes to creating content—give me steel and bricks and wood any day—but I love watching Mel turn an idea into a video. She tells stories and entertains, all while teaching people about concepts she understands the way I understand how the angles of a building can draw a person in and make them feel emotions like longing and comfort and discord. "You could talk about how we're all part of the planet, then tie in little clips of us doing things while we're down here."

She peeks at me over her shoulder. "Well, I have been secretly recording all of you since yesterday."

"Hey!" Bryan says. "You better show my good side."

Mel bursts out laughing, and I swear I can see some of the tension slide off her shoulders. A strand of hair sticks to her neck and my fingers reach to free it before I can stop them. Mel leans into my touch, and a different kind of excitement, one that I feel deep in my belly, makes me suck in a breath.

"So, the video will be about how we're all members of this planet and we're just here trying to understand it?" Mel asks.

The idea is amazing, pardon the unsanctioned use of the word, but Mel's voice holds a hint of uncertainty.

"Yes!" we all shout.

"I think this could be really cool," she whispers.

"We'll make sure it is," Jess says. They smile at each other and I really hope this means whatever friction was building between them is finally over. Because even if it's true and Mel does like me, they've been friends for years and I'd rather be kicked out of the Bestie Brigade than come between them.

The river moves fast, but not so fast that there's actual rapids. Mel pulls out her phone and records everything in front of us, then leans back until her head's resting on my knees. The camera's pointing straight up and her ponytail falls against my bare leg. This kind of physical contact is nothing new for us, but after Jess's comment, everything feels different. More sensual. And it's happening in front of her parents and Jess and Theo and a warrior goddess named Tamara.

"Everything out here is so extra," Mel says. She tilts her head farther back until our eyes connect. "I feel so small compared to how grand it is, but then I also feel like I can take on the world. Does that make sense?"

My throat's too dry to speak, so I nod.

Resist the urge to brush the loose strands of hair off her face.

To press my lips against the soft skin next to her closed eyes.

Where did that come from?

A splash beyond the other boat, followed by screaming, makes us jump.

"Did someone fall in?" Theo leans forward over the front of the boat. Waves slap against the side of the other boat and the girls squeal as water splashes inside.

"Theo! Get back!" Mel's out of my lap and pulling on Theo's arm. He sits as waves much bigger than what we've seen out here move toward us.

"Looks like a rock slide," Tamara says. I twist around and she points up the canyon wall at a small ledge a couple hundred feet up. "It's a totally normal thing. The canyon is constantly evolving. We smooshy humans have to hope we don't get in the way when it happens."

Mel snorts when Tamara says smooshy. I guess even warrior goddesses can be silly sometimes.

"You can't be surrounded by rocks and expect them not to fall," Bryan says.

"Do you think it'll happen again?" Mel asks as the waves get closer.

"The safest bet is to always be ready for it." Tamara's focused on the approaching waves and misses the excitement in Mel's eyes. She must assume Mel's afraid of getting killed by rocks.

Which is one hundred percent my fear.

"Hold on!" Margo shouts seconds before the waves hit our boat.

No one's ever confused me for an experienced boater, but even I can tell that the water splashing against the rubber boat isn't a threat. Maybe of getting wet, but not of capsizing us. We rock from side to side and Theo curses under his breath, but a moment later the waves are gone and it's like it never happened.

"Let me know if you see any more rocks falling," Mel says. "That would be an epic video." She chews her lower lip between her teeth. She does that when she's working on an idea. It's the first time I've seen her do it since she suggested the centrifugal force video, and I get a burst of excitement for what she'll come up with.

I crisscross my finger over my heart and swallow the fear that's stuck in my throat. "I promise."

Fortunately no more rocks fall from the canyon walls for the rest of the boat ride. We have to paddle against the current on the return trip, and I'm ready for a nap when we get back to the beach. But as soon as my feet touch sand, it's clear that's not happening.

"Anyone up for a swim?" Naomi asks. Her gaze bounces from her friends and us and lands on Hunter for a beat longer.

"That sounds great!" Mel rushes to Hunter's side and loops her arm through his. "If you're nice, I'll even let you throw me in the air like you used to."

He rubs the top of her head and laughs. "You're a little bigger than the last time we did that."

She squeezes his bicep. "Aww, come on. Show off those muscles." She tosses a wink at Naomi, who blushes but doesn't look away.

Operation Amazing is in full effect.

And I'm not getting a nap.

Since we're already wearing swimsuits for the boat ride, we dump our things in a pile and wade into the water. The bottom of the river is rocky and muddy, and the current pulls at my legs. My gaze drifts to the life jackets in the boat. The murky water's barely up to my knees but I'm not comfortable going in much deeper.

Theo and Hunter run into the water and dive in with a splash, while Mel and Naomi wade in behind them. Even the parents join us, sinking down to their shoulders. Sage and Neb seem lost in their own little world. Neb keeps pointing at the sky and Sage watches him like he's the most fascinating person in the world.

A pair of sheep with big twisting horns appear on the opposite shore. They watch us for a moment like they're deciding if we're a threat, then lower their heads to the river and drink.

Theo pops out of the water and points. "Do those swim?"

Mel grips my arm, her fingers digging in hard. "Probably." She and Theo stare at each other with wide eyes, then back at the sheep. "We've had a running joke about wild animals since our first camping trip and last time I checked, he's still terrified of anything with cloven feet."

I burst out laughing, and Theo narrows his eyes at me.

"I think they're more worried about getting a drink than swimming across the river to attack you," Naomi says.

Theo points two fingers at his eyes, then at the sheep. "I'm watching you."

"You okay with this?" Jess tiptoes over the rocky bottom until she's at my side.

"The water feels great."

"That's not what I asked."

The best part of best friends is they understand the weird things that make you who you are. No judgment, just unconditional support. Despite being from California, the state with over 800 miles of oceanfront land, I never learned to swim. "I'm a little nervous."

"I'll stay with you if you want to go in deeper."

I drag my fingers over the surface. "Is there a current?"

"It's a river, so yeah."

"Maybe I'll stay here."

Almost like a bestie beacon was flipped, Mel swims toward us. She stays low in the water with her hands on the bottom until she's on my other side, then she flips over to sit. "We can be your swimmies."

I laugh through my nose. "My what?"

Mel looks up at me, and the earnestness in her eyes makes my belly do a backflip. "Those plastic inflatable things they put on your arms when you're learning to swim. Jess and I can be that for you. Right?" She smiles at Jess, who moves closer to my side.

"Absolutely."

"Please don't embarrass me," I say.

"In front of who?" Mel pushes to her feet and now her wet skin is pressed against mine. She's a little cold from the water but I feel like I'm on fire. "My brother and the parentals? Neb and Sage, who don't seem to be aware that anyone else is even in the Grand Canyon?" She squeezes my arm tightly. "We've got you."

We wade deeper into the water. The current's swift and rocks jab at the bottom of my feet, but soon we're deep enough that we can sink into the water.

"Let yourself float," Mel says.

"If I knew how to do that, I wouldn't need the help." My voice comes out sharper than I mean to, and I suck in a breath. "Sorry. This is freaking me out. The past two days have been a zip code away from my comfort zone."

Mel studies me for a beat, then the corner of her mouth curls in a smile. It's sexy and charming and I've completely forgotten what I was upset about. "It's all physics. The buoyancy of the water in your body counterbalances with the buoyancy of the river and you float."

I raise a brow.

Mel touches a fingertip to my temple. "Relax like you're in the bathtub. The water will keep you up."

"And we're not going anywhere," Jess says.

They hold onto my arms but the instinct to stay in control is too strong. What if I relax like they're saying and the current sucks me under and I'm swept away to the Pacific Ocean?

"Steph, I promise we won't let go," Mel says.

I take a deep breath, then my feet lift off the river bottom on their own, and some outside force tilts my head back until I'm looking at the sky. A lightness I've never experienced fills my chest. "This is incredible," I whisper.

"You're floating!" Mel says.

My legs stretch toward shore. I'm pretty sure their grip on my arms is what's keeping me from sinking, but the smiles on their faces makes me keep that thought to myself. I peek at Mel. "So are you two gonna ferry me around the rest of the afternoon?"

"Next up: doggie paddle," Jess says.

We laugh, and a burst of pride slides next to the lightness. I don't know if we're fixed, but right now, I couldn't imagine things being more perfect.

13
MELODY

Swimming in the Colorado River with my two best friends was near perfection, even if the big-horned sheep on the other side of the river were a little too close. Jess seems to believe me that she could never be a third wheel and Steph, well, the more time we spend together, the more I'm convinced she likes me.

Even though today was a lot more relaxing than yesterday, my legs feel like they weigh a thousand pounds. As soon as we're back at the campsite, we crash in our tents for a nap, but thoughts of choosing a school and tormenting myself for making a mistake, even though I said I was okay with it, won't let me sleep.

And of course I can't stop wondering what it would be like to kiss Steph—and how Jess will react if we do.

After half an hour of rolling back and forth, I give up. "I'm going to the bathroom," I whisper into the air. Their steady breathing answers.

Bryan's sitting at their picnic table when I return, and I pause before he sees me, my feet frozen on the hard dirt. This is my chance to find out the truth.

"Couldn't sleep?" he asks.

I shake my head. "If there was a way to let my legs sleep while the rest of me was awake, I'd do that."

He gestures at the bench next to him. "I think that's called sitting."

I laugh through my nose and sit on the bench opposite him. "Why aren't you napping?"

"Wish I could. My mom says I fought naps from the time I was two and I've never been able to since then."

"Huh." I'm not sure what to do with this glimpse inside his childhood, and a twinge of guilt stabs me for not wondering about his life prior to meeting Mom. He obviously came from somewhere, but I've been too wrapped up in how their relationship and marriage affected me to really get to know him. "You grew up in Michigan, right? What was it like?"

He shifts so his elbows rest on the table between us. He holds his right palm toward me and points at the outside edge of his hand. "I'm from a small town in west Michigan right along the big lake." When I tilt my head in confusion, he laughs. "Twenty years in California and I still forget that people aren't familiar with Lake Michigan. Most Michiganders call it the Big Lake because there are thousands of smaller lakes all over the state."

"So you're pretty used to being on the water."

His gaze travels past me to the river gurgling beyond the campsite. "You could say that. I've been swimming since I could walk and learned to canoe not long after at summer camp. Been looking for ways to be on the water ever since."

"But you and Mom hardly ever go to the ocean." Farmers markets and free concerts in the park, yes. But I don't think they've ever taken a beach day.

He glances over his shoulder at his tent before leaning closer to me. "Don't tell anyone, but I'm not a fan of the ocean."

I sit up straight. "How can anyone not like the ocean? It's where life first formed, and it connects us to the rest of the world, and—"

"And it's filled with salt water." He pretends to shudder, and I smile. "I prefer my lakes unsalted."

"Interesting." And it is. But I hate how charming he is when he's clearly been lying to us. I need to spit the words out and get it over with. My smile falls. "Can I ask you something?"

He holds out his hands, palms up.

My fingernail traces a scratch in the picnic table. "A couple weeks ago. I overheard you on the phone. Talking about moving money around. And—" I clear my throat. Swallow hard. Look him in the eyes. "What aren't you telling us?"

He drags a hand over his face and lowers his head.

My heart pounds. "What are you hiding from Mom?"

His shoulders shudder as he takes a deep breath. He doesn't deny it. But when he looks up, he's smiling. "We thought we could surprise you."

I lean back. "We?"

"It's about your college decision." My hands fall to the table with a thump, and his hands go up. "Hear me out. I know you feel obligated to take the scholarship at your second choice school, and I commend you for that. But that isn't your only option."

"What do you mean?"

"Your mom has been looking at loans to pay for you to go to Oregon. With both our salaries, the payment will be more manageable." He pauses, like he's waiting for his words to sink in.

And they take a minute.

Because if I heard him right—my mouth falls open. "You two are going to pay for my tuition?"

He nods, and my instincts urge me to say no, to tell him it's impossible, that we don't take handouts.

But this isn't a handout. He married Mom. He's my stepdad. They said "what's mine is yours" in their vows, which at the time I thought referred to the remote control and air fryer, but what if they meant bigger things, like helping her daughter avoid of a lifetime of student loans?

Tears burn my eyes as I realize what this means. "I can be a Duck?"

He nods, his eyes shining back at me. "If that's what you want."

My breath wooshes out of me. "Omigod. I don't know what to say."

"Say thank you."

"Thank you." It's not enough. Those two words will never be enough. "And I'm sorry I thought you were lying."

A smile spreads across his face. "Technically I was keeping a secret from you, so you weren't far off."

Realization that Bryan is as good of a person as I thought, and that he wasn't hiding anything or deceiving Mom, works its way through me. I take a deep breath. She's in love with a wonderful man and I get to go to the University of Oregon! All my daydreams about walking through campus and hanging out with friends and becoming an actual scientist are closer to happening.

And Steph. I get to spend the next four years with Steph.

If that's what she wants.

I'm filled with the need to move, to take action, to do something. To find out if she feels the same way about me as I do about her. If she thinks about me when I'm not with her, and even when I am, and if she's dreamt of us going to the same school, too.

"We're family now," Bryan says, snapping me back to the conversation. "I hope you know you can count on me."

"Thank you," I say again. I move around the table and throw my arms around his neck. It's not the most graceful as far as hugs go, but that's not the point. Family doesn't need to be graceful. "I'm gonna..." I point at my tent. I'm going to burst if I don't share this news.

He smiles. "It's nice to see you this happy."

Jess and Steph are still sleeping when I unzip the tent, but it only takes a couple loud exhales and shuffling in my bag for them to wake up. "I have news," I say, settling onto my bed, then share the joy-bomb Bryan just dropped on me.

Steph scrambles to a sitting position. "You can go to Oregon?" The happiness shining in her eyes makes my heart flutter, and for a moment we're the only two people in the universe.

"I'm really happy for you." Jess's voice is flat, and the sadness on her face brings my joy crashing down around me.

I reach for her hand but she pulls away.

"No, it's okay." She gives us a weak smile. "My despondence over my future is a separate thing from my happiness for yours. I truly am happy." She raises her brows and nods once more. "Truly. I just need a minute with this news."

"Do you want us to leave you alone?" Steph asks.

I expect Jess to protest, to tell us to stay, but she whispers, "Sure," to the floor.

Steph gives me a wide-eyed look and we hurry out of the tent and toward the picnic table, where Bryan's no longer sitting. "Is she gonna be okay?"

I stare at the closed tent flap. "I think so. I hope so. But this is happening. All we can do is try not to shove it in her face."

Steph glances at me, then quickly away. Pink colors her cheeks. "This?"

I replay my words in my head.

Oh.

"Um, I meant school? But, um..."

Her lips curl into a smile. "I don't think I've ever seen you at a loss for words."

Because I never am. If there's one sure thing in life, it's that Melody Thompson has a comeback for everything. "I—" I still don't know what to say. Because if I answer truthfully, I'll push us past the boundaries of friendship into something that could be wonderful and exciting and amazing, but could also blow up in my face.

She reaches for my hand. Laces her fingers through mine. Steps closer until the toes of our shoes touch. "I agree that we shouldn't shove this in her face."

My heart pounds so loudly it drowns out all other sound. My body flushes and my stomach flips, along with all the other stereotypical responses that happen when the person you're crushing on leans toward you with her eyes on yours and her lips slightly parted.

"Who's ready for dinner?" Mom shouts.

Steph and I leap apart. The foot of space between us feels wider than the Grand Canyon and yet a spark of energy still connects us.

"Mel, can you help me pick up the boxes?" Mom asks.

"Sure?" My eyes haven't left Steph. She's staring at my mouth like she's not sure what almost happened.

Or maybe she's thinking about kissing me.

The way I am about her.

Mom nudges my side with her elbow and laughs. "It wasn't a complicated question."

"Um, yeah. Sure." I try to telepathically tell Steph that we'll continue this later, but my brain is fritzing.

We walk toward the canteen and I peek inside the dining hall. Long tables with enough wooden chairs to seat groups bigger than ours fill the room. It's rustic and dated, but it's cozy and I kind of wish we were eating at least one of our meals in there.

When we reach the line for food, we grab the stacked boxes and head back toward the campsite. Mom's usually chatty and her silence makes it feel like she's restraining herself. I turn to her and say, "What?"

"What what?" she says. It's not like her to not spit out whatever's on her mind, and to do it firmly and directly.

Sometimes it drives me crazy, but I love her for it.

Some of my friends seem to take pride in not getting along with their parents and refuse to admit when they're right about anything, but that's not my relationship with Mom. Even though Hunter transferred back home his freshman year of college, he was busy with classes, so for the last few years it's felt like it was me and Mom against the world. At least until Bryan came along.

"Bryan said he talked to you about Oregon. About the tuition."

"Yes. It's incredible. It doesn't quite feel real."

"He also shared that you thought he was hiding something from us."

Heat burns my face. "I'm sorry I accused him of lying.

I should have asked what it was about instead of letting my imagination run wild."

She brushes her knuckle against my cheek. "There's been a lot of new in your life lately, with more to come. I'm proud of you for asking him directly, and for looking out for me." Tears brighten her eyes, which makes my eyes water.

"I'm glad you're happy, Mom."

She stops in the trail and studies me. "Thank you." Then she pauses so long I go crazy wondering what she's trying not to say. "Mel, I can't tell you how proud I am of you. We've had some rough moments over the years, but you and Hunter are proof that good can come from a pile of shit."

A laugh bubbles up my throat. "Did you just call Dad a pile of shit?"

"Metaphorically. But he hasn't offered to help, so he's earned that title."

I've long given up on wishing my dad cared more for me, but it still stings to hear it said out loud.

Mom smiles at the sky above us. "I want you to be happy. If that's 750 miles away in Oregon, then I'm glad we can make it work."

For as much as I've dreamed about going to Oregon, I hadn't really thought about how far I'll be from home. And how far from Mom. All the times I said I was too busy to join them for a "fun excursion" flash through my mind, and I simultaneously regret those childish reactions and am filled with a yearning to spend time with her while I can. "I'll miss you."

"I'll miss you, too." Her voice catches and she smiles. "But this gives me an extra reason to visit Nancy."

"I don't know how to say thank you enough."

"Get a good education and be happy. That's all I want for you."

"I'll do my best."

The others are waiting at the campsite when we return. We pass out the boxes that are identical to last night's, and Steph settles on the bench next to me, her leg achingly close to mine.

By the time we're done eating, my knee is resting against hers, but to look at us, you wouldn't know anything is happening.

Is anything happening? It hasn't been that long since my last relationship and I'm definitely not clueless about flirting, but I've never dated someone who I know as well as Steph. Someone I see all the time, whose expressions are as familiar as my own. Someone who's really affectionate and touches people a lot without it meaning anything.

But the spark between us is real. I'm sure of it.

I slide my leg closer until we're touching from hip to ankle, and she hooks her ankle around mine. She glances at me from the corner of her eye, a soft smile playing on her lips, and my heart nearly leaps out of my chest.

A quick glance at the other tables shows no one is paying us any attention. Then my gaze falls on Jess, who looks away as soon as I make eye contact. Steph's elbow brushes mine and I swear I've never felt more conflicted in my life. I want to ask Steph to go for a walk or to the bathroom, anything to get her away from the others, but I told Jess she would never be a third wheel and if I single out Steph, that's exactly what I'll be doing.

Before I can decide what to do, Jess gathers the trash from our table and says, "Theo, want to help me clean up?"

His hand pauses mid-air. He was about to take a drink of water and now he gapes at her with his mouth open. "I'm sorry, I realize you're still getting to know me. That's not a thing I do."

Uncertainty flickers across her face, but she pushes it away with the smile she uses when she really wants something. "Please? It's not like we have to wash dishes or anything."

"Okay, fine." He grabs the trash from his table while Jess collects everything from the other, and they head for the lodge.

I don't know if she did this to get away from us or to give us a chance to be alone, but I'm taking it.

"Do you want to—" I start.

"Wanna go for a walk?" Steph asks.

"Yeah," we both say.

I don't bother telling anyone where we're going because I'm afraid they'll see on my face exactly what I'm thinking. We follow a path the opposite direction of the lodge, passing other campsites until we reach a rock the size of my car at the edge of the river.

Without a word, we climb up. Steph goes first, extending her hand to help me, even though she scaled it easily. But now we're holding hands, so maybe that was her intention.

"Jess seems less upset than earlier," I say.

"I don't want to talk about Jess."

Oh.

Steph lowers in one movement so she's sitting cross-legged and tugs me down next to her. "I'm really glad you convinced me to come on this trip."

My heart rate slows as I sit. Okay, we're just talking. "I'm sorry I didn't realize how freaked out you were. By the hike and the boat."

She laughs through her nose. "I'm kind of a mess, huh?"

"Hardly. Your quirks make you perfect."

Her head snaps toward me. I wish I could pull the word back into my mouth, but then she smiles. "I think you're pretty damn perfect, too."

My thoughts jump back to two nights ago in the stairwell of the hotel. When she said she wanted to be single. Sitting together at the edge of the Colorado River at the bottom of the Grand Canyon, with the almost full moon shining brightly in the sky, it doesn't feel like she wants to be single.

I need to know for sure.

"So, the other night," I begin. "When you said you weren't upset about Brooklyn—"

"Because I wanted to be single," she finishes.

"Yeah."

Steph unfolds her legs and shifts closer so our bodies are almost touching. Almost. "I thought that's what I wanted." She pauses. Her tongue grazes her lower lip and I'm transfixed. A grizzly bear could crash through the trees and I wouldn't be able to stop staring at her.

"But it's not?"

She shakes her head. "I think I was afraid."

"Of what?" There are so many ways she could answer, but I have to know.

Her eyes shine in the low light. "Of losing you as a friend."

I grab her other hand and twist so we're facing each other. "Steph, you could never lose me as a friend. Why would you even think that?"

Her chin tucks against her chest, her focus on our hands. "It was really hard when I first moved to Bakersfield. It wasn't like when I moved in elementary and kids became best friends because they both like grape bubble gum."

"But I do like grape bubble gum."

A smile spreads across Steph's face. "Don't think I didn't notice." She rests our clasped hands on her knees and butterflies race through my belly. "You and Jess are everything to me. I don't want things to get messed up and have to finish high school alone."

A strand of her hair falls against her cheek. I loosen my hand from her grip to tuck it behind her ear, and her eyes flutter closed for a second. "Do you honestly think we'd ditch you with two months to go? Especially now that we're both gonna be Ducks? That's one hundred percent a busted myth."

She quirks her brow.

"I'll never stop watching Myth Busters."

"I would never ask you to." Her smile falls and her lip catches between her teeth. She takes a breath. Exhales slowly. "Can I ask you something else?"

My heart pounds. "Sure?"

"I have a myth—well, more like a theory—that I need your help confirming."

I cock my head, confused.

"That you'd be okay if I kissed you."

— 14 —
STEPHANIE

Mel's eyes widen.

Regret slams through me. This was a mistake. She doesn't like me like that. She's just being nice because I'm in a vulnerable mood.

But we don't usually hold hands like this. And now the corner of her mouth is curving into that adorable smirk that's turning me into a puddle.

"I'd like that," she says.

Part of me wants to ask again. To make sure she's really sure.

But overthinking things has never done me any favors.

With one hand supporting me on the ground, I lean forward and trail my fingers over the edge of her jaw until my hand cups her cheek. Her eyes close and we both inhale. Exhale. Shut out the voice in my head telling me this could ruin our friendship and focus on how beautiful she looks in the moonlight. How I think I've wanted this since before I ended things with Brooklyn.

If I'm being honest, I've wanted this since long before that.

"You okay?" Mel whispers.

Heat flames my cheeks and I'm grateful she can't see in the low light. "Sorry. I've wanted this for so long—"

"That it's built up to something huge?"

I nod. Of course she understands. She always sees the situation from the other person's point of view.

Or maybe she's nervous, too.

"I promise if this sucks, we can forget it ever happened," I say, even though that's the last thing I want.

She laughs softly, her breath tickling my lips. "It's not gonna suck." Then she closes the space between us and we finally kiss.

We stay like that for a moment, our lips pressed softly together, my heart pounding, everything in the world around us frozen in this instant, then she sinks into me and truly kisses me. She unfolds her legs so she can lean closer and her hand slides up my arm, over my shoulder, and settles on the back of my neck. Her fingers play in my curls as her mouth moves against mine, and my brain spins. I've kissed plenty of girls since my first kiss with Sonia in eighth grade, but none have ever felt like this. Like I've jumped off a cliff and found my way home.

She breaks the kiss and I take a slow, shaky breath to hide how hard I'm breathing.

But she is, too.

"That," she says. "Absolutely did not suck."

I press my forehead against hers. I can't stop the smile that spreads over my face. "So why did you stop?"

"I needed to catch my breath."

If it's possible for a heart to explode from happiness, I think mine's about to. I take another breath, exaggerating for effect, and she laughs.

This is everything I could have hope for. That taking things to a new level wouldn't be awkward because of our friendship, and the things I love about her would make everything even better.

Like. Not love. I'm not ready to think about that yet.

Before I can spiral any more, she pulls my mouth to hers. She's less cautious this time, and when her lips part and her tongue slides against mine, I don't hold back.

We don't pull apart until the cold from the rock seeps through our clothes and we start to shiver against each other.

"They're probably getting worried about us," Mel says. I kiss the edge of her mouth, then her jaw, then move to her neck until she lets out a small sigh. "I don't actually want to go back..."

"We can go back," I whisper against the hollow of her throat.

Neither of us mention the fact that we're sharing a tent, and that if we're quiet, we can continue this for as long as we'd like.

She stretches out her legs before standing. When her hand slips into mine and tugs me to my feet, it feels natural. Like the way it's always been, but even better. Before she can climb off the rock, I pull her into my arms and tuck my head in the spot on her throat where my lips had just been.

"Should we keep this from Jess?" Mel asks. "Just for now?"

I sigh against her skin. "She'll figure it out the second we're back."

"Probably. But if she doesn't?" She pulls back to look me in the eyes. "I'm not saying this should be a secret. Not at all. But—"

"No, I get it. This will make her feel even more left out."

Mel brushes her lips against my cheek and holds me closer. "She's totally going to figure it out."

We're careful to keep space between us when we return to the campsite, but Jess's eyebrows climb so far up her forehead that I'm sure she already knows.

"There you are!" Margo says from near the fire. She's sitting close to Bryan on a blanket on the ground. Sage is on Neb's lap and the others are spaced around the fire, talking. "We were about to send out a search party."

"Sorry," Mel says. "There's a cool rock near the river and we lost track of time."

I swear Theo whispers, "Make-out rock," but I can't be sure.

We find a couple spots on the picnic table near Sage and Neb.

"I bet it's the rock I found earlier," Neb says. "We were scouting for a good place to watch the lunar eclipse and thought that could be a contender."

"We could probably hike higher up," Sage says. "But it's happening pretty late and I don't want to try to navigate those trails in the dark."

"Preach," I say, holding out my fist for her to bump. We tap knuckles and laugh. "I barely made it here in the daylight."

"I'm hoping we can find the perfect spot on our hike tomorrow," Neb says. His eyes shift to Sage when he says the word perfect, but she doesn't seem to notice.

Mel clears her throat. "Neb, do you think you could help me with some videos tomorrow? I'm still working out the actual idea, but it'd be beyond cool if I could feature a real scientist."

Sage claps her hands. "I love this idea! Babe, you'll be so great."

Neb dips his head like he's embarrassed. "Yeah, of course."

"Don't worry," I say. "I was nervous the first time Mel asked me to be in a video, but she's a pro."

"Aww, thanks." Mel bumps her elbow against my arm and sparks shoot through me. She must feel it too because she inches away. "Neb, I promise I won't make you do anything silly."

"So no dancing?" he says. "I might act like a grandpa, but I know half the posts on that site are about viral dances."

Mel and I laugh. "No dancing," she says, then leans closer to me. "Now I just need to figure out what the hell this video will be about."

The conversation drifts and soon people crawl into their tents. Jess comes over to us and points at herself, then the lodge. "I'm heading to the bathroom, so…" She trails off, and guilt hits me in the gut.

She totally knows.

Mel jumps to her feet and we follow her to the tent to grab our bathroom stuff. No one says anything as we walk, and the bathroom is crowded with other campers so we can't exactly have a conversation there either.

When we're back in the tent, Jess turns her back to us as we undress, and I'm suddenly self-conscious. I've changed in front of them hundreds of times, but now that Mel and I have kissed, taking off my clothes has a totally different meaning.

Mel must think it too, because she faces a different direction, and that's how me and my two best friends end up with our backs to each other as we get ready for bed. Our flashlights point at the ceiling from the floor, making weird shadows on our faces and the sides of the tent.

"Neb promised to help with the video tomorrow," Mel says to Jess.

"Have you figured out the topic?" Jess asks.

Mel tugs her sweatshirt over her head and sits on her bedding, which is between mine and Jess's. "I like the idea about watching the lunar eclipse from the deepest spot in the earth. It can be something about extremes in science. Or how the things we witness every day are part of a huge evolutional process and we're only here for a split second of it."

Her mind fascinates me. I climb into my sleeping bag, careful not to brush against Mel.

"Like an interview? Just having him talk?" Jess asks.

"Anything but dancing," I say, and Mel laughs.

Jess's nostrils flare and I realize too late that she wasn't part of that conversation and doesn't know why it's funny. I wave a hand in the air. "Neb made her promise not to make him dance." My voice falls flat. It's like my words tipped the balance from Bestie Brigade to Third Wheel Outcast.

"I'll help however I can," Jess says. A smile curls her lips but it seems forced. "And we'll make Jordan Fricking Beebe wish he'd never heard of you."

A frown darkens Mel's face, but an instant later she reaches over to give Jess a high five. "Yeah we will!" Then she turns to slap my hand and the world moves in slow motion. Her tongue grazes her lower lip as she leans closer, hand stretched out in front of her. Everything inside me comes alive when I reach to touch her palm. The memory of her lips on mine, our arms around each other, the feel of her breath on my skin, makes me want to pull her the rest of the way toward me. I can't remember wanting someone this badly and knowing that even though she's right in front of me, I can't have her.

At least not yet.

Our slap misses the mark and we barely touch.

"That was weak," Mel says, but it comes out breathy, not her usual sarcastic tone. Her eyes hold mine for another second before she crawls into her sleeping bag. "Okay if we turn out the lights?"

"Sure," Jess and I reply.

The tent goes dark.

And then there's silence.

At every sleepover the three of us have ever had, we've talked long into the night. Didn't matter if we were tired or someone had a stomachache, we'd analyze anything and everything until we finally passed out from exhaustion. And there were always videos and selfies, even if we didn't plan to do anything with them later.

But we've barely taken any pics on this trip. At least not of the three of us.

If there's an argument, Jess fixes things. If she's hurting, we need to step up.

Tomorrow. Tomorrow I'll make sure she feels included.

After an eternity, the sounds of breathing fill the tent. Disappointment hits low in my belly. What, were Mel and I going to make out after Jess falls asleep? That feels creepy and inappropriate. It's totally better if we wait until we're back home to see where this thing goes.

Then slowly, slowly, a zipper sounds.

A moment later, Mel's breath warms my ear. "This feels really disrespectful," she says. "But I couldn't fall asleep without one more kiss." Her head moves over mine, but it's impossible to see her face in the dark.

I pull my arm out from my cocoon and reach for her face. My finger pokes her in the eye and she stifles a squeal. We freeze, waiting to see if Jess reacts, but her slow breaths continue.

Biting my lip to hold in a laugh, I slide my hand into Mel's hair and pull her closer. Our lips meet clumsily, but it doesn't matter.

Nothing matters except this.

She tastes like toothpaste and her hair smells like campfire and the combination of these two scents burns in my brain for eternity. Her hand trails over my face, brushing over my closed eyes, my jaw, my throat, and she deepens the kiss.

I try to stay quiet, but it's too easy to get lost in her.

When the sleeping bag next to us rustles, Mel rests her cheek against mine, her heart pounding in a beat just as fast but opposite of mine. "Good night," she whispers before crawling back to her bed.

"Good night." I zip my sleeping bag up to my neck in an attempt to trap her heat and her scent next to me, and fall asleep with my fingers pressed to my lips, imagining hers still there.

Bright sunlight wakes me. Jess and Mel are still sleeping, and I'm relieved Jess hasn't fled like yesterday morning. My vow from last night comes back to me. Our number one mission today is to make Jess feel included.

I unzip myself and escape to the bathroom. Sage and Naomi are already in there, whispering near the sinks.

"Good morning." Naomi's red curls are bigger than mine but she manages to balance them on the top of her head in a way that probably took two seconds but looks cooler than anything I could ever put together.

"Morning." I smile at them and point at her messy bun. "You need to teach me how to do that."

"It's witchery," Sage says with a smirk. "I've watched her do it hundreds of times and still can't figure it out."

"That's because your hair is so fine a bobby pin barely stays in it," Naomi says. "Come here." She motions me over and pulls the hair tie off my wrist. "May I?" she asks, nodding at my forehead.

"Sure?"

She slides her hands through my hair, gathering it at the top of my head. "The trick is to only pull your hair halfway through the hair tie, then grab some of the excess on the second loop, then do that once more, depending on how big the elastic is."

"You're speaking Greek," Sage says, and I laugh.

Naomi tugs a couple pieces and spins me around so I'm looking at the mirror. "See? It just takes a little practice."

My hair's not as long as hers so my bun's not nearly as big, but it's perfectly messy. The dark brown streaks from underneath give the purple curls depth as they swirl together at the top of my head. "I look like an ice cream cone."

They burst out laughing.

"But a beautiful ice cream cone," Sage says.

My cheeks flush. "So you two have been best friends since high school?"

"Feels like longer," Sage says. "But yeah. Naomi's helped me through a lot of shit."

Naomi slides an arm around Sage's waist. "You know I'd do anything for you."

They exchange a look that has me doubling down on my vow to show Jess how important she is to us.

"You ready for the hike today?" Sage asks. "Neb's excited to help with Mel's video, and I'm sure the scenery will inspire them."

"I hope so," I say. "Mel's hiding it well, but she's freaking out about posting a video with a mistake and having it called out by Jordan Fricking Beebe."

"That's the guy who duetted her?" Naomi asks. I nod, and she scowls. "Sometimes I wonder what I see in the opposite sex."

"Life's a lot easier not worrying about them." I may not have the skills to style the perfect messy bun, but I have no doubts when it comes to my sexuality. "For me anyway." Her smile fades and I rush to keep talking. "I'm sure the perfect guy's out there for you." I touch her arm and catch the corner of my lip between my teeth. "And it'll be amazing."

Naomi's eyebrows shoot up and she points back and forth between me and Sage. "I don't know what you're planning," she pauses before giving me a wink. "But don't let me stop you."

I let out a squeal and they both laugh. We may have only met a couple days ago, but they both seem like really genuine people and if I can help Naomi find happiness, I'll do it.

They wait for me to use the bathroom, then we head back to the campsite. The parents sit around a small fire drinking coffee, but no one else is up. I crawl into our tent and sit on my bed, too excited to fall back asleep. So instead I take deep breaths and yawn and fake sneeze until Mel and Jess roll toward me.

"Omigod, what?" Mel groans, her eyes still closed.

"Naomi just approved Operation Amazing!"

Mel's eyes pop open and Jess sits up. "Keep talking," Mel says.

I repeat the conversation and when I'm done, the three of us are holding hands and bouncing on Mel's bed.

"I know exactly how to kick this to the next level," Mel says. She squeezes my hand, then reaches for her shoes and climbs out of the tent.

"Sounds like it's gonna be an interesting day," Jess says.

She seems more tired than upset, but I feel awkward because of Mel. "I really hope we can figure out Mel's video."

Jess glances away.

That was the wrong thing to say.

"She always manages to make things work in the end," Jess says.

It's a loaded statement, and a true best friend would push her to talk, but this thing with Mel is so new I don't know if I'm ready to defend it yet. "I hope so."

I dig out my hiking clothes to change and Jess leaves for the bathroom. I mentally kick myself. I promised I'd make her feel included and she's starting the day alone.

Outside, breakfast's already on the table. Mel's sitting with Naomi and Sage and they're talking and laughing with their heads close together, so I grab food and sit at a table with Theo.

"Can I ask you a question?" I say.

"You may ask whatever you'd like. Whether I answer, that's a different story." He waggles his brows and I straighten. "I'm kidding. I'm an open book. What's up?"

I nod toward the lodge, toward the bathrooms. "Is Jess okay? She isn't really talking to us but I know she's upset. I don't want to say the wrong thing and make it worse, but I hate that she feels left out."

Theo sets his bacon on a napkin and rests his elbows on the table. The few times I've been around him, he's always been jokey and tried to make people laugh, but right now he looks serious. Like a teacher. "I don't want to betray her confidence, but you're right to think she feels left out."

"Usually I'm the one feeling like the outsider."

He cocks his head and waves a hand at me. "I don't believe that for a second. You seem like you have your shit together more than most kids your age."

"Okay, outsider might be an exaggeration. But Mel and Jess have been best friends since way before I showed up and I hate that I'm coming between them."

"How are you coming between them? I thought you're the Bestie Brigade?"

"You know about that?"

"Mel shares a lot with me." His smile is soft and my senses perk.

"Did she tell you about...?" I don't say the words but sort of point at myself and blush.

He rubs his hands together. "Did you two finally kiss?"

Now my face is definitely red. "Finally? How long was this a possibility?"

His smile gets so big that his mouth opens wide enough to see his molars, then he shakes his head and acts serious. "She's only mentioned it recently, but you'd have to be blind not to see that you're attracted to each other."

"I thought I was being so careful." I scan the others. Does everyone know, or is Theo just hyper-aware because he spends all day with horny preteens?

"I'm fairly certain the parents are clueless, so your tent situation is safe for now."

I didn't think it was possible to blush harder, but my face could set the table on fire. "We're not—I'm not." I shake my head. "That's not a thing. Especially with Jess in there."

"Which brings us back to the dilemma at hand."

I appreciate that he doesn't dwell on what Mel and I may or may not be doing behind closed tent flaps. Sure, I've thought about what it'd be like to do more than kiss, but I'm in no hurry to get her clothes off.

"Have you talked to Jess about you two?" he asks.

"The first night here she asked if I liked her." It feels weak saying it out loud. I'm better than this.

"Keeping it from her is only going to make the situation worse." He picks up a piece of pineapple and pops it in his mouth. "It's okay to admit you still don't know where this is going. But not telling her isn't cool."

"Sage was right. You are helpful."

He presses his hands to his chest. "Aww, thank you." Then he boops me on the nose with his finger. "I like you for Mel. You don't bullshit around and you're wicked cool."

Before I can respond, Margo claps her hands to get everyone's attention as Jess returns to the campsite. "The Benji and Ronny train leaves in half an hour, so finish up breakfast and do whatever you need to do to get ready."

"Mom," Mel groans with a hand over her face. "You're embarrassing yourself." Then she catches my eye and her smile makes the rest of my body as warm as my face.

"Yeah," Theo whispers. "You're totally subtle."

Jess hesitates next to our table. "Am I interrupting?"

Theo jumps to his feet. "And Theo McGinnis exits stage left." He curtsies before grabbing his trash, then leaves us alone.

Jess takes his empty seat. "What was that about?"

I spit the words out before I lose my nerve. "We need to talk."

She folds her hands in her lap. "That's never a good opening."

"No, it's not bad." A thousand words jumble on my tongue, none of them the right ones. "You were right the other night. About me and Mel."

Her brows lift but she doesn't say anything.

"I do like her. And—" I swallow. Take a breath. Take another breath. "And we kissed last night."

Her gaze drops to the table. "I figured as much."

My mouth falls open. "You heard us?"

Her eyes get wider. "You were kissing in the tent? With me in there?"

My face warms again. I'm gonna die of heat stroke at this point. "It happened when we went for a walk. But then only once in the tent." I flatten my hands on the table. "I don't want there to be any secrets between us."

"I don't want to hear the sordid details."

"There aren't any." Her lips curl into a smile and a whoosh of breath leaves me. "I promise I'll keep that to myself."

"Keep what to yourself?" Mel says from behind me. Jess must have seen her approach but didn't warn me, and now I'm even more flustered.

"About you two," Jess says with a smirk.

Mel's eyes nearly bug out of her head and she nods slowly. "Oh! Oh. So we're talking about this." She sits next to Jess, and I don't know if it was strategic to sit next to her and not me, but I'm glad. "Yes, um, this is a thing."

Jess reaches for both our hands. "I'm happy for you. Really. I'm a little sad for me because of course you're going to share things that I won't be a part of, but—" She makes a point of looking us each in the eyes. "I am one hundred percent okay with that. I just don't want to lose my best friends."

"You won't," Mel says.

"Never." I climb out of my seat and hurry to the other side of the table, then wrap my arms around them. Slow clapping from across the campsite makes us turn.

Theo gives us a thumbs-up.

"That guy has the subtlety of a sledgehammer," Mel says.

"Maybe we can use that to our advantage," Jess says.

We follow her gaze to the edge of the campsite where Hunter and Naomi talk quietly.

Mel claps. "Operation Amazing is a go!"

$$\sim\!\!\sim 15 \sim\!\!\sim$$

MELODY

"This hike's a little over a mile," Ronny says. "But it's still challenging."

"It follows the Colorado and cuts in and out of caves that have been here since before even the Havasupai," Benji says.

They stand side-by-side at the trailhead next to the sign marked River Trail. Their casual athleticism is mildly intimidating but despite their no-nonsense style, they clearly enjoy their jobs.

But how could you not when it means you get to be in nature every day?

Ronny starts down the trail and Benji motions for us to follow. "I'll pick up sweep." He moves to the back of the line.

Steph hurries to be right behind Ronny, so Jess and I follow. My legs feel mostly recovered from the hike down the South Kaibab Trail two days ago, but my pack is heavy with enough water for the day and food for lunch.

Steph seems determined to keep Jess between us, and Jess seems more like herself than she's been the whole trip.

The trail winds back and forth from the river. In some spots it's so narrow we have to hug close to the canyon wall, then it widens enough that I don't feel like I'm going to fall into the river a hundred feet below us. The views from the bottom of the canyon are different from on the hike down. When we first left the trailhead, adrenaline and the spectacular vistas carried us through the first few hours, and this time it's a relief to know we only have to hike a mile before we get to relax.

Hunter and Naomi are close enough behind us to catch bits of their conversation. And based on my brother's topic of choice, he needs our help.

He's rambling about a book on rock formations that he helped edit when the start of an idea for the video hits me. I stop so suddenly that he runs into me, which bumps me forward and makes me trip over my own feet. I yelp as I stumble toward the ground, but a quick hand under my armpit stops me before I faceplant on a rock.

"Mel, you can't stop like that!" Hunter yells.

"Omigod, are you okay?" Naomi asks, elbowing him.

Jess, who's still got a grip on my arm, pulls me to my feet. "What happened there?"

"Sorry!" I grab Jess's shoulder and pull her in for a hug. "I don't know how you reacted so fast, but thank you."

By now the entire group has stopped and Mom's pushing her way to the front of the group. "Mel! Did you fall? Are you hurt? Do you need to take a break?" She runs her hands over my arms and neck and forehead, searching for nonexistent wounds.

"Mom, I'm fine. Jess caught me before I fell."

"Did you twist your ankle? An injury like that could make it almost impossible to hike out tomorrow."

"We could always strap her to a burro," Hunter says with a laugh.

I point at him. "There will be no burros."

"Mmm, a burrito sounds so good," Steph says.

I smile at her. "Let's do that when we get back to reality." Then I realize I basically asked her on a date in front of everyone.

Jess takes a tiny step back and I fight the urge to explain it away. If Steph and I are going to be together, going on dates will be part of that.

If Steph is surprised, she doesn't show it. "It's a date."

Okay then.

Hunter gives me a peculiar look, which I return with a cheesy grin, even though the video idea completely vanished from my brain.

"So everyone's okay?" Ronny looks at me with mild concern.

"Yep, ready to go," I say.

We reach the end of the trail in less than an hour and toss our packs next to a massive boulder. I'm walking toward the river's edge when Hunter joins me.

"I didn't mean to yell at you back there," he says. "I wasn't paying attention to you and was afraid I'd be the reason you'd hurt yourself."

I raise a brow. "So who were you paying attention to?"

Pink colors his cheeks.

This is going exactly as I hoped. But instead of taking the direct approach, I lean on his need to give brotherly advice. "Can I talk to you about something?"

He kicks a stone into the river. The current swallows the splash, barely giving it time to make a ripple. "Of course."

"How do you know when it's worth risking a friendship for something more?" He's the last person I would go to for actual romance advice, but my brother is like the most stubborn horse in the world. If I ask him about Naomi directly, he'll buck and pull and run away, but if I get him talking about my situation, he'll be drinking from the river in no time.

Or however that metaphor goes.

He glances at Steph and Jess, who are sitting far enough away along the river's edge that they can't hear us. "You like one of your friends?"

I nod. "And I know Steph likes me back. But putting yourself out there is scary. What if it doesn't work out and we stop being friends?"

His brows furrow. "Is this really about Steph?"

My head bobbles up and down and my eyes widen innocently. "Yes. Absolutely." Then I give him a sly smile. "Why do you ask?"

"Because I know you and it feels like you're using your situation to tease information out of me."

I bat my eyes at him. "What information could I possibly tease out of you?"

His gaze flicks over my shoulder, just for a second, and I follow to where he looked. To Naomi.

I try to swallow my smile, but he notices.

"I see," he says.

"See what?" My eyelashes flutter again, and he laughs.

He focuses back on me and rubs his neck. "Why don't you stop with the games and tell me whatever's on your mind?"

"I think you should get back together with Naomi."

"I see," he says again.

"That's lazy writing," I whisper, ducking away as he reaches to tousle my head. "What? You're always complaining about writers who repeat words or phrases, even if it's for effect, and that's literally what you just did."

"Fair point."

I step closer to him and rest my head on his shoulder. The river churns below us, the waves crashing against the canyon walls and sending water arcing into the air where it catches the sunlight. "I want you to be happy. You seem happy with her. You always have. And I know things didn't work out before but that was because of college and timing or whatever. From where I'm sitting, that's not an issue anymore."

"She's still in school."

"Yeah, at UC Berkeley, which you loved. And your job is remote. Last time I checked the definition of remote work, you can do it from anywhere."

He stiffens. "So, what? I'm supposed to move back to Berkeley and we live happily ever after?"

"Why not?"

"Life isn't a fairy tale. Things don't work out just because you want them to."

"They can if you want them badly enough." I poke his leg and he sighs. "Start simple."

"Simple," he repeats.

"Kiss her," I whisper, dragging out the words.

He laughs. "How are we having this same conversation five years later?"

"Because I refuse to stand by while you let her get away." Yeah, I pushed him to kiss her on the camping trip when we first met Theo and Naomi, but I can only do so much. "If you still have feelings for her, you need to do something about it. Now."

His eyes grow wide. "Now?"

I shrug. "You've got something better to do?"

"Here I thought my little sister needed my advice on her budding relationship, but apparently I was wrong."

"Ew, don't say budding."

He raises his brows.

"Go talk to her."

He taps my chin with his finger. My heart feels ready to overflow as he meanders over to where Naomi's talking with Sage, Neb, and Theo. Naomi smiles in response to something he says, and even more importantly, when he looks at the river, she gives him a very unsubtle once-over.

I hurry to Jess and Steph. "Phase whatever of Operation Amazing is complete. I basically told Hunter to make things happen with Naomi and to move to Berkeley to be with her."

Jess barks a laugh. "That's a bit aggressive for him, isn't it?"

I sit between them and stare out at the water. "Yes, but his approach is clearly getting him nowhere."

"What's the next phase of the plan?" Steph asks. "Or is our work done?"

I look past her to check on Hunter's progress. He and Naomi have separated themselves from the others and are sitting on a rocky outcropping, alone. "Almost. I still want to give Naomi whatever nudge she might need, but after that, it's up to them."

"I love this for them." Steph smiles and holds her hand to her chest. "The beginning of a relationship is so exciting, and it's even more exciting since they both probably thought they'd never get another chance together."

My heart gallops. I want to touch her lips, to feel her smile and share her gooey feelings, but I'm literally wedged between her and Jess and kissing Steph right now really doesn't sound like the best plan. "I hope they can make it work."

"Since that's basically solved," Jess says. "Should we talk about the video?"

Anxiety tightens my chest. I'm not typically an anxious or nervous person—I think Hunter got our family's share of those traits—but trying to figure out the perfect response to being called out for making a mistake and having my intelligence questioned has got me second-guessing everything I do. "I really like the idea of tying the human experience to the layers of the canyon and how deep we've traveled. How everything is related and if you only stay at the surface, you'll never truly know anyone."

"That'll blow JFB outta the water," Steph says.

"I can tie it into science by comparing it to accepting the things that happen around us. Gravity, centrifugal force." I make a point to enunciate the word centrifugal clearly. "And digging deeper to truly understand a concept."

"Not to point out the obvious," Jess says, "but that has the added bonus of belittling the way he runs his account without ever naming him."

I rub my hands together. "Ooh, I like that!" Another thought hits me. "How do I use Neb with all this? I've got a real life scientist—"

"A hot real life scientist," Jess adds.

"Yes, yes. I've convinced him to help and I want to make sure it's worth his time."

Steph snorts. "Make him explain the lunar eclipse without a shirt."

"Thirst trap!" Jess yells, causing the others to look our way.

Laughter bursts out of me and I cover my face. "Omigod, Jess."

She leans into me, laughing. "You laugh, but sex sells." She points at Neb, but fortunately they're standing far enough away that it isn't clear who she's pointing at.

"You've recorded a lot of footage, right?" Steph asks. When I nod, she continues. "You could probably do a whole series from down here. Maybe have him talk in more than one video, but make his focus be on the eclipse."

"Like a guest star," I say.

"Ha, stars." This time Jess points at the sky. "I see what you did there."

Steph turns to face me. "You have me and Jess on all the time, so it wouldn't be weird to have other people too."

I clap my hands together. "I've got it! I'll record him while the sun's still out wherever we're planning to watch the eclipse, then again during the eclipse. Then I can edit the video to cut back and forth between the two timelines." People rarely watch more than a couple minutes of someone talking. The platform is all about fast edits and motion.

"That's gonna be bomb," Steph says.

"I should talk to him about it now." I rest my hands on their shoulders to push myself to my feet.

"But what about the response video?" Jess asks. She looks uncertain, like she isn't sure if she should push on this, and it's what I love about her. That she pushes without being pushy.

I tap the side of my head. "I'm sorting it out in here." I join Neb and the others and am explaining my plan for the eclipse video when a group of hikers join us at the river's edge. There are three women and four guys, all about Hunter's age, and they have the same lean muscles and determined looks as our guides.

Theo approaches them with the easy smile that's as much a part of him as his dark hair and quick wit. By the time the rest of us make our way over, he's got them all laughing. "New friends!" he says. "Meet my old friends." He points at each of them as he says their names. "Cally, Blake, Mike and Mica—I'm still puzzling over that one. Alex and Kurt. And Topher."

"And Topher," the new friends say in unison, and laugh.

"Always just Topher," says the sandy-haired guy wearing a neon orange jacket.

"Aww, Toph. We love you even if no one else does," says the girl with long dark braids. Is that Mike or Alex?

We all say our names and there's hand shaking and head bobbing, then the parents come over and it almost feels like a party.

"You all camping down here?" Blake, the shortest of the three guys, but definitely the cutest, eyes our bags.

"How'd you guess?" I ask.

"Doesn't seem like you have much gear."

"Your bags don't seem very full," Steph says, and a spark of pride warms me. She's not obvious about pushing back, but she catches that he sort of implied that as females, we need more gear than they do. Or that we're heavy packers. Or maybe I'm overthinking this.

Cally slides her arm through Blake's and points at Alex and Kurt, the two who look the most rugged. "These two convinced us to hike down and back in one day."

Naomi's eyes go wide. "I know Benji said people do that, but people really do that? How?"

Cally laughs. "That was my reaction, too."

"The official sites warn you not to." Kurt grips the straps of his backpack like he's anchoring himself to the ground. "But it's doable if you plan ahead."

"And it helps when you've got tree trunks for legs." Alex, the one with the braids, says. She seems to be with Kurt. Or if not, the look she gives him is scandalous.

Topher thrusts out his leg and flexes. "Hey, I've got tree trunks too!"

They laugh again, and I get the feeling he's their comic relief the same way Theo is for us.

Theo, whose gaze lingers on Topher.

Interesting.

"We're just stopping for lunch," the blonde woman named Mike says. Her voice is softer than the others' but she doesn't seem intimidated by the rest of them. She seems secure next to her partner Mica, who's been scanning the area on alert since they arrived.

"Perfect," Mom says. "We're about to eat, too."

"Ooh, great! Let's picnic together!" Cally says. As if on cue, they strip off their packs and unload their food. We follow suit, and soon we're seated along the rocks at the edge of the river, our groups intermingled.

Cally and Blake settle near us.

"Where are you from?" I ask.

"Boulder," Blake says.

"Colorado," Cally says. "But I grew up in Vermont."

"Those sound cold and snowy." Steph shivers next to me, and even though I know she's pretending, I want to wrap an arm around her.

"We're skiers, so it tracks," Cally says, darting a smile at Blake, whose mouth falls open.

"Excuse me?" He freezes with a piece of jerky halfway to his lips.

Steph, Jess, and I exchange confused looks.

"I do not ski." Blake points at his chest. "I'm a snowboarder."

"I've never done either," I admit. Snowboarding has always sounded fun but I've never had a strong desire to be cold on purpose. I blame living in southern California.

"Oh, you should try it sometime!" Cally's face lights up. "It's so freeing. I love being part of nature and flying through the air—"

"Hold up," Jess says. "You do jumps?"

Blake gives Cally an adoring look. "Crazy sick jumps."

Cally blushes. "I competed in slopestyle on the junior circuit for a couple years. I tried out for the Olympic qualifiers, but I wasn't fast enough."

My eyes go wide. "That is beyond cool."

Steph nudges me. "You should get them on video too."

"You're making a video?" Blake asks.

"She's super popular on TikTok," Jess says. "MeltyPoint. It's all about science."

Cally nods slowly. "That's really awesome. Alex would dig that. She's an environmental scientist and is planning to single-handedly save the planet."

"You doing something for the eclipse?" Blake asks.

I point at Neb, who hasn't left Sage's side, even with all the extra people. "He's our resident science guy. We're planning an alternate timeline thing where we shoot in the same location during the day, then later during the eclipse."

Blake's head bobs up and down. "I can't wait to see it."

"You're gonna follow me?"

He fist-bumps my shoulder. "Well, yeah. Life's all about random connections. You never know who you'll meet when you least expect it." He gives Cally a soft smile and I add them to my relationship goals list.

"Yo." Kurt, the biggest of all of them, stands, looking like a Greek god. "If we're gonna get outta this thing before the eclipse, we need to keep moving."

Steph rubs her hands down her thighs. "I can't believe you're doing the full hike in one day. My legs have barely recovered from the hike down."

Blake points at Kurt. "He wanted to do rim to rim, but we convinced him to go easy on us."

Cally laughs. "More like Topher threatened to bail on the trip." They stand and slip the straps of their packs over their shoulders. "This was really cool."

I jump to my feet. Is it too soon to hug? We barely talked but they have such a chill vibe that I don't want it to end. "Good luck with the climb." I nod at the trailhead.

"Maybe leave us some breadcrumbs for tomorrow," Jess says with a laugh.

Blake beams at her and she blushes. "You got it."

Cally holds out her arms. "Is it too soon to hug?"

"We love hugs!" Steph says, and we embrace Cally and Blake in a huffle.

We follow them to the rest of the group. Theo and Topher

are deep in conversation, and the others exchange knowing looks behind their backs.

"What?" I mouth to Cally.

"Toph's got a gift for connecting with people. He could meet his soul mate on a ride share."

My heart does a little flutter. "Theo's the same way."

The two seem oblivious that we're all watching, until Mica nudges Topher with his knee. "Dude, time to roll."

Topher looks up at him and blinks as if coming out of a trance. Theo has the same captivated look on his face. For as long as we've been friends, I've rarely seen this gentler side and I wish I could bottle the hope and excitement oozing from him.

Topher says something too low for us to hear, then Theo pulls out his phone and they exchange numbers.

Jess smacks my arm and I mouth "I know" at her. Of course Theo would meet someone at the bottom of the earth.

The guys stand, more hugs get thrown around, then the group marches down the trail and out of our lives.

Except based on the smile on Theo's face, this won't be the last we hear from them.

— 16 —
STEPHANIE

We hang out by the river for a little longer, then the non-parental adults head off by themselves, leaving us with the parents. Mel and Jess walk along the edge of the river to shoot more footage, and I can't help but think Mel's trying to avoid her parents.

I'd give anything for my parents to try more.

It still doesn't feel real that they're getting divorced. Probably because I haven't been home since they told me, but even though they're always fighting and don't even seem to like each other anymore, part of me hoped that since they made it twenty years together, they would make it twenty more.

"You look like you could use a friend," Nancy says from a few feet away.

I shrug. She seems nice and all, but I'm not really in the mood to share with someone I barely know.

"Well, I could use a friend." She gestures at the rock I'm sitting on. "Can I join you?"

"Sure." I scoot over and she sits with her knees pulled up to her chest.

"It's weird when your friendships change," she says. My head snaps up, but she hooks her thumb over her shoulder at Margo and Bryan. "For years, Margo and I have been the dynamic divorced duo, conquering imposter syndrome and single-mom stereotypes with one arm tied behind our backs."

I laugh despite my mood, and she smiles back.

"Of course I'm happy for her. Who wouldn't want her best friend to be happy? But sometimes change can be hard."

An uneasy feeling stirs in my chest. I'm not jealous of my friends. "Why are you telling me this?"

She rubs her palm back and forth over the rock. "You seem like you have things you need to get off your chest." The concern in her eyes combined with the way she bites her lower lip almost makes me burst into tears. I press my knuckles to the corner of my eyes and let my hair fall in my face.

I nod at Mel and Jess. "I can talk to my friends."

"I didn't mean to ambush you. Theo and Naomi are always telling me to go easy, but when I see someone hurting, I want to help." She glances at me before looking out over the river. "It's okay if you'd rather not talk to me. But please know that I'm here if you need an impartial ear."

She's right. Talking to her would be easy. I won't see her again after this week and from what Mel said, this is kind of her specialty. And she's divorced, so she knows what's coming for my family. But I'm afraid that if I start talking, if I say my fears out loud, I won't be able to stop talking and all those fears will come true. About my parents, and screwing up my friendship with Mel, and if I truly have what it takes to be an architect.

"I'll leave you alone." She pats my knee and climbs off the rock.

"Wait." I twist around to look at her and she stops. "You can stay."

She sits back next to me and we watch the river. I've learned that I can sit in silence longer than most other people, something that drives Mel crazy, and after a few minutes, Nancy clears her throat. "So you're going to the University of Oregon? Do you know what you want to study?"

Responses about architecture and designing buildings and being on campus with Mel pile on top of each other, but that's not what comes out of my mouth. "Right before we left, my parents told me they're getting divorced."

She sucks air between her teeth. Several moments pass before she speaks, and I like that she doesn't rush to tell me it'll be okay. "That's hard."

"How will my family be a family after this?"

"Family is what you make it." She takes a breath. "I'm not going to sugarcoat this. It's going to be difficult. For all of you." She shifts so she's facing me and crisscrosses her legs. "But this doesn't change who your parents are to you. They're still your mom and dad and they still love you exactly the same."

Everything goes blurry as tears fill my eyes. "That's more or less what they said to me."

"You're old enough to understand that relationships are tricky. People change, and if the person you thought was your perfect match at one point in your life doesn't change with you, the relationship will stagnate."

Could that happen with me and Mel? She understands me better than anyone in the world, even better than my parents, but I'm not so naïve to think that the person I like when I'm barely eighteen could be my soul mate.

"My advice to you, if that's okay?" She waits for me to nod before continuing. "Focus on your relationship with your parents and try not to worry too much about the future. The relationship that's broken is theirs, not yours, and as much as you care for them, this is out of your hands."

"Thanks." Deep down this is all logical, but hearing her words helps my brain accept it. "If I'm honest, my parents haven't been happy in years, but they're my parents. I never imagined they would split up." Everything is going to change. When I get home from this trip, it might be the last time they're both waiting for me. They'll probably be in two different places when I'm on break from college.

Our house will never be the same.

A tear runs down my cheek. I wipe it away with my sleeve and stare at the wet spot. "I feel really selfish. This is hard on them, too."

Her lips curve into a gentle smile. "It's human nature to be selfish. Don't beat yourself up over that." She taps my knee with a finger. "It's when you stop being self-aware that you should be concerned."

Mamá raised me to always think about how my actions affect others, so I don't think that's gonna be a problem. "How do I talk to them about this?"

"Same way you talk to them now." A hawk soars in front of us, its cry echoing over the river, and swoops low to the water. We watch it fly away, then she turns back to me. "We're constantly encountering things that have the potential to change us. I'm not going to assume this is the first challenge you've faced in your life, but it's important that you stay true to yourself. That's the best way you can help your parents."

I hadn't even thought about me needing to help them, and I feel even more selfish. "Thanks. My head's been swirling since they told me and what you're saying helps me make sense of everything."

"I'm glad." She nudges my arm with her elbow. "Now I need to apply that advice to my own life."

"Is—is there anything you want to talk about?" I doubt I could say anything that will actually help, but I feel a connection with her and at least I can listen.

She studies me for a moment, her eyes shining in the bright sunlight. "That's very sweet of you to ask. I'll be okay. I have wonderful children and a career I love. My life is very fulfilling. The rest will fall into place when it's meant to." She pats my knee again. "And yes, I know it sounds like I'm convincing myself. I work a lot with manifesting goals."

I cock my head. My self-help knowledge is limited to what Mel's shared, and this is new to me.

"Basically it means stating out loud what you want, and repeating it many times. The energy that you put out into the world folds back in on itself and, according to the theory, helps your goals become reality."

It sounds like what Papá calls woo-woo basura, but hearing it from Nancy makes it feel more real. Like you really can just say what you want and it'll happen.

I mean, that's kind of what I did with Mel. I admitted to Jess that I liked her, and now we've officially moved past the friend zone. "I could get behind that," I say.

Just then, Mel calls my name from near the shore of the river.

"Go join your friends. But know that I'm here if you need to talk."

"I really appreciate it." I give her a side hug before hopping off the rock.

I catch up to them near the river's edge.

"We thought we'd hike this way a bit." Jess points farther downriver.

"Not really a hike," Mel says. "Just a casual walk. But I want to check out a row of hoodoos near the next bend in the river."

It can't hurt to try to manifest. "Things will work out with us," I whisper to myself. I link my arms through theirs, but I have to let go pretty quickly because the trail is too narrow to walk side by side.

When we reach the spot she was talking about, Mel stands with her hands on her hips and looks around. The walls of the canyon go straight up like skyscrapers. There's the occasional ledge or gap in the stone where plants have sprouted, but it's mostly straight rock. The first time my parents took me to downtown Los Angeles, I couldn't believe how high the buildings stretched into the blue sky, and I have that same disorientated feeling now.

"You really get a sense for how deep we are here, you know?" Mel says.

"What if you start by recording the sky, then pull down in fast speed to us here at the river?" Jess points at the formation at the bend up ahead. "You can use a lot of the footage you already have from the hike down to show the variations in the rock wall."

"You're really good at this," I say to Jess. "At visualizing the big picture of things."

Her cheeks color and she kicks a loose rock with her toe. "Yeah, but that doesn't translate into a career."

"Are you kidding?" Mel says. "That's like strategy and event planning and chief operating big deal person. There are tons of ways you can use those skills."

Jess visibly bristles. "I know college is what you both want, but I really don't think it's right for me."

Mel reaches for her arm. "I didn't meant to imply that. I'm just saying that there's a lot of things you're good at and a lot you can do in the future." She turns in a slow circle, staring up at the sky. "But nothing has to be decided right now. This place is the perfect reminder that slow and steady can make as much of an impact as racing full speed toward a goal."

I snap my fingers. "What about that!"

They both face me, brows raised expectantly.

"For the video. You can show the hiking footage and all that in triple time, then do a super fast drop to the bottom where we are, then slow it down to a freeze frame or almost slow motion."

Mel bounces on the ball of her feet. "Because science isn't fast. We make mistakes when we rush. Experiments can be flashy and cool, but the knowledge behind them takes patience and persistence. And hard work."

"This would be a cool way to dig at JFB without mentioning him," Jess says.

"And you could tie in how much time and research you put into your videos," I say, nodding. "But without being in your face about it. He tries to play it like you're a silly girl who doesn't know what she's talking about, and he couldn't be more wrong." Anger builds inside me as I think about how easily assholes like Jordan Fricking Beebe can tear someone down with barely a thought.

Mel nods slowly, watching us. "Yes. But what's the hook? I can't start with 'I'm a girl and I work hard at science,' but I also don't want to go Morgan Freeman voiceover and talk about how the earth was formed billions of years ago."

"We could totally have Neb do the deep voice intro." I laugh. "And you've already got that hook. You're a girl who works hard at science and who's fascinated by the world around us."

"What if you start by lying on the ground looking up at the sky," Jess says. "You can talk about how overwhelming it is being here at the bottom of the canyon surrounded by millennia of evolution, but how your curiosity about how things work makes you want to know more. And then you explain that's how a lot of science experiments start."

"Jess, you're fricking brilliant," Mel says. "We can finesse the exact wording as we go, but I already have a lot of footage that could work with this idea." She lays on the ground between us and stares up at the sky. "It really is overwhelming being here." Her gaze falls on me and pauses, and my pulse kicks up. "Come down here," she says.

Jess and I lay on either side of her, but I'm guessing my fingers are the only ones she twists through hers. I press my arm against hers as we stare at the stretch of blue above us.

"It feels like the sky is farther away down here," I say.

Mel squeezes my hand. "Technically it is. The atmosphere is roughly sixty miles above the surface of the earth. We're over a mile below the surface. The same way the oxygen gets thinner the closer you get to space, in theory the oxygen levels should be different down here."

"So we should have extra energy or less energy?" I lift my legs in the air and let them fall to the ground. "Because I gotta tell you, my energy levels are not the greatest right now."

Mel points her phone at the sky but flips the camera so it's pointing at her face. "Get closer." We squish into the frame and she hits record. She doesn't say anything as we stare into the camera, then she flips the orientation so it's pointing at the sky. After several beats, she hits stop, then flips it again. "I wanted one without me talking, but now I'll try to get philosophical."

Jess and I giggle. This is one of my favorite parts about being friends with Melody Thompson. She can pull an idea from nothing and, five seconds later, turn it into something that's smart and relatable while still down to earth. Really down to earth in this case.

I giggle again and she turns her head.

"What?"

"Just making stupid jokes."

"Nothing you say is stupid. Out with it Stephita."

My nickname coming from her mouth makes me tingle all over. It speaks to an extra level of familiarity that we're just beginning to uncover. "I was thinking that your videos are popular because you're down to earth—"

"Now we're really down to earth," Jess says with a laugh.

I lean up onto my elbow. "Yes! Exactly."

Mel rolls her eyes. "I can't take you two anywhere."

I nudge her with my elbow. "You got this."

She pushes to her feet and stretches her arms over her head. Turns in a circle with her face tilted to the sky. "It's so beautiful out here. I feel like anything I say will trivialize it."

I brush my knuckles against her bare leg. "So say that."

Mel looks down at me. The mix of emotions on her face makes me want to pull her into my arms, but I smile instead.

"Also, do the slow spinning thing again and we'll record it," I say. "That was a cool shot from this angle."

Jess records her, then hands the phone back to Mel.

"Let's see what I can pull out of my ass." Mel flips it to selfie mode, and plasters on a smile. "Hey, it's your favorite tokker, MeltyPoint, coming at you from the bottom of the earth. Ugh, no." She taps the screen and lowers her phone. "That was awful."

"It wasn't awful," Jess says. "Stop overthinking it and just talk."

"You're always saying everything can be fixed in editing," I add. "Just spit out what's on your mind."

Mel laughs. "Minus JFB."

"Yes," we reply, nodding.

"Okay." Mel smooths back nonexistent stray hairs, clears her throat, and hits record. "For as long as I can remember, I've loved figuring out how things work, how systems react to each other, and why our world behaves the way it does. For the past couple days, I've been camping in the Grand Canyon—" She flips the camera and pans in a quick circle to show the canyon walls. "This place is like a living science experiment. The layers—" She stops the recording and yells at the sky. "Why is this so hard?"

I scramble to my feet. Rest a hand on her arm. "You're putting too much pressure on yourself. Stop worrying about JFB and do what you do best."

Her eyes go wide. "That's it!"

"What's it?"

"Pressure!"

Jess and I exchange confused looks.

"I'm not following," Jess says.

Mel waves her arms at the canyon surrounding us. "This! The canyon! The layers and the river and all the history. Thousands of years of pressure created it. Pressure carved out the river."

"Technically it was erosion," I say softly. I don't want to interrupt her flow, but I don't want her to make another mistake.

She points at me. "Yes, erosion, like bullies wearing down on you. Pressure, erosion, and conflict make us who we are. It can make us stronger and push us to change in ways we don't expect." She rests her hands on her hips. "Even Jordan Fricking Beebe. I can't stand him but his friction pushes me. Challenges me."

"So we need to find places that represent that pressure?" Jess asks.

"We don't need to find it," Mel says. "It's all around us." She clears her throat, holds up a finger to us, and points the camera at herself. "This place is like being surrounded by a science experiment. As we hiked to the bottom of the canyon, it was impossible not to feel the history, the thousands and thousands of years that created this natural phenomenon." She flips the camera toward the canyon walls and the rock formation at the bend in the river. "The layers in the rock are visual evidence of the world long before we were here, and this river, which right now seems as calm as a backyard stream, is what caused it all. The constant pressure carved where we're standing."

She taps the screen and looks at us. Her cheeks are flushed with excitement, and she's so beautiful here in her element that it takes my breath away. "Is it too off-brand to talk about social pressure?"

"It might be a tiny bit off brand," I say, swallowing hard. "But I think it's necessary. You're talking to young girls who could totally use advice on how to deal with the toxic men of the world."

"And it's the perfect way to handle JFB," Jess says. "Everyone's expecting a response from you, and calling out his behavior and comparing his ass to the largest crack in the world is both hilarious and appropriate."

Mel slaps a hand over her face. "Omigod. We're in JFB's ass crack."

We burst out laughing. The sound echoes off the walls of the canyon until it fades in the distance.

"I hate that I've let him spend so much time in my head. The goal of my channel is to make people happy while informing them about science." Her lips tighten into a thin line and her jaw clenches. "I don't know why haters feel the need to tear me and other creators down."

"Because people suck." I step closer and risk catching her pinkie finger with mine. "At least most people."

That earns me a smile. "Let's go a little farther along the river," Mel says.

We follow her down the trail until we're finally staring at the hoodoos that brought us here. They seems taller up close—taller than my two-story house—and wider around than any tree I've ever seen. I run my hand along the rough surface and a piece breaks off.

I jump back, eyes wide. "I didn't mean to break it!"

Jess laughs. "I don't think you can break the Grand Canyon."

Mel points at me. "Yes!" She taps her screen again and pans up the formation. "This place shows us that even with the most intense pressure the world can throw at us, we won't break. We'll change and become something even more beautiful than before." She continues panning, capturing my face when she says beautiful.

A blush crawls up my neck until I'm sure I'm totally red, but I don't care.

"Let's keep moving," Jess says.

We round the bend in the river and stop in our tracks. The canyon opens in front of us, stretching farther than seems possible. The reds and golds of the rock glow in the afternoon sun while the river flows quietly next to us. Mel leads us single-file down the narrow trail until she finally stops near a smaller formation. She tilts her face toward the clear blue sky. "I'll have to research everything that's created under pressure. Diamonds, obviously. Maybe pearls. But I'm sure there's other things that people are familiar with that will make the concept relatable."

I kick a loose stone closer to the formation. "You could include emotional pressure. Like divorce or relationships."

"That's a cool idea." She seems distracted as she inches closer to the rock wall, and I try to ignore the sting at how casually she dismissed my idea.

"I'm really glad the Brooklyn thing didn't come between you and Mel," Jess says.

A dull roar whooshes through my ears. My mouth goes dry. "What Brooklyn thing?"

Jess's eyes widen and she clamps her lips shut.

I put my hand on her arm. "Jess."

She glances at Mel before meeting my eyes. "I thought you knew. It was forever ago and barely a thing and—"

"Just tell me."

Jess's face pales. "Brooklyn was Mel's first kiss."

My breath catches and something twists in my gut.

Surprise.

Hurt.

Jealousy.

The older you get, the more people you kiss. It's easy to forget the unmemorable ones, but no matter how awful it is, you never forget your first kiss. Or who it's with. Which means every time I've mentioned Brooklyn over the past few months, Mel chose to keep this from me.

"I swear I thought you knew," Jess whispers.

"There's an opening here," Mel calls over her shoulder.

Jess moves to her side but I hang back a few feet. The crevice isn't super deep, but it's dark and narrow and makes the giant walls around us seem less stable. And right now I need a little space from Mel.

My chest tightens and I step back until I'm on the other side of the trail.

Jess puts her face right in the opening. "It's like a crack in the earth that holds secrets older than the universe."

Mel leans in with her phone held out in front of her. "No!" They drop to their knees, their shoulders tight against the opening.

"I think I can reach it," Jess says.

Their voices are muffled, so I move closer. I can guess what happened without asking, but I ask anyways. "Is it your phone?"

Mel looks at me over her shoulder. The panic in her eyes is worse than when she forgot about a physics test—which she still aced—but all I can think is that she's been lying to me for months. "It bounced too far inside," she says.

Jess pulls off her bag and wiggles farther into the crevice.

"Be careful!" My shout echoes into the opening. "Maybe we should go back to the campsite and get something to help reach it."

Mel's gaze jumps from me to the darkness that holds her phone.

"It's not like anyone's gonna steal it," I say. My voice sounds flat but she gives me a small smile.

"You're right." She rests a hand on Jess's back. "Jess, get out of there."

"I've almost got it." Her voice sounds like it's far away, echoing deep into the soul of the canyon.

Mel stands and brushes off her pants. "Jess, it's okay."

"Get out of the creepy crevice," I say.

Mel tilts her head. "You think it's creepy?"

I wave a hand at the crevice, which looks like it's swallowed Jess. "It's a crack in the foundation. It undermines the integrity of the entire structure."

Just like the secret she's been keeping from me.

Mel taps her finger to my nose before I can move away. "You're going to be an amazing architect."

I feel like my heart is breaking. "Amazing?"

She lifts a shoulder. "I said what I said."

We turn back to Jess. She's flat on her belly and only her ankles stick out of the opening. Mel nudges her shoe against Jess's. "Come on!"

"Almost there!"

This time the echo is cut short by a rumbling noise above.

I jerk around and squint at the sky. "Is that a plane?"

Mel gasps. She points above us, her eyes wide. "Rock slide!"

"Jess!" I scream.

Jess cries out and Mel and I dive for Jess's legs and pull. She crawls backward toward the opening but rocks the size of avocados rain on the trail all around us.

Pelting our shoulders and backs.

Landing on Jess.

I cover my head with one arm and pull Jess with the other. Stones pepper my arms and neck. I try to shield Jess but it's happening too fast.

A hand on my arm pulls me back.

Tears streak Mel's face. "If we're all dead, there won't be anyone to get help."

Dust fills the air as the rumbling stops.

"Jess!"
She's not moving.
Not crying.
Not anything.

— 17 —
MELODY

Jess's feet stick out from beneath the rocks. Without a word, Steph and I drop to our knees and throw rocks from Jess's back and legs and arms. She's got little cuts all over but it's the fact that she hasn't moved that's so scary.

I shout her name again and a sob rips through me. This can't be happening.

When we've cleared the rocks, we pull Jess the rest of the way from the crevice.

"Are you sure we're supposed to move her?" Steph asks.

"I have no idea." Careful not to put any weight on her, I brush her hair from her face. Her eyes remain closed. I lean closer and her faint breath warms my face. "She's breathing!" I touch her cheek and her eyes flutter open. "Oh, thank god."

Steph crowds next to me. "Are you hurt? What's hurt?" She gently touches Jess's back and legs. Jess winces when Steph gets to her ankle.

Jess pulls her arm out from beneath her and holds up her hand.

My phone.

My stomach heaves.

This is my fault.

Jess almost died because of me.

Fresh tears burn down my face. "You shouldn't have done that."

Steph gasps behind me. "Jess, why'd you do that? You could have died for a stupid phone!"

Something unnamed pricks my heart at her words but I focus on Jess.

"You would have done the same thing." Jess pushes the phone toward me and that's when I see the kaleidoscope of fractures splintering the screen. It looks like it'd crumble apart if not for the rubber case.

Another wave of nausea sweeps through me. My phone is my life. "How am I gonna record—" I snap my mouth closed.

"Your priorities need adjusting." Steph's voice is colder than I've ever heard it, and I feel like she knocked the wind out of me.

Is that how she really feels?

"We need to get her out of here," Steph says.

"How?" Jess whispers.

"Let us worry about that," I say, even though alarms clang inside me. We're at the bottom of a canyon. It's not like we can call an ambulance. "Can you roll over?"

She rolls to her side and we help her lean against the canyon wall. As soon as she's upright, blood trails from her hairline down the side of her face.

"Jess, your head is bleeding!" Steph reaches for Jess's face but stops herself. "Hold on, I'm sure I've got something in my bag for that."

"I think I need—" Jess slumps toward us and I catch her head before it hits the ground again.

"Oh no, oh no, oh no," I repeat over and over again. "Jess!" I shimmy my bag off my shoulders and swing it around to tuck under her head as she goes limp.

Steph dabs at the blood on Jess's forehead with a tissue and we stare at each other with wide eyes.

"We have to carry her," I say.

"Or should one of us go back and get the parents? It's not too far."

"That's probably a better plan."

"I'd say I'll text you when I get there, but..." Steph waves a hand at the entirety of the canyon. "Wait! The walkie-talkies!" She points at my bag. "You have one, right?" She doesn't wait for me to answer. She gently lifts Jess's head and swaps my bag for hers, then nudges it toward me.

The walkie-talkie is tucked in the front pocket, right where Bryan put it, and a new wave of guilt twists my stomach. I'm pretty sure I rolled my eyes when Bryan insisted I take it. "I have no idea what the range is on these things."

"Just try," Steph says. There's a tension in her voice I've never heard.

I wish I could rewind to ten minutes ago and do everything differently. But I can't. So I turn the knob and hold down the button like Bryan showed me. "Um, hello? Mom? Bryan?" The silence that follows feels big enough to fill the canyon. My fingers ache to reach for Steph, but when I glance at her, she looks away.

After several moments, I try again.

"Shouldn't there be static or something?" Steph asks.

I turn it over and gasp. A crack runs the length of the device and water seeps from the bottom. "I think it's broken. But why is it wet?" I grab my bag, and find my answer. Dents cover my steel water bottle. One of them actually punctured the bottle and the water's leaking into my bag. "My water's gone too."

"Let's check the other bags," Steph says.

Jess's bag is buried under a pile of rocks, and before I unbury it, Steph groans. "My bottle's cracked too."

A silent prayer escapes my lips as I unzip Jess's bag. Stick my hand inside. And pull out her shattered water bottle.

I toss it in front of us and Steph slumps against the rough stone wall.

"You sure you don't have a secret stash of water someplace?" Steph asks.

My head snaps to her. "What's that supposed to mean?"

Steph holds my gaze, her jaw clenched, but then her lower lip quivers.

"Steph, what's going on?"

A tear mixes with the dirt on her face. "Why didn't you tell me you kissed Brooklyn?"

I fall back on the hard ground. Someone could've offered me a million dollars to guess why Steph was upset and I would never have thought of this. The words 'how did you find out?' threaten to spill out of my mouth, but I catch them before they make this situation even worse. "I was going to. I wanted to. When the two of you first started dating, you seemed really into her and I didn't want to ruin that for you."

She sniffs and drags a hand across her face. "And there was no good time in the past two months for you to mention, oh, by the way, my first kiss was with your girlfriend?"

"I should have told you. I'm sorry." I push to my feet and step toward her, but she stiffens, so I hold out my hand. "I don't want this to come between us."

She stares at my hand like I just slapped her. "You don't get to decide that."

Her words are like a kick to the chest, then her earlier comment about my priorities floods back and I sit hard against the wall near Jess. Why is Steph allowed to be mad and I'm not?

The sun breaks through a cloud, making it feel ten degrees hotter than it was when we got here. Jess is still breathing, which is more than I can say for Steph. Her face is getting redder and redder and—

"Have you drank any water?" Just because I'm mad doesn't mean I'm not worried about her.

Her eyes flick to her busted bottle on the ground. "I had some at lunch."

I reach for my phone that's not in my pocket. "It's been hours since then."

She shrugs and moves beneath the shade of a small tree. "I'll be okay."

"One of us needs to go for help," I say. "Jess could have internal bleeding and we can't just sit here while she dies."

Steph looks up to where the rocks fell from, then back to the trail. "I'll go."

"Are you sure you're okay going by yourself?"

"We don't have much choice."

"Thank you." I reach for her hand but she takes a step back and stares at Jess for a moment.

"I'll be back as fast as I can." She glances over her shoulder as she hurries down the trail, then she rounds the bend and is gone.

Leaving me alone with my unconscious best friend, holding a bloody tissue against the side of her head.

I hate feeling helpless. I've always been the friend who figures things out then jumps right in without worrying about the consequences. Which is how we ended up in this situation.

Steph is right.

If it wasn't for my obsession with making the perfect video, we'd be back with the parents, safe in a clearing where rocks don't fall and best friends don't almost die.

She could still die.

The cut on her face doesn't seem deep, and she's breathing normally, but she's definitely not awake. The heaviness in my chest gets worse with each passing minute. This is all my fault. If I hadn't been so fixated on my phone, Jess wouldn't have gotten hurt. The three of us would be laughing and joking and flirting.

Except now Steph's mad about Brooklyn. Jess is the only one who could've told her, and I can't exactly be mad at her right now.

My heart sinks further as Steph's words loop in my head. Telling me my priorities need adjusting. Is that what she really thinks? I thought she supported my videos, understood how important it is for me to have a purpose beyond myself, but maybe she hasn't been completely honest.

It's not like this is the first time one of us has said something less than kind, but we always apologize right away.

And I don't know how to regain her trust about Brooklyn. I never meant to keep it from her, but I waited too long when they started dating and it never seemed like the right time.

Now that the dust from the rockslide has settled, everything looks exactly as it did when we arrived. The river gurgles, a light breeze swirls, and a hawk hovers overhead. Probably wondering if we'll be its next meal.

And Jess still hasn't moved.

We've got to get her out of here.

Tears slide down my face and panic shoves all rational thoughts out of my head. I'm about to throw Jess onto my back when shouts come from farther down the river.

"Jess, we're saved!" I stand, careful not to bump her makeshift pillow, and I wave my arms. "Over here!"

Steph half-runs up the path with my brother and Naomi and the rest of their crew. Neb's face pales when he sees us. Sage grabs his arm and something unspoken passes between them, then he rushes toward Jess. Everyone else stands in a half-circle behind him while he kneels next to Jess and runs a hand over her head.

"He's trained as an EMT," Sage says.

Neb feels her pulse and listens to her breathing before feeling her arms and legs. "What happened?"

I point at the pile of rocks near the crevice. "She was almost crushed by that. I don't know if a rock hit her head or if she hit her head when she fell." Another sob chokes me and relief that someone else is in charge makes my legs give out beneath me.

Steph glances at me, then quickly looks at Neb. "She was awake right after, then passed out when we pulled her out of there." She doesn't mention my phone but our argument hangs between us.

Theo's eyes nearly pop out of his head. "When Tamara said there could be falling rocks, this is not what I pictured."

"You and me both," I say.

Naomi and Hunter both move toward me, and Hunter is the one to pull me close. "It's going to be okay."

"You don't know that." I lean into his shoulder, grateful we're not alone anymore.

We watch as Neb cradles the back of Jess's head in his hand and feels her neck with his other hand. "Nothing seems to be broken. It looks like her ankle's sprained. And she's definitely got a concussion." He peers at the cut on Jess's face. "I don't think there's anything here to fashion a stretcher, so we'll have to carry her." He looks up at Hunter. "You able to help?"

Hunter nods. "Yeah, of course." He stretches his arms out in front of him and rolls his shoulders back.

"I'd pretend to be offended you didn't ask me, but you made the right decision," Theo says.

"You may need to work in shifts," Sage says.

Hunter flushes but doesn't object. I love my brother, but he's not known for his physical prowess, and carrying a lifeless teenager on an uneven trail doesn't sound easy.

Neb lowers himself so he can slide an arm under Jess's head, then scoops her legs with his other arm. She moans softly as he stands. "I can get her like this for a bit, but we need to start walking."

Hunter pats Neb's shoulder as we walk. "Let me know when you need a break."

Theo rushes in front of Neb and points out every rock, twig, and lizard so Neb can avoid tripping, and Hunter's right behind him looking like he's ready to help the second Neb gets tired. The rest of us exchange worried looks. I didn't pay attention to whether or not there was a doctor or nurse at the lodge, but they have to have someone to help when people get hurt.

Steph's next to me on the narrow trail, but avoids touching me. "She's gonna be okay, right?" Her voice sounds off. Scared and shaky like mine, but there's a layer of uncertainty, like she's not sure she even wants to talk to me.

I don't know how things flipped so quickly. How she suddenly feels like a stranger. My breath comes fast and I fight more tears. "I don't know."

Jess's head bounces against Neb's arms, but I can't tell if her eyes are open.

"It has to be good that nothing's broken, right?" Steph asks.

"I think so," I say. "But if she's too dizzy to walk, how's she gonna get out of here tomorrow?"

"Not to undrama your drama," Hunter says from behind us. "But they can probably bring her up on a donkey."

I whirl around and Hunter walks into me. "What do you mean she can ride a donkey?"

He points in the air, presumably toward the trail we'll be hiking tomorrow. "The donkeys we saw on the hike down."

"Dibs on riding up on a donkey!" Theo shouts from the front of the line.

"I don't think your teacher salary will cover that," Naomi shouts back.

"And I thought you were afraid of large animals?" I ask. And how would Jess stay on the donkey? I guess she won't be unconscious so she can hold on, but will they have to strap her on like a piece of luggage?

"I'm tapping out." Neb lowers to the ground, still holding Jess against his chest. Hunter swoops in to take over and even though he doesn't seem as steady as Neb, we keep moving.

After several minutes, Neb clears his throat and moves closer to Hunter. "Have you got her all right?"

Hunter squints up the trail. "I don't think it's much farther."

"I'm not a sack of potatoes," Jess says with a shaky voice.

"Jess!" I rush to her side and run my hands lightly over her forehead.

"I'm not dead," she says, a smile lifting the corner of her mouth.

"I'm very, very glad."

Steph rushes to her other side. "Please don't ever scare us like that again." Her gaze bounces from Jess to the trail to the canyon walls.

Everywhere but me.

"No more rockslides. Got it." Jess lifts a finger to punctuate her point and her arm flops onto her belly.

"Take it easy," Neb says. "No sudden movements."

Jess nods and closes her eyes. "Got it."

"Hunter, you ready to switch?" Neb asks.

Hunter doesn't even try to pretend he's not tired. "Yes."

They carefully shift Jess back into Neb's arms and we keep walking.

The pressure in my chest lightens a tiny bit, and I work my way to Naomi's side. Neb is at the front of the line behind Theo, far enough away that he shouldn't hear. "So what happened with Neb that he learned all the EMT stuff?"

Naomi looks at Sage instead of me. "You want to tell the story?"

Sage's face grows serious. "Not long before we met, Neb was hiking with his dad in the woods and his dad collapsed on the trail. Neb didn't know what to do. He called for help but it took a long time for paramedics to find them."

My hand flies to my mouth. "Omigod!"

Tears shine in Sage's eyes. "He died from an aneurism before they got there."

"So he watched his dad die?" I couldn't imagine. My relationship with my father is nonexistent, especially since he started a new family on the opposite side of the country, and even though the random cards and calls are awkward, I like knowing that he's out there living his best life. Or at least I try to convince myself of that last part.

Sage nods. "Then the summer when we met, I had a panic attack in the middle of a crowd. He rescued me but was mad at himself that the only thing he knew how to do was to carry me out of there."

Sage smiles. "Well, yeah. He's still good at the carrying part. But he went through EMT training as soon as he started college. It's come in handy more than a few times. "

Naomi elbows her. "I'm pretty sure Neb would carry you out of the canyon if you asked."

Sage flutters her eyes dramatically and they giggle.

Naomi sighs. "You've got yourself a sciencey fireman lumberjack all rolled into one."

We look at Neb. He could totally be a fireman rushing through a burning building with a victim in his arms.

Sage rests her head against Naomi's. "Have you tried manifesting a relationship?"

I poke Hunter's arm. He scowls at me, so I nod at Naomi and he shakes his head, but not before I see his smile.

They giggle again and I swear Hunter straightens his back and flexes his shoulders.

We round a bend in the river and finally see the campsite. The parents are sitting around the campfire and bolt to their feet when they see us. Mom must have her child-radar on because she's already sprinting toward us, Bryan and Nancy right behind her.

Mom rushes to Jess, running her hands over her face and shoulders, and gasps when she sees the blood on Jess's forehead.

"What happened?" Nancy asks as Bryan takes Jess from Neb. They're both big guys and transfer her pretty easily, but she covers her face with her hands.

We quickly relay the story. Neb updates them on Jess's condition and Bryan radios into the lodge to alert them that there's been an injury.

Mom turns to me and Steph. "Are either of you hurt?"

I pull up my sleeves. Bright red scrapes race down my arms, but I'm not bleeding. "Nothing serious."

Mom pulls me against her, then reaches for Steph and hugs us both. My body reacts to Steph's closeness before my brain reminds me what she really thinks about me. Mom kisses us both on the forehead and smooths our hair like we're five years old. "We'll get you cleaned up, too."

"The lodge has basic med services," Bryan says. "We'll get you all checked out and reevaluate the plan for tomorrow."

"We were thinking she could ride a donkey," I say.

Bryan glances at Mom, who shrugs. "A mule could be an option."

Concern about my phone niggles the back of my mind, but

I tell it to shut up. Yes, it's broken, but the chip is probably okay and I can use other phones to record the rest of the footage.

The adrenaline that carried us at the start of the hike is nonexistent by the time we get to the lodge. Bryan carries Jess directly inside, with Steph and me close behind. The woman at the counter uses a walkie-talkie to let the medical person know we've arrived, and a few minutes later we're crowded into a small office stocked with bandages and pill bottles, with Jess propped on a small cot beneath the single window.

A woman with a black pixie and colorful tattoos covering her arms comes in. "I'm Janine. The med tech here at Phantom Ranch." She snaps on plastic gloves and shines a light in Jess's eyes. She doesn't look much older than Sage and Naomi, but I suppose you need to be young to do that hike on a regular enough basis to work down here. She cleans the cut on Jess's head and covers it with a bandage, then moves her attention to Jess's ankle.

Jess flinches as Janine squeezes her ankle and rotates her foot.

"You've got a mild sprain. In normal situations it'd heal in a week, but life down here makes injuries more complicated."

Janine wraps a compression bandage around her ankle, then hands Jess several gauze bandages. "Stay off your foot as much as you can. The cut is superficial so should heal easily enough in the next week or so." She runs her fingers over Jess's forehead. "Try to keep the canyon grit out of it if you can." She looks at Bryan. "Are you her father?"

He shakes his head. "One of her guardians for this trip."

She nods and rests a hand on Jess's shoulder. "You've got a mild concussion and will need to be monitored for the next twenty-four to forty-eight hours to make sure your symptoms don't worsen."

"Monitored?" Jess's voice is scratchy. "I'm not a child."

Janine gives her a soft smile. "Standard procedure no matter how many wrinkles you've got. Do you feel nauseous at all? Or dizzy?"

"The dizziness has mostly gone away. And I haven't felt sick."

"That's all good news." Janine turns to Bryan. "If a couple of you are able to rotate shifts overnight, she should be feeling right as rain by the morning."

"Just in time for the hike out of here tomorrow," Jess says.

Janine purses her lips. "Ooh, that's gonna be dicey. Any chance y'all can swing a mule?"

I snort at the visual of literally swinging a mule.

"We can make that happen," Bryan says.

Jess sits up, then winces. "You don't have to do that. It's gotta be expensive." She pushes her legs off the edge of the cot. "I'm sure I can manage."

He moves closer and stops her with a gentle hand on her shoulder. "We're not having you get injured again. End of discussion."

Jess nods, and Janine tosses her plastic gloves in a trash can. "I'm in cabin 204 if something turns overnight, and I'll start bright and early so I can see you before you head up." She turns her attention to me and Steph and pauses. "You two got a bit banged up, too. Need me to look you over?"

Steph and I hold out our arms at the same time, turning them over to show we're okay. "Nah," I say. "Jess got the worst of it."

Janine inches closer to Steph. "You look a little under the weather." Before Steph can react, Janine shines a light in her eyes. "Drink more water."

"Yes, Ma'am," Steph says.

"Good girls." Janine tucks the light in her back pocket. "You slack packing out of here?"

Bryan cocks his head. "Um, no?"

Janine nods. "Thought I heard there's a big group heading up in the morning. All good." She leans close to Jess and peers in her eyes. "You say something if you start to feel worse. None of this 'I'm too cool to ask for help' garbage."

Jess nods slowly. "O-okay."

Bryan helps Jess to her feet. She wobbles a bit, and Bryan hooks his arm through hers to support her.

"Thank you," we all say as we head outside.

Back at the campsite, everyone fusses over Jess until she's resting in a makeshift nest near the fire. Neb checks on her once more, then turns to me. "Do you still need help with your video today?"

I shake my head. "I'm not doing it."

"What?" Jess croaks.

"You're more important than any video." I glance at Steph and she looks away. "You almost died."

"Yeah, and if you don't make the video, I'll have almost died for nothing."

"Jess, I'm serious." The fear from earlier sweeps through me, making my hands tremble. I reach for her arm and press my cheek to her hand. "You don't know what it was like seeing you unconscious."

"I'm serious, too. When will you have another chance like this?" Jess looks from my eyes to everyone standing around us. "Just make sure it's the best video you've ever created and it'll all be worth it."

I let out a breath. "Okay. Neb, I guess we're still doing the video."

His smile makes me flush, despite everything swirling in my head. It's genuine and inviting and makes whoever he's focused on feel like the most important person in his world. "Just let me know what you have in mind."

"Assuming we don't have to airlift Jess out of here." Steph's voice comes out harsh and I cut my eyes at her.

"They can't do much for a concussion except monitor her," Neb says.

Naomi grabs my hand. "It's okay to do the video while also worrying about Jess."

Jess has always been super involved with my videos—from coming up with ideas, to giving advice about edits, and of course starring in them—so I know Naomi is right, but I still feel guilty. I face Neb. "Is it okay if we film at that big rock?"

The same rock where Steph and I kissed. But right now Steph's acting as cold as the rock surrounding us.

"Sun's getting low," he says. "If we're going to record anything, we better do it now."

"I want to watch!" Naomi claps her hands in excitement, and after saying our goodbyes to the parents and Jess, I lead the rest of our group to the rock where Steph and I kissed. She follows us on the trail, but I have to wonder if we'll ever kiss again.

I climb to the top and look down at Neb while the others watch. My confidence feels shaky but I force those emotions back. "I want to record you here, now and during the eclipse. I'm picturing cutting back and forth between the two time frames, so I'll basically have you do the same thing for both."

Neb crosses his arms across his chest and nods. "I like it. Do you have a script in mind, or should I just spew about the eclipse?"

I nod. "Spew away. Space is not exactly my area of expertise. But try to throw in some big arm movements so it's not just you talking."

Neb pinwheels his arms backwards and we all laugh.

"Something like that."

"You got this babe," Sage says. "But let me fix your hair." She joins him on the rock, and he pulls her to his chest and kisses her.

"I want someone to look at me the way those two do," Naomi whispers next to me. "Or the way Steph looks at you."

My head snaps toward her and heat rushes to my cheeks, even though I don't know if Steph will ever look at me that way again. "I think you do."

Her eyes go wide.

"There's a certain someone who's related to me who hasn't stopped watching you since we got to the hotel." That last bit may be a stretch, but based on the expression on Naomi's face, the exaggeration has the desired effect.

"I can't deny there's still something there," she says. "But we tried before and it didn't work."

"Forgive me for pointing out the obvious, but you were kids. Basically my age." If Steph and I get past this fight, our age could still doom us, but we won't be hundreds of miles apart like Hunter and Naomi were. "And yeah, you still live far apart, but Hunter's job is remote. He could move anywhere."

Her finger twists through her curls. Her gaze lands on Hunter, whose struggle is real. He's staring across the river like he's trying not to watch Neb and Sage, but also trying not to stare at Naomi.

"Poor guy doesn't know what to do with himself," I say. "Just kiss him and see where it goes."

Naomi throws an arm around my shoulder and laughs. "What would I do without you?"

"Not my brother," I whisper, ducking out of her arm as she gasps.

"Melody, he's ready for you!" Sage calls.

Neb's standing in the center of the rock in a wide stance with his hands on his hips.

"Maybe not so super-heroish," I say with a laugh.

He scowls at Sage but breaks into a grin. "I told you."

She shrugs and jumps off the rock. "You look hot."

He throws her a look that makes me and Naomi sigh, then clears his throat.

I pull out Jess's phone and the lock screen makes my heart lurch. The picture's from a costume store near home, where Steph found pirate hats for us to try on and we yelled "Bestie Brigade!" as Jess took the picture. That moment feels so far away. Now Steph won't look at or talk to me and I almost killed Jess.

Tears burn my eyes but I blink them away. I can get emotional later. Right now I need to stay focused.

I open the video app, aim the phone at him, and nod.

"The most obvious difference between a solar and lunar eclipse is which object is cast in shadow." Neb moves his arm through the air, blocking the sun with his fist. "With a solar eclipse, the moon passes between the sun and earth, preventing the sun's rays from reaching the earth. With a lunar eclipse, the earth passes between the sun and moon, and we block the light from reflecting off the moon's surface." His voice is solid and he gestures at the sky with the confidence of the superhero Sage tried to make him imitate. Since I'm below him, the canyon wall and hints of the sky fill the frame behind him.

He pauses and I hit stop. "Neb, that was awesome! I like to do lots of short clips, so take a breath and we'll record more."

"He's really good," Naomi says.

I nod. "This is gonna be epic."

We record a couple more clips, then Sage climbs back up on the rock and slides an arm around his waist. Naomi, Hunter, and Theo stroll near the river, and I wish Steph would move closer to me. Instead, she wanders between everyone else, looking as lost as I feel.

"This has been fun," Theo says, waving at everyone who's paired off into couples. "but I'm heading back."

"Theo you don't have to leave," Naomi says, but it's the least convincing I've ever heard her. She and Hunter lean side by side against a rock formation and he looks more content than I've seen in a long time.

"We'll go with you." I say, and I trail behind Steph as we follow Theo to the campsite.

Jess is still nestled in her blanket cocoon near the fire while the parents linger nearby.

"How are you feeling?" Steph asks Jess. We crouch next to her and she gives us a weak smile.

"My head hurts and I'm covered in bruises, so fantastic?"

I run my fingers through her hair to look at the bandage. "I'm so glad you're not dead."

She snorts a laugh. "You and me both." Her lips slide into a frown. "I'm worried about tomorrow."

"You're not excited about the donkey express?" Steph laughs

but it feels forced, like she's pouring all her energy into being sweet to Jess and not looking at me.

Jess adjusts the blanket nest, then sighs in frustration. "I don't want it to look like I'm trying to get attention."

"No offense," Steph says. "But I've been meaning to tell you that getting caught in a freak rockslide in the Grand Canyon is a bit desperate, even for you."

This time Jess laughs for real, then presses a hand to her head. She swats at Steph with the other hand. "No making me laugh."

"Girls, you should really let Jess rest," Mom says.

"What fun is that?" I ask.

Mom gives me The Look and I raise my brows back at her, although with a smile that says I'm sorry. "Bryan and I think it might be a good idea if Jess sleeps in our tent tonight."

"What?" Jess twists to look at Mom and grabs her neck. "Ow."

Mom nods as if Jess made her point for her. "Jess, sweetie, you need to be observed for at least the next day to make sure you don't take a turn for the worse, and we can't do that unless you're with us. Bryan and I will take shifts staying up."

Jess's eyes go wide. "So I'm supposed to sleep with you staring at me?" Her lips pull back in a grimace. "Sorry. I don't mean to be ungrateful. But that seems weird."

"And won't that make you too tired for the hike tomorrow?" Steph asks.

Mom sighs. "This is the best solution we can come up with."

My stomach flips despite myself. Before the accident, I would have been beyond excited for this opportunity to be alone with Steph, but now I don't know what to expect. She can't ignore me forever, and with no one else around, hopefully we can finally talk.

But that scares me, because what if our relationship, and our friendship, end tonight?

— **18** —

STEPHANIE

Dinner's over and we're hanging around the fire while the moon creeps higher in the sky. It's been dark for at least an hour and Mel's fidgeting so much I want to grab her hands.

Except I don't know if I'm allowed to do that anymore.

Or if I even want to.

"Should we go back to the rock now?" Mel asks the group. "I don't mean to sound like a five-year-old, but I don't want to miss it."

"We've got time," Neb says. "People think an eclipse is a blink-and-you-miss-it event, but to the naked eye, the sun and moon appear to move at an incredibly slow pace. The eclipse could start while we're sitting here and we'd still have enough time to get to the rock." He glances at Naomi, who fights a smile, like they're hiding something.

"What was that look?" I whisper before I remember Mel and I aren't talking.

Mel shrugs. The way she chews on the corner of her mouth means she's holding back whatever she's thinking.

Is this how it's gonna be the rest of the trip?

The rest of high school?

And college?

"They're not going to make me stay here while you all go to the rock, are they?" Jess asks. She used the bathroom while we waited on the other side of the door in case she needed help and has been sitting with us on the picnic table since dinner. She seems like herself again since eating, but the parents haven't stopped not-so-subtly staring at her.

"Absolutely not," Mel says. "We'll get you there."

Jess smiles—the first genuine smile I've seen from her since she first asked about me and Mel.

We're quiet after that. So quiet that the others notice.

"Is everything okay?" Margo asks Mel. Nancy and Bryan watch from the corner of their eyes, and I swear Naomi and Sage lean forward.

"Yeah, just tired," Mel say. "I think I spent all my adrenaline earlier and I'm trying to save whatever's left for the eclipse."

I've always admired Mel's ability to think on her feet and sound convincing while doing it. Even though she won't look at me, I'm grateful she didn't tell everyone what's really going on.

How with one lie she's made me doubt her, and with one thoughtless comment, I made her hate me.

The worst part is, I don't believe what I said. Mamá's constantly telling Papá that he needs to get his priorities straight, something that should have been a sign they were heading for a divorce, and I was thinking about them and our family breaking up right before Jess told me about Brooklyn. Right before she got hurt. The comment flew out of my mouth and by the time the dust settled the damage was done.

And now I don't know how to fix it.

After what feels like forever, Bryan and Neb declare that it's time to go. We pack up water, snacks, and blankets to sit on and head down the trail. Neb insists on giving Jess a piggyback ride, and Bryan walks close by like he's ready to catch her if she slips.

Hunter and Naomi walk side by side, their hands close enough that they're basically holding hands. Even if they haven't officially gotten back together, Operation Amazing seems to be a success.

Mel walks ahead of me, and her silence is torture.

Moonlight shines on the rock, welcoming us, and we gather in a half circle around it.

"So now we wait?" Jess asks.

"Basically." Neb looks at Mel. "You've got three minutes max for the video right?"

Mel nods, brows raised. "It's actually longer now, but most people stop watching after a minute so I try to keep them shorter."

Neb puts his hands in his pockets, then quickly shifts so his arms are over his chest. "The eclipse moves too slowly to get in one shot. You'll want several as it makes its way through the progression."

Mel leans against the rock and stares up. The moon's high above us, the stars covering the sky around it. "Let's get the first one now."

Neb climbs up the rock way faster than I ever could and assumes his superhero pose. Sage and Naomi giggle, and he rolls his eyes. "I'm not doing this for the video."

"Too late," Mel says. "Already got it."

"Dude, you look good," Theo says. "And Mel's a pro so you'll look even better when she's finished."

"Aww, Theo." Mel smiles up at Neb. "Give me ten seconds of setup, like maybe about waiting for the eclipse, and don't use your arms."

Neb nods and spews something about planetary alignment.

Mel gives him a thumbs-up, then she's back at my side. "This is going to be so epic!"

"Let's find someplace to sit. You all need to rest your legs for the hike tomorrow."

We settle Jess between us and Mel watches the footage while we stare at the sky. "I don't want to waste the battery, but I want to make sure I don't need to reshoot."

"That must have been what it was like before digital cameras," Jess says. "Can you imagine having no idea if a picture turned out, or if your eyes were closed, until you got the pictures developed?"

Mel shudders next to me. "No."

The others sit on blankets and jackets and the quiet makes me sleepy.

"How much longer until it starts?" Theo asks.

Mel shrugs. "I'm counting on Neb to let us know."

Jess leans back on her elbows, and Margo immediately crosses the clearing and crouches in front of her. "How are you doing?"

Jess wobbles her hand back and forth. "Okay. My head still hurts, but it helps that it's so dark out here."

Margo touches Jess's chin, then smooths her hair away from her face. "Well, you holler if you feel like you need to lie down. Bryan's super geeked about the eclipse but it won't be the end of the world if I have to miss it."

Mel gasps and presses a hand over her mouth. "Mom! Are you saying you don't think everything Bryan likes is the most interesting thing ever?"

Margo laughs and shoves Mel's knee. "You hush. Couples don't have to like all the same things. The magic comes when those differences make you perfectly complement each other."

Mel nods. "Nice recovery."

"I'm totally writing that down," Jess says. "You know, for when I finally meet someone."

Margo's words repeat in my head. I obviously know that two people don't have to agree on everything to be compatible, but I hadn't thought about how those differences can be what makes a relationship work.

But it can also be what tears them apart. Like my parents. Or me and Mel. One lie, one unthinking moment, and now our relationship might be doomed. Is our friendship ruined, too? Tears burn my eyes and I wipe them with my sleeve before anyone notices.

"Mel, you ready for another clip?" Neb asks. He's already on the rock and points at the sky. "It's starting."

The moon looks the same as it did before, except one edge is a little fuzzy, like someone smudged the outline.

Mel scrambles to her feet. "On it!" She glances at me as she gets up, and for a moment we're back at last night, all the nerves and butterflies from right before we kissed. She opens her mouth like she's going to say something, but instead points the camera at Neb.

"Right now the moon's passing into the penumbral shadow, which is the partial, outer shadow cast by the earth." Neb raises his arm partway and looks to the sky. "What we see down here depends on how the earth aligns with the moon and sun."

"Okay, that's good for now," Mel says, then she's back by my side. She wiggles back and forth and whispers to herself. "This is seriously going to be so cool."

We stare at the sky as the moon is slowly erased.

"I thought it would be faster," Jess says.

"The eclipse itself can last an hour or two because of how much bigger the earth is than the moon," Neb says. "So it takes a while for it to fully manifest."

"I don't want to say this is boring, because it's super cool," I say to the group. "But I didn't picture us just sitting here."

"Y'all should be grateful I retired my mooning pants after college," Theo says.

Naomi groans. "Only because you could lose your job for indecent exposure."

Theo shrugs. "We all have different motivators for growing up. That was mine."

"I love you, dear brother, but if I never see your bare ass again it will be too soon."

Mel bursts out laughing as Neb covers his face with his hand. "Agreed," he says.

Sage rubs Neb's arm and laughs. "The first time Neb and I saw each other, it was preceded by Theo's butt."

"I love you, Theo," Mel says. "But I agree with everyone else."

"I am hurt." Theo crosses his arms over his chest. "Hurt!"

Mel gets to her feet and gives Theo a hug. "You're still one of my favorite people."

"Only one of them?" He raises a brow, then gives me a wink. "I see how it is."

The moon slips farther into darkness, and Neb stands. "Ready for the next one?"

He and Mel record another ten seconds, but instead of sitting back down, they whisper near the rock.

Jess leans close. "What's going on with you two?"

"I screwed everything up and now she hates me." The tears are back and this time one sneaks down my cheek.

Jess wipes it with her sleeve. "What the heck happened while I was unconscious?"

"I said she needed to get her priorities straight." I catch myself before sharing the specifics. I don't want Jess to think Mel was more concerned about her phone than Jess being hurt, because that's not true.

"She is a bit obsessive about the videos," Jess says. I catch her eye and she smiles. "But it's cool she's so passionate about it, you know?"

"It's one of the bazillion things I like about her. But I'm also upset about Brooklyn." It's possible Jess doesn't remember telling me. Don't head injuries sometimes make you forget things from right before the injury?

Jess grabs my hand. "I'm really sorry for telling you that way. I totally thought you knew."

"I should have known. That's not something friends should keep from each other. But—"

Mel bounces over to us, fighting back a smile.

"What?" Jess whispers.

Mel giggles. "I can't say. But omigod."

"Not fair!" Jess laughs, then presses her fingers to her bandaged head.

"You'll find out soon," Mel says. "And it'll be beyond epic."

As the moon slowly disappears, she and Neb record a couple more clips. Even though we've been watching for what feels like hours, when the earth's shadow covers the moon and it glows a coppery red—the umbra, Neb informs us—we all gasp.

"The exact color of the moon during the eclipse is dependent on debris in the atmosphere," Neb says.

"Space dust!" Naomi shouts.

Neb laughs. "More like volcanic sediment, but sure."

Moments later, a ring of light shines around the moon like something out of a Tolkien movie.

"Mel, now!" Neb says, then turns to Sage. "I need an assistant for this one."

Sage looks at Naomi before taking his hand. "Oh, okay."

He helps her climb the rock and positions her so she's facing him. He nods at Mel, who gives him a thumbs-up. "I think you all know how special eclipses are to me." He touches the center of his chest and Sage covers his hand with hers. "My dad and I had a special connection and when he died, I thought that was lost."

"What. Is. Happening?" I whisper to Jess. She gives me a wide-eyed look and shakes her head.

"Sage, finding you, loving you, has made me happier than I ever thought possible."

Sage covers her mouth with her hand and glances at Naomi, who has a smile plastered to her face.

Neb lowers to one knee and everyone gasps. Sage wobbles on her feet. Then he reaches into his pocket and pulls out a small box. And opens it. "Sage Winters, will you marry me?"

Sage drops to her knees and buries herself in his arms.

Now everyone's screaming. She must have said yes because they're hugging and kissing and crying. Happy tears fill my eyes and my heart clenches. I want that happiness. To be so complete with someone that they're my everything.

Neb pulls Sage to her feet and picks her up so her legs swing out behind her.

And Mel records it all. When she joins me and Jess, I've never seen her smile so big. "That's what he told me earlier. He's been planning all along to propose during the eclipse, and when

I asked him to do the video, it made it even easier to have me record it."

"Guys, the eclipse is still doing its eclipsey thing," Theo says. The edge of the moon has reappeared, like it's coming back to life.

"Ooh, we're not done," Mel says.

I want to pull her into a hug, to feel her pressed close against me, but I don't know what's allowed anymore.

She approaches Neb and Sage, who sit side by side on the rock and seem lost in each other. Sage slides off the rock when Mel holds up her phone, and they record another clip.

When the eclipse finally ends and the moon is back to its usual full self, we grab our things and return to the campsite. Other campers must have been watching, too, because the bathrooms are crowded with people brushing their teeth and doing their bedtime routines. The three of us wait outside for our turn, Mel pacing in small circles while Jess and I lean against the side of the building.

"What if the video doesn't turn out the way I want?" Mel asks.

"Mel, you recorded a fricking eclipse," Jess says. "How can it not be good?"

An awkward silence fills the air. Normally I'd jump in with encouragement, but my words jumble in my mouth.

"If it doesn't turn out the way you expect, it's because it'll be even better," Jess says.

"It's just that I can see what I want so clearly. If it falls below that expectation, I'm gonna be disappointed," Mel says.

Her words punch me in the gut. I've failed to meet her expectations one day into our relationship. I'd already imagined us as a happy couple on campus, but I ruined it. Now I don't know if we'll even be friends anymore.

"It's gonna be fricking epic," Jess says.

"It is gonna be epic," Mel repeats.

"Epic," I say. My voice lacks its usual strength. Mel glances at me, then quickly looks away. It's the first time I've spoken to her in hours and the word hangs between us.

"Look," Jess says. "I can't deal with you two being like this." She waves her hand at me and Mel as a group of women exit the bathroom. Jess lowers her voice. "Mel, I don't blame you for what happened. I'm the one who crawled inside the Grand Canyon's ass crack."

My lip twitches and Jess turns to me. "Steph, I know you feel bad for what you said. And Mel, I'm sorry I blabbed about you and Brooklyn, but I thought Steph knew because it was years ago. Now, can you please figure this out so we can go back to being the Bestie Brigade?"

Jess's words are like a pin in my anger balloon. It's not like Mel kissed Brooklyn three months ago. It was years ago, long before we knew each other.

Two more women leave the bathroom, and Mel catches the door before it closes. She holds it for us and we line up at the sinks to brush our teeth, with Jess between us. I try to keep my focus on the sink in front of me, but my eyes keep wandering two mirrors over. On the third time, Mel's eyes meet mine and I catch a hint of a smile before I look away.

The moon is still high in the sky as we walk back to the campsite. Neither of us have responded to Jess's demand to make things normal, but the tension that's surrounded us since the accident feels a little lighter.

"Jess," Mel says. "I'm really sorry you have to sleep in the tent with my mom and Bryan. I don't want to do that and I'm related to them. Well, her." She clears her throat. "Them."

"It's okay," Jess says. "Honestly, when those rocks came down I thought it was over for me. Then I thought they were going to have to air-lift me out of here. So sleeping in their tent so they can make sure I don't die in my sleep or whatever is not a big deal."

"Jess!" I stop on the path and the next thing I know we're in a huffle. Mel's arms are light against my back, but she doesn't pull away. "I know we joked about it, but did you really think you were going to die?" We're terrible friends for not realizing that Jess was being strong because she didn't want to be the center of attention any more than she already was. Because that's how she is.

"Jess, I'm so sorry we didn't know!" Mel adds. "We're awful friends."

Jess laughs into our hair. "No you're not. None of us had rockslide on our bingo card. You handled it the same way I would have."

"You would have done more," I say. And she's doing more now. Getting us talking, trying to fix our friendship before it's too damaged to repair.

"Well," Jess says, and something about her tone makes me look up. She's smiling and the moonlight catches a twinkle in her eye. "What if I said I did all this so you two could be alone in the tent?"

Mel snorts and I burst out laughing. "You may be selfless," I say. "But I don't believe you manifested a rockslide."

It feels good to laugh after so many hours of tension.

Mel glances at me, and for a second we feel back to normal. Then her smile fades and the sinking feeling I've carried all afternoon returns.

We've had a million sleepovers, but this will be the first time I'm sleeping next to her while thinking about doing more.

Those thoughts could become reality. But we have to be on speaking terms first.

— **19** —

MELODY

For a moment, I thought we might be okay, then the hurt from when Steph basically said she doesn't value the most important thing in my life came rushing back and now I don't know what to do with these conflicting feelings. I'm tempted to get advice from Naomi but I'm already in the tent, pretending to organize my bag. Naomi would probably tell me to talk to Steph and be honest about how she hurt me, because we can't move forward until we get past this.

Steph clears her throat. "Am I allowed to ask what you're thinking?" The sadness in her eyes nearly undoes me, and my words trip over each other.

"Yeah. I mean, of course." The corner of my mouth lifts and she smiles back. "I'm pretty sure I saw my brother kissing Naomi right before we closed the tent."

Steph's eyebrows shoot up. "What!?" She squeals, then slaps her hand over her mouth. "Really?"

I wave at the tent wall toward Hunter's tent. "I mean, the moon only provides so much light so I can't say for sure, but if they weren't kissing, they were hugging with their faces."

Steph laughs. "Do you think they'll kick Theo out of the tent?"

"And make him bunk with his mom? He may never recover."

There's a pause, like we've exhausted all there is to say, and I hate this awkwardness. I take a quick breath and contemplate what I should have asked hours ago. "How are you doing with your parents? You haven't said anything and I don't want to pry, but I also don't want you to think I don't care and so I've been stuck in a loop in my head."

She blinks, like the change in topic surprises her, and presses her lips together. "It sucks. I'm trying not to think about it. Naomi's mom actually talked to me a little."

I start to lean closer, then pull back. "I'm sorry that I haven't been the friend you need."

"You—you've always been there for me," she says. "There's been a lot going on. And honestly, thinking about it makes me panicky and sad and that's not how I want to feel right now."

"I still feel like a selfish dick."

She turns her face toward mine. If I leaned forward, I could tuck my face against hers. "You're not," she says.

"Can we—can we talk about earlier?"

Her head bobs. "Yes. Please." She reaches for my hand but pulls back before making contact. "I know how important the videos are to you, and your mission for your account. I was scared about Jess and thinking about my parents and it just kind of came out."

I tug at the sleeve of my sweatshirt. It's what I wanted to hear, but my heart insists it isn't enough. "People don't blurt out things that aren't already in their head."

Her eyes widen. "Please believe me. Mamá says that to Papá all the time, and I was thinking about them when Jess got hurt." This time she does grab my hand. Her skin is warm against mine and I try to focus on her words and not the flurry of emotions in my chest. "I really admire what you're doing with your account. And hearing from Neb that scientists are watching is like total validation that you're doing something special."

"That is pretty cool."

Her gaze drops before meeting mine again. "I can't take back what I said, but you're my best friend and—and I like you. Like, really like you." Her voice catches and she blinks quickly. "Our friendship means so much to me that the thought of losing you makes me afraid to even try for something more, and I can't help but think that I'm right."

My stomach drops. The lump in my throat makes it hard to speak, but I force out the most honest thing I can. "I don't know what I'd do without you in my life. I'm so very sorry I didn't tell you about Brooklyn. I'm not going to make excuses or pretend I forgot because no one forgets their first kiss, but it was forever ago and she and I haven't talked in ages."

Steph tucks a piece of hair behind her ear. "When Jess told me, I was really upset because it felt like you've been lying to me this whole time. But it was a long time ago and I believe that you didn't mean to turn it into a thing."

I let out a breath. "The possibility of this"—I point back and forth between us—"has made me happier than I've ever been. We're going to have fights. All we can do is promise to be honest with each other. I'm not perfect." I flip my hair and give her a small smile. "Despite what the Melties may think."

Steph's eyes crinkle as she smiles.

"And I'm going to screw up. I'm sorry if I made you feel less important with all the video stuff. But you matter. More than you know."

She grabs my other hand and rests them both on our crossed legs. "So you're not worried this could ruin our friendship?"

I let out a slow breath. "Of course I've thought about it. You're too important to me not to. But people are always saying that the best relationships are the ones that start out as friends. And you're the best friend I have."

"What about Jess?"

"I'm not attracted to Jess."

A smile spreads over her face as she focuses on our hands. "Not what I meant, but I hear you."

"So you like me?" Asking the words so simply is scary and makes me break out in a sweat, but I want to make it clear that I'm in this one hundred percent.

She nods. "I think I always have."

Forget backflips. My heart does a back handspring with a roundoff and waves its hands at the end. "Then we have to trust that the rest will work itself out. I wouldn't start something with you if I didn't think there could be a future for us. And that's even without us both studying at Oregon."

"I still can't believe we're both going there." Steph tugs me closer until our knees touch. Then our faces are so close I can feel her soft breath on my cheek. "If we're going to do this, there is one thing you need to know."

My eyes focus on hers and I swear I can see her hopes and dreams and everything she wants. "What's that?"

"I'll never be a Myth Busters superfan."

I burst out laughing, then her lips are on mine and everything falls into place. There's something comforting about being with someone who makes me feel safe, who I know without a doubt cares for me and has my best interests at heart.

She pulls away and I press my forehead to hers. The air feels thick with intention. We're practically adults and we're alone without any risk of parents checking on us. We can do whatever we want. But this is still very new and I've never been one to jump into bed with someone right away.

And my heart still feels bruised. "Is it okay if we, if we don't..." I don't know how to say I'm not ready for what being alone in a tent means.

"We don't have to do anything you're not comfortable with," Steph says. "Just being here with you is more than enough."

"I want more," I say. "But I need a little more time."

If she's disappointed, she hides it well. "I'm glad you don't hate me."

My head tilts. "You didn't actually think that, did you?"

She picks at the zipper on her sleeping bag and bites her lip. "Maybe?"

I reach for her cheek and her eyes meet mine. "I can't promise I'll always say the right thing, but I can promise I'll never hate you."

Steph nods. "Same."

We rearrange our sleeping bags so they're zipped together, then lie facing each other.

"Tell me one of your favorite things," Steph says.

You. "Um, you already know everything I like."

"I don't think I do."

A thousand responses flip through my mind. It's hard to think of anything but her. "The moment when I lie down at night and my body accepts it's time to go to sleep. I'm in go-go-go mode all day, and that moment"—I squeeze her fingers—"this moment, is when I'm finally calm."

She leans closer and brushes a kiss near the corner of my eye.

"What about you?" I say. "What's a favorite thing I don't know?"

Her eyebrows rise like she didn't expect to be asked in return. A smile curls her lips. "My hair."

I snort a laugh and shake my head. "I already knew that."

Her face grows serious and her finger tucks a piece of my hair behind my ear. "Your hair. I love how it always smells like strawberries, even when we're in a dusty canyon and sleeping in a tent."

We watch each other in the darkness until she finally pulls back and we settle onto our mats, falling asleep with our fingers laced together and our breath on each other's faces.

I wake in the middle of the night with the desperate need to pee. I whisper to Steph where I'm going, then tiptoe out of the campsite to the bathroom, where I find Naomi and Sage. "Is this where all the cool kids hang out?" My voice echoes off the tiled walls and I cringe at the sound.

"Just catching up," Naomi says.

They giggle, and Sage turns her hand to catch the light in her engagement ring. The stone is a dark gray brown and seems like it has swirls of light coming from inside it.

"What kind of stone is that?" I ask.

"Labradorite," Sage says. "It symbolizes strength and shielding."

I press my hand to my heart, and Naomi pretends to swoon next to me.

I nudge her with my elbow. "You totally kissed Hunter, didn't you?"

Her cheeks flame red, something I've always found endearing about her, and she laughs. "Perhaps." Then she nudges me with her elbow. "What about you? Things with Steph seem to be going well?"

This time I blush. "Yes. They are." Thank goodness.

Naomi snorts. "Theo was hot pissed when I made him sleep with Mom."

"Ha! That's what I guessed!"

"Do I want to know how involved you were in making this happen?" Naomi asks.

"We had a whole plan but I have no idea if we actually made a difference," I say. "You two obviously care about each other. Operation Amazing just gave you the nudge you both needed."

Naomi plants her hands on her hips and her mouth falls open. "Operation Amazing?"

Sage bursts out laughing. "Omigod, that's so perfect."

My toe traces a square of linoleum. "So how do you know when the person you like is the one? That it's not just infatuation or hormones or whatever?"

"You don't at first," Sage says. "The hormones are what bring you together, but you need to have friendship and mutual respect for it to be a healthy relationship." Naomi's hinted at some of the problems in Sage's past, and she speaks with a determination that comes from experience. "For me, with Neb, I was attracted to him right away but it took time for me to fully trust him."

Naomi reaches for my hand. "Listen to your gut. You have good instincts and that will guide you in the right direction."

"So will I be seeing you at Thanksgiving?" I ask with a smirk. Naomi's eyes go wide as Sage laughs. "Too soon?"

Naomi sighs, but I can't tell if it's a sigh of excitement or frustration. "Probably."

"Probably too soon or probably we'll see you at Thanksgiving?"

Her face scrunches up. "Both? But hopefully yes to Thanksgiving." Sage and I jump up and down and Naomi covers her face with her hands. "I hate being the center of attention. I like to help other people."

Sage throws an arm around Naomi's shoulder and winks at me. "Well, we like to help you."

"And we want you to be happy." I wrap my arm around her other side, then add, "And my brother's happiness is important, too."

We fold into a hug and my bladder screams.

"Okay, but I really have to pee."

A few hours later, the sounds of rustling tents and low voices wake me. Steph's arm is draped over my waist, her head tucked against my chest, and I don't want to ever move.

"I'm not ready for the hike." Steph's voice is thick with sleep and she tightens her grip on my body. I settle into her arms, remembering moments from last night. When she reached for me after I went to the bathroom, her breath hot on my neck until I fell back asleep. Now that we've fully crossed the friend-line, I don't want to leave our cocoon.

"I'm excited to get back to the land of WiFi," I say into her hair. "I'm just trying not to focus on how high we have to climb to get there."

She adjusts so we're looking at each other. "Do you think Jess is okay?"

My lips clench together. "We would have heard if there was a problem, right?"

"I think so."

"When I went to the bathroom in the middle of the night, there was a faint light in their tent but I didn't hear anything."

Steph's eyes go wide, then she exhales. "So she most likely didn't die in her sleep."

I push her shoulder as a shudder passes through me.

"Omigod, stop. I don't even want to think about that possibility. I'm sure she's okay."

"Do you think you have enough footage for the response video?"

JFB's face rolls through my mind, and I immediately shut down those thoughts. This isn't about him anymore. "I'll get more as we leave."

Steph kisses the tip of my nose and my eyes flutter shut. "It's gonna be amazing."

My eyes fly open. "Speaking of amazing!" I fill her in on the latest with Hunter and Naomi and we're speculating what we'll wear to their wedding when Theo sings right outside our tent.

"Wakey, wakey! Eggs and bakey!" The sound of the tent zipper makes us spring apart, but since we connected our sleeping bags, our springing options are limited. "If you're sleeping longer than me, you definitely need to get up." His head pokes inside but his eyes are closed. "Are you decent?"

"As decent as we're going to be," I say.

Steph gives me a wide-eyed look.

"He won't tell anyone," I whisper.

He fake gasps when he opens his eyes, and his mouth widens into that adorable Theo smile that I love so much. "You little minx."

"Shush!" Even though Steph and I only kissed, I can't fight the grin that spreads over my face.

He climbs through the tent opening, careful to keep the flap mostly closed, then zips it shut. He sits cross-legged near our feet and rests his chin in his hands. "Now I understand why you're luxuriating in here while everyone else is packing."

Red streaks over Steph's cheeks. "Have you seen Jess this morning?"

"Does she seem okay?" I lean forward like his answer will come faster if I move closer.

Theo glances back and forth between us. "She seems tired, but okay. She's sitting at the picnic table watching the others tearing down the tents."

I exhale loudly and lean back on my hands.

"You're not tearing down a tent," Steph says.

He raises a brow and cocks his head. "Manual labor and I do not mix. Besides, I need to conserve my energy if they expect me to walk out of this canyon."

"Same." I hold out my fist and he bumps it.

"But seriously," he says. "Your mom sent me in here to wake you up, so you better disassemble whatever's going on here"—he waves a hand at our sleeping bags—"unless you're ready for a big reveal."

"Definitely not." I sit upright and shoo him toward the door. "Off you go."

"Thanks for the warning," Steph says.

"Any time, ma petite." He unzips an opening barely large enough for him to squeeze through, then disappears outside.

Moments later, Mom calls my name and reality crashes around us.

"I don't think we can put this off any longer," I say.

Steph raises a brow. "Telling everyone or leaving the tent?"

"The second one," I say.

"It feels like we're in our own little world in here."

"I don't want to leave," I say. "Actually, that's not accurate. I'm really looking forward to civilization. But I don't want to leave this." I lean forward to kiss her jawline and she sighs.

"If you want us to stay a secret from your mom, you have to stop doing that."

I lean back on my arms. "Maybe keeping it a secret is pointless. Yeah, we've got the hotel room tonight, but they're not gonna make everyone change rooms to keep us apart."

"Do you think we'll still be able to have sleepovers?"

That question flitted through my mind a couple times, but I don't know the answer so I kept pushing it away to worry about another time. "I don't know. This is new territory for me."

She smiles. "Me too."

"Mel, seriously!" Mom shouts from very close to our tent.

We jump out of the sleeping bag and move to opposite sides of the tent. "Coming!" Then we burst into giggles.

Ten minutes later, the tent and everything that was in it are crammed inside our packs, ready for the long hike ahead. We're sitting at a picnic table with Jess between us, and even though she swears she feels okay, I can't shake the image of her lying facedown on the ground. Neb and Sage are at another table doing what can only be called canoodling, while Hunter and Naomi are doing a less obvious version. Theo's wandering around the campsite looking a little lost while the moms leave to get breakfast. Bryan follows them with an expression on his face like he's holding in a secret and might explode if he doesn't get away from us.

"That was super weird," Jess says.

"Was he like that overnight?" I ask.

She shakes her head and winces a little. "Nah, he went to sleep right away while your mom casually stared at me. If they switched guard duty, I missed it."

"Hopefully they don't make you sleep with them tonight," Steph says.

Jess raises a brow. "Wouldn't that work out better for you?" Her voice has a slight edge, but she swallows it and smiles weakly.

I hook my arm through hers. "We would never sacrifice you to the parental gods so we can be alone."

Steph smiles when I say 'we.' I didn't mean to label us an us, but it feels good to say it out loud, even if it's only to Jess.

Theo sits at our table with a thunk and exhales dramatically. "Please save me." The three of us tilt our heads to the side and he waves a hand at the two couples. "I can't take any more of... that."

I reach for his hand across the table. "Are you gonna text that Topher guy?"

He quirks a brow and a smile lifts the corner of his mouth. "Possibly."

"Where does he even live?" Steph asks.

"Colorado."

"That's super convenient," Jess says.

He shrugs. "I never say no because something seems inconvenient. The best stories come from the challenges."

"Ooh, I like that," Jess says. "You gave me a lot to think about the other day, but looking at challenges as a positive puts them in a different perspective."

"Theo," I say. "You try to pretend that you're all fun and games, but you're the sweetest guy I know."

Theo points at Bryan, who's hustling up the path toward us. "You might change your mind when you find out his secret."

I sit up straight. "You know why he's acting so weird?"

"After one year of teaching middle school, my eavesdropping skills are on point. I can hear conversations from across a classroom. The parentals didn't stand a chance."

Steph smacks her hand on the table. "But you're not gonna tell us?"

Theo smiles. "Let him have his moment."

Bryan's practically skipping by the time he stops in front of the table. His eyes gleam and he's smiling so hard his dimples show, and it's more than a little endearing. "I have a surprise!"

Naomi and the others join us at our table. "What's up?" she asks.

Bryan bounces from one foot to the other. "We're slack packing!"

Steph, Jess, and I exchange confused looks and shrug at him.

"In English," Theo says.

"We've hired mules to carry our gear out of the canyon!"

I clap my hands together. "Omigod that's amazing!"

"That's a thing?" Naomi asks.

"Can one carry me?" Theo asks.

Jess sighs. "I think I'm the only one getting the Virgin Mary treatment."

We all burst out laughing, and Bryan rubs his hand over his stubble. "Since we'll still need to carry water and snacks on the hike, we'll need to get creative with our gear. I brought a few empty packs but there's not enough for everyone."

"We can switch off carrying them," Neb says. He brushes a kiss on Sage's forehead. "I'll carry your water."

Theo makes a gagging sound and Naomi shoots him a dirty look.

Bryan claps his hands together the way Mom does when she's making a point. "Let's get moving!"

We're shoving clothes from one bag to another when the moms get back with breakfast.

"Ronny and Benji were eating when we picked this up," Nancy says. "We're meeting them in fifteen minutes, so eat fast!"

I give Mom a panicked look and she nods at the mess of bags. "We can sort out the clothes at the hotel tonight," she says.

Steph and I consolidate our day essentials into my bag, add hers to the donkey pile, then get to work inhaling breakfast.

Mom sits next to me as I'm finishing my eggs. "I know these camping trips aren't your favorite thing in the world, but I'm so glad we did this. You'll be out of the house in six months and it's important to me that we have this time together." She wipes a tear from her eye. "That you have this time with Bryan."

I stand and pull her into a hug. "I do appreciate these trips, Mom. And I can't believe I really get to go to Oregon."

"We're a family. Families do what they can to make each other happy." She doesn't mention Dad, but my mind leaps to New York and his new family and how he no longer has time for us.

I squeeze her harder. "Thank you."

She hugs me back, then kisses my cheek. "Now finish up so we can get going."

It's a mad dash to hit the bathrooms and refill our water bottles at the lodge, then we join our guides on the path.

"Everyone ready?" Benji asks.

"As ready as we'll ever be," Hunter says.

"Good," Ronny says. "Because we just got word that a storm's rolling in."

20
STEPHANIE

Everyone starts talking at once.

"What kind of storm?" Neb asks. His normally relaxed face scrunches up like he's ready to go into battle.

"Rain. Some wind," Benji says.

"Should we wait it out?" Margo asks. "Or stay an extra day? I don't want to risk anyone getting hurt."

"Or stranded on the trail," Bryan says.

"We should be fine," Ronny says. "Worst case, we'll get wet."

Her voice isn't as confident as usual, but I decide to trust her. Because what else can we do?

"I vote we hurry up and try to beat it," Hunter says.

"I think we're all with you on that one, dear brother," Mel says.

"The mules are on the other side of the lodge," Benji says. "Grab your stuff and let's head out!"

We hurry along the path to the other side of the lodge and are greeted by a row of mules—not donkeys like we thought— whinnying and flicking their tails.

"I'm supposed to ride one of those?" Jess says.

Ronny rests a hand on Jess's shoulder. "The one with the saddle."

Jess's face pales. "I thought they'd be... smaller. I'm gonna be high off the ground and the trails aren't very wide."

"The trails are plenty wide, and the mules are used to carrying hundreds of pounds up and down these trails," Ronny says. "They're more stable than we are."

Theo takes a small step toward the mule with the saddle, then stops. "Think of it this way: they move so slow that if you fall, it shouldn't hurt."

Naomi smacks the back of his head. "Is this how you encourage your students?"

He ducks away before she can hit him again. "I'm a realist. Better to address your fears head-on." He faces Jess. "Would you rather I sing you tales of valiant warriors riding beasts of burden into battle?"

Jess laughs. "That's something I'd like to witness. But right now, real is good." They fist-bump, and Naomi throws her hands in the air.

"Let's move, everyone," Bryan calls.

A couple guys covered in flannel and dust secure our packs to the mules with a complicated system of leather straps and rope.

Jess is the last one loaded onto a mule—a sentence I will never get used to saying. "Does he have a name?" she asks.

One of the flannel guys scratches the mule's ears. "Her name's Darla."

"Darla the Donkey," she says. "I like it."

"She's a mule," the guys says. "They aren't interchangeable."

"Okay," Jess says. "But she'll be Darla the Donkey when I tell this story back home."

The other flannel guy does a low whistle and the mules clomp toward the trail.

Slowly.

"Aren't they gonna slow us down?" I whisper to Mel. I'm grateful not to have to carry our packs, but if we're trying to beat a storm, we're gonna need to go faster than this.

"Their pace might be slow, but it's steady," Benji says from behind us.

"Like the tortoise and the hare?" Nancy asks.

Benji nods. "People tend to start fast but they need lots of breaks. These girls will stop for water when we do, but other than that, they'll keep trucking until they get to the stables at the top."

Ronny points up the trail. "We're taking the Bright Angel Trail. It's longer, but it's not as steep and makes for easier climbing."

When we reach a metal bridge over the river that looks a lot like the one we crossed three days ago, we pause.

"I'm gonna miss this," Sage says. "You can almost see our rock from here."

Neb leans down to kiss the side of her neck, and I flush remembering my kiss on that rock, too.

My fingers brush Mel's. "I'm really glad I'm here."

"Me too," she whispers.

"And I want to say again that I'm sorry for yesterday."

She shakes her head. "I'm sorry too. But I don't want to dwell on that. Yeah, it hurt, but I understand where it came from. I promise I'll try not to let my videos dominate every part of my life."

When a building's foundation cracks, it can tear apart the entire building if it's not fixed soon enough. I hope our fight isn't our first crack, that our relationship will survive, because her words give me hope that I can get through anything with her by my side.

Mel touches my cheek. "And like Theo said, challenges can make us stronger."

I laugh. "Hopefully we can channel that strength for the hike."

I don't know where she gets the strength, but Mel doesn't let anything faze her. If something knocks her down, she pushes her way back up. If she's scared, she ignores her racing heart and does what needs to be done.

My belly flutters and daydreams flood through me.

Being roommates with Mel.

Being more than roommates with Mel.

Studying together.

Laughing together.

Being together.

We take a couple more pictures, including a selfie with Jess and Darla, then say goodbye to the river and continue up the trail.

It's a lot easier without our bags. The mules are at the back of the line, along with the two flannel guys, who apparently come with the mules, and Darla leads like the queen she is. Mel and I walk a few feet ahead of Benji since they won't let us be next to Jess.

The trail starts out flat so I try to soak in the beauty of the rocks and the sky far above us, but with each step, I move farther away from the safety I felt with Mel in the tent and closer to the reality of my parents getting divorced.

"You okay?" Mel asks.

"Is it that obvious?"

She smiles softly. "I'd like to think I'm at least a little tuned into your mood."

"I'm not looking forward to getting back to real life." Her smile falters and I reach for her hand. "It has nothing to do with you. I'm very excited about us. It's my parents."

Her lips tighten and she nods. "I wish there was something I could say or do that would magically make it easier, but I can't."

I squeeze her hand. "I know you would. This sucks, and the only way to make it stop sucking is to go directly through the suck."

"I'm putting that on a T-shirt," Jess says from atop Darla.

"Only if Mel sells them online."

Mel nods, her eyes bright. "I can definitely make that happen."

"Speaking of going through the suck," I say. "How are you feeling about the video response?"

"I haven't been able to review the footage since I used a bunch of different phones, but I've been thinking through concepts and I'm pretty sure I know how it's going to come together."

Something in my chest flutters. Mel's creativity is amazing, and it's even more fascinating to watch up close.

"I'll shoot a few more clips today to make sure I have what I need, then I'll need to put it together at the hotel."

"Don't lie," Jess says. "You'll have that thing done before we leave the parking lot."

Mel blushes. "Ha, maybe."

"River Resthouse is in about a half mile," Benji says. "There's bathrooms there, and after that the hike gets serious."

I fight back a groan. I knew what to expect when I agreed to come on this trip, and there's no avoiding the hard work it's gonna take to make it out of the canyon.

"Those clouds are unreal," Mel says. The white fluffy clouds that have followed us since we arrived have been swallowed by dark clouds that look like they mean business. If their business is soaking us and making the hike miserable.

"I hope we can beat the rain," I say.

"It would be almost cathartic ending in the rain," Mel says. "Like it's cleansing us from our past selves and we're emerging renewed or refreshed."

"I don't know about refreshed," Theo says from in front of us. "But I see your rebirth analogy." He reaches for a fist bump and Mel trips over a rock.

"No injuries on the way out of here!" Jess shouts.

We settle into a single-file line and soon reach the first stop. "Five minutes," Ronny shouts from the front of the line. "We need to keep moving."

After a frantic rush through the outhouses, we're back on the trail. Benji wasn't kidding about the hike getting serious. A series of switchbacks with railroad ties laid into the trail greets us almost immediately. Our pace is slow and steady like it was on the way down, except now we have the occasional snort from the mules. It's definitely easier without the added weight of our packs, but with each step forward, the weight on my shoulders feels heavier.

Everything's gonna be different when I get home. The end of senior year is supposed to be happy and full of celebrating, and I'm sure it still will be, but I'm not looking forward to it anymore. Even though we haven't lived there very long, our house is my safe place, and now that's ruined. One of them will move out and I'll be reminded that it couldn't hold their marriage together.

Nancy's words play through my head. To focus on my relationship with Mamá and Papá and let them worry about what happens between them. Because their relationship has nothing to do with me.

Maybe if I repeat that enough times, I'll believe it.

The group is quiet as we climb, climb, climb. Mel and I take turns carrying the pack with our water, and when it's my turn, the weight makes me want to collapse in the dirt. Now and then a conversation between the moms drifts back, but soon even they're silent, the only sounds the huffs of the mules and the guides pointing out rock formations as we get higher.

After what feels like hours, we reach the next stop. A small sign reads *Indian Garden – Toilet*, and we drop our bags and collapse onto rough stools made from cut-up logs. No one talks. Mel and I share an energy bar with Jess, who tries to insist she doesn't need it, and we're on our feet again way too soon.

The clouds continue to darken. The path turns and several of us gasp. I know we're in a canyon and it's really deep but there's a literal wall of rock in front of us.

"How are we supposed to climb that?" Mel asks.

"I thought this was the easier trail?" Naomi says.

"It's longer," Neb says. "But it is easier than the South Kaibab."

The different colored layers of rock dip and spike along the wall, like a mural depicting the history of what's happened in the canyon. But being this close to something so old doesn't make the idea of having to climb it any better.

But I feel ready for the challenge. My parents' divorce is going to change me, there's no getting around that, but just like this hike, it doesn't have to break me. It can make me stronger.

And I'll have Mel by my side as I figure it out. Our fight didn't break us, and we'll be stronger because of it, too.

Naomi stares at the wall of rock. "That's easier?"

"I'm with my sister on this one," Theo says. "I agreed to a hike, not a climb."

"We aren't going straight up the face," Ronny says, rolling her eyes. She and Benji haven't been with us the whole trip but they seem like they're ready to be done with our group. "The switchbacks get more intense through here, but I promise it's a level you all can handle."

We take another break at Three Mile Resthouse, and my legs protest when we start again. When we stop at Mile-and-a-Half Resthouse, they flat-out refuse to cooperate. I rub my knuckles over the front of my thighs to loosen the muscles, but they start to cramp.

Mel's mom appears at my side. "How much water have you had?"

I gesture at the Nalgene bottle dangling from my pack. Water reaches the four ounce mark, which means I've drank sixteen.

Margo's eyes go wide. "Is that your first bottle?"

I scrunch up my face. "Maybe?" We bought new bottles in the lodge to replace the ones that broke, but she's right. I haven't even finished the first one.

"Steph, sweetie, you should be finishing your second or third by now." She unclasps my bottle and hands it to me. "Drink up." Then she reaches into her pack and pulls out a bruised banana. "And eat this while we walk."

"Should we be concerned about that?" Nancy points at the sky. The wall of dark clouds creeps over the canyon like a blanket slowly getting pulled toward us.

Ronny's jaw clenches. "That will make things a bit trickier. If you've got rain gear, now's the time to get it out."

She and Benji pull out ponchos while the rest of us look at each other with wide eyes. When we repacked our bags this morning, I put all my clothes in the other bag with Mel's stuff, so now all I have is what I'm wearing. And from the looks on everyone else's faces, I'm guessing they're in the same boat. Or mule.

"I've got nothing," Hunter says, and the rest of us murmur our agreement.

"Well, then let's keep moving," Ronny says.

Our pace speeds up, even as the trail gets steeper. Benji announces that we're halfway to the next stop when the raindrops start.

"Mel, you should get this." Jess says. We turn back to face her, and she nods at the sky and holds out her phone.

It's like someone split the world in half. One side is pale blue with traces of white clouds, and the other is a grayish purple. The line between them looks almost too perfect to be natural.

Mel starts recording as a crack of thunder explodes above us. Darla the Mule makes a strangled noise and jumps forward, knocking into Mel, who's leaning toward the edge of the trail.

Before I can react, lightning streaks across the sky and she tumbles out of sight.

— 21 —
MELODY

A scream rips out of me.

My arm catches on a tree root, the force nearly ripping my arm out of the socket and slamming my body into the side of the slippery stone wall. I'm dangling from my arm when shouts echo across the canyon.

I scramble against the stone, sending loose rocks tumbling down down down. My toe catches on something strong enough to support my weight so I'm able to take the pressure off the root, which looks like it's gonna rip from the wet ground any second.

My life must have a greater purpose, otherwise I'd be dead.

Bryan's face appears over the edge, followed by Benji and Steph.

"I'm here!" I shout into the air.

A strong hand wraps around my wrist, the grip solid despite the rain. Pain shoots through my shoulder and a sob tears out of me.

I'm not going to die.

Not here.

I barely have time to take a breath and I'm yanked toward the sky. The canyon does her best to keep me—clawing at my chest and legs as I try to find a toehold—and in one swift motion, my chest hits horizontal ground. My legs dangle over the edge, the hard rock digging into my thighs, but I'm safe.

Hands grab my armpits and I'm dragged onto the trail. I roll onto my back and the rain covers me, washing away my tears. A second later, Mom's on top of me, cradling my head beneath her arms. When her eyes meet mine, her tears nearly undo me.

"I thought I lost you," she whispers.

My breath catches in my chest and I start to sit up, but Ronny appears next to Mom and gently presses my shoulders to keep me on the ground. I wince at the contact. "Is anything broken?"

I bend my knees and arms. "I don't think so."

She squeezes my knees, then my ankles. "Any pain?"

"Just my shoulder."

She gently pokes my shoulder and white-hot pain makes me gasp. "It might be dislocated. Someone grab a shirt for a sling."

"Did you hit your head?"

"I don't think so, but it happened so fast I'm not sure."

She slides her hand under my neck to feel my spine and nods to herself. "Unfortunately we can't linger. Are you able to keep walking?"

"I feel like I fell off a canyon, but I should be okay."

A smile twitches the corner of Ronny's mouth. A long-sleeved shirt appears and Ronny helps me sit, then loops it around my neck and secures my arm against my chest. "Your balance might be a little off. We can strap you to a mule if it gets to be too much."

My mouth falls open, and she winks. As soon as she backs away, I'm slow-motion tackled by the rest of the group. I wave them off. "We can do this later. Right now we need to beat that." I point at the sky, which has grown darker in the last few minutes.

Hunter tucks me against his chest and holds me. Even after three days in a tent, he smells like home, and my breathing slows. "Please don't scare me like that again."

"I'll do my best," I say into his shoulder.

I'm barely on my feet when Steph pulls me into a hug. "I thought you were gone!" Her heart pounds against mine, calming me even more.

"Darla is so sorry!" Jess cries while stroking the mule's ears.

I gasp. "Your phone!"

Her eyes widen and we turn to where I fell. The rain has turned the trail to mud but there, at the edge, is her phone. A crack runs through the middle of the screen, but it's not at the bottom of the canyon.

"Looks like we'll be buying two phones when we get back," Mom says.

"I'm really sorry."

She lifts my chin with her finger. "Those are just things. You're safe, and that's all that matters."

Steph wipes off Jess's phone and the screen lights up. "It's only the screen." She hands it to Jess, then faces me, but whatever she's about to say is cut off by Ronny.

"Let's keep moving!"

Mom and Steph stay close as we walk, providing a barrier between me and the drop off. My fingers follow a line in the canyon wall, the solid rock anchoring me.

Benji gently fist-bumps my hand. "You totally veggie belayed."

"What?"

He points at the brush at the edge of the trail. "You used the vegetation to climb. Veggie belay."

I burst out laughing, and pain shoots through my ribs. "Ow!"

Steph bumps her hip against mine. "Check that off the bucket list."

My feet drag over the wet earth as the storm opens up over us. Rain soaks through my clothes and turns the dusty trail to mud, weighing down my boots and making each step more difficult. Ronny and Benji keep staring at the massive cloud overhead, but so far there hasn't been any lightning.

Not like there's anywhere to hide if there is.

I lift my face to the rain. My brush with death fills me with a sense of clarity, a renewed sense of purpose. It sounds cliché, but follower counts and trolls like JFB suddenly seem trivial. Worrying about them will only slow me down from reaching my goals.

Steph swears she didn't mean what she said about my priorities, but whether she meant it or not, she has a point. I excused my obsession with making videos because they have a purpose, but I can be successful without letting it overwhelm my life.

Steph grabs my hand at some point, and her grip anchors me. The canyon really did bring out the best and worst of all of us, and I'm grateful she's still by my side.

Except for the occasional pep talk from Benji to "keep going, we're almost there," no one has spoken for at least an hour. Even Darla seems defeated, her head hanging low and her ears pinned back from the rain. Or maybe she feels bad for almost killing me.

Steph nudges her phone into my hand. "The view is pretty amazing from here."

A smile tries to creep over my face, but I don't have the energy. Even so, I take her phone to replace footage that's hopefully still on my shattered phone, and see that she's right. We're close enough to the top that the full scale of the canyon, the Grand Fricking Canyon, spreads out before us. The rain somehow makes the colors of the canyon walls more vibrant and even with the sky pelting us, the scene before us is spectacular.

Now my smile is real.

"Thank you," I say to Steph, then glance at her and Jess. "I think I want to change the focus of the video."

"Okay," Steph says, lengthening the word as she squeezes my hand.

"But everything I've thought of sounds weak compared to what I had planned."

"What about focusing on the rain?" Jess asks. "Something about how it could have ruined the trip—and yeah, it obviously did because of you almost dying—but it also washed away all the crap and left this amazing view."

An idea sparks fast and a surge of adrenaline rushes through me. "Jess, remind me to give you a promotion!"

She pumps a fist in the air and the three of us laugh, and I press my slinged arm against my ribs.

I totally know what I'm going to do.

When we reach the Bright Angel Trailhead, Theo collapses onto the ground and does the equivalent of a snow angel, except face down and in the mucky dirt. "I've never been so happy to see the horizon!" His voice comes out garbled and we all laugh.

"There's still a quarter mile to the lodge," Ronny says, all traces of amusement gone from her voice. Not that there was much to begin with. She must be as tired as the rest of us.

"Group huffle!" I say. We're soaked to the bone and covered in mud, but I don't care. We conquered, and survived, the canyon and I want to celebrate.

And maybe the body heat will distract me from my growing anxiety about reading all the comments I've missed and needing to creating a masterpiece.

"What the hell is a huffle?" Theo asks.

"Bring it in!" Naomi yells. Hunter hasn't left her side and he's the first one to wrap his arms around her. Neb and Sage quickly join them, while the rest of us come together in slow motion.

"Hurrying is not a thing right now," Steph says. "I'm surprised I'm still standing."

"Can someone help me?" Jess says. She swings a leg over Darla's side, but seems hesitant to drop to the ground.

Benji rushes to help her, then she drags him toward the group hug. Arms collide and soon we're doing this weird bounce without jumping with our heads pressed forward. Laughter lifts from the center.

"Ronny, get in here," Nancy says, and another set of arms slides over my shoulders.

I feel safe and loved and proud and exhausted and—and this needs to be documented. "Picture!" I shout. Several hands hold up their phones. "Neb, you've got the longest arms," I say, and we crowd around him, our faces aimed at the sky and the rain. I'm smiling so hard my cheeks hurt and I wish I could live in this moment forever. "Switch to video! Everyone keep smiling."

He does as I say, moving in a slow circle to capture everyone.

"Let me get a picture of all of you," Benji says. He and Ronny untangle from the group, grab a phone from an outstretched hand, and step a few feet away. We crowd into a more traditional pose in front of the canyon, our exhausted smiles proof that we made it.

Mom slides her arm around me and squeezes. My ribs protest, but I hug her back. "I cannot express how grateful I am that you're safe," she says. "When you disappeared over that edge, my world stopped."

I lift my face to look in her eyes. Tears stream down her cheeks and her lips form a wobbly smile. "I'm okay, Mom."

Her hand traces around my eye and down my cheek. "Don't ever doubt for a second how important you are to me."

Tears blur my vision as I nod.

Hunter joins us, wrapping his arms around me without saying anything, while Bryan hesitates a few feet away. I smile at him and wave him over. "Family huffle."

His long arms encircle the three of us, and for the first time since he married Mom, it truly feels like family.

We break apart for selfies and couple shots. Jess, Steph, and I take our turn posing, then Jess steps away and Steph slides her arms around me while Jess takes our picture. "I can't believe this is over," she says.

"Over, but not over," I say. She cocks her head and I lean my forehead against the side of her neck. Strands of her wet hair cling to my cheek. "The hike is over, but this. Us. We're just beginning."

I feel her smile against my face. "Are you going full cheese on me?"

"Maybe."

Her arm tightens around me. "Good."

After another round of hugs with Ronny and Benji, we drag ourselves to the lodge to use the bathrooms, then make the final trip to the hotel.

((●))

A hot shower is a luxury I will never again take for granted. Bruises bloom on my chest and thighs, and the scrapes on my hands and sore shoulder make bathing a little slower, but I feel content.

At peace.

I emerge from the bathroom in a cloud of steam, a towel wrapped around me and my wet hair hanging loose. Steph makes a weird noise from the opposite side of the room which Jess, who's passed out on one of the beds, doesn't seem to notice.

Mom and Bryan suggested keeping Jess in their hotel room, but we swore a blood oath to poke her every hour to make sure she's okay. Even though it would have meant me and Steph having a hotel room to ourselves.

"Should I get dressed in there?" I hook a thumb at the bathroom. I've never given a second thought to getting dressed in front of the two of them, but being naked in front of Steph has a very different meaning now.

Steph grabs her shower stuff. "You can have the room." She pauses next to me. Her eyes skim over my bare shoulders before meeting mine. "It's weird that this part is weird, right?"

I nod, grateful that she understands and I didn't accidentally offend her. "Obviously it's nothing new, but it feels more..." I inhale slowly, trying to calm my racing heart while I think of the right word. "Intimate."

Steph leans closer and brushes her lips against mine. "That's not necessarily a bad thing. But we're not in a rush." Then she taps my nose with her finger. "Let's promise to be honest with each other, about the good and the not so good. I really want this to work, so we have to share the awkward stuff, too."

"Deal." I press my lips to hers and stay there for a beat.

She closes the distance between us, then quickly jumps away. "I don't want to get you dirty." She heads for the bathroom and stops with a hand on the doorknob. "My phone's on the nightstand. I want to see magic when I come back out here."

I bounce on my toes, the thrill of kissing Steph colliding with excitement for the video. All I have to do is translate the visual in my head into an actual story. I throw on clothes, decide to let my hair air dry, and shove the pillows from the empty bed against the headboard. Settling into my nest, I get to work.

The others already sent Steph videos I took on their phones, plus their footage from the hike down, so I've got a lot to work with. My finger hesitates on a selfie Jess took minutes before she got hurt. Jess is ahead of Steph and me and she's making a kissy face at the camera, while we're lost in each other, thinking we're being subtle. But Jess not only knew, she documented the moment.

I download my favorite video editing app and upload clips from the hike down South Kaibab Trail, the boat ride, a couple of the stars, and finally the climb out in the pouring rain. Anyone can put together a travelogue—the real magic is in the editing and the voice-over. Yeah, you want cool shots, preferably in a rapid-fire edit, but the video alone doesn't tell the story.

At least not for me.

The clips come together quickly, and while the footage isn't exactly what I'd choose, it's hard to screw up shots of the Grand Canyon. I play it without sound a couple times, and realize it needs more of me. Switching to Steph's photo album, I swipe though her pics, lingering on the selfies of us when we emerged from the canyon barely an hour ago, until I find a video of me in the rain, then another of me laughing on our hike shortly before Jess got hurt. In both I'm staring at the sky in amazement, and the expression on my face brings me back to that moment, to when I felt wholly present in that precise second of my life.

Steph was right. My priorities needed a reboot and this trip, and everything that's happened in the past few days, has made that clear.

I select the pics and videos to upload and keep swiping until I see a picture of me looking like I'm about to cry. It was right after we got back to the campsite after Jess got hurt, and even though I hate remembering how sad I felt, it's perfect for this story.

I add the picture and two more videos, and watch it a couple more times, the narration piecing itself together in my head. After a couple deep breaths, I hit record and start talking.

"I love science—especially physics—because there are rules that control how things in the world happen and how we react to them. It's fascinating how a shift in tectonic plates thousands of years ago can turn into this." Onscreen me points to the layers of rock in the canyon. "The Colorado River carved into the rock long before any of us were here, and it proves that no matter what obstacles you face, there's always a way around it." Cut to a shot of us on the boat on the river. "Or through it."

"But things don't always work out the way we want." I debate including a picture of Jess injured, but decide against it. I'd hate for her to think I'm trying to cash in on her accident. I glance at her in the other bed, wishing I could see inside her brain to make sure she's truly okay, and opt for a pic of her on Darla just as the rain came crashing down onto us. Then I add a couple seconds of us hiking in the rain, followed by me with my face to the sky, soaking in the rain and mud and everything.

I hit pause to clear my throat, then continue. "What makes us who we are is how we respond to those external pressures. Do we carry it with us, leaving scars that we'll have for the rest of our lives?" Cut to me lying on my back right after I fell, the stripes of the canyon walls gleaming behind me. "Or do we let them roll off our back, not forgetting the pain of those moments, but not letting them stop us from reaching for our goals. Our dreams. Who we're meant to be."

My thumb hits the save button and I play the video. When I first started making videos, I fumbled through the editing functions in the online app, but using a separate video editor allows me faster cuts and I can sync the audio file to hit the exact visual beats, making the video feel more professional. That's my dream, my goal. To be viewed as a professional who doesn't let the Jordan Fricking Beebes of the world slow me down. I may not be able to stop what they say, but that's on them. I choose to rise above that crap.

I add the group photo from the trailhead, followed by the pic of me and Steph, when the shower turns off. My eyes dart to the bathroom. Even though Steph's been in a million of my videos, and we're usually touching in them, this picture clearly screams that we're a couple, and I should get her permission before including it.

I'll make sure she's good with it before I publish.

"So if it seems like the world is full of haters who want to tear you down, rise up!" I pump my fist even though I'm only recording my voice. "Because trolls are always gonna troll, but you are amazing and you'll elevate to a whole new level of epicness."

I end with a panoramic shot Theo took on the hike down, glad I can include something from him, then hit save again.

When Steph emerges from the bathroom, I've nearly chewed off my thumbnail watching it for the third time.

"Can I see?" Steph asks, pointing at her phone in my hand. A cloud of lavender follows her as she sits on the bed next to me.

I roll toward her and tuck my head against her neck. "You smell good."

She laughs, the sound vibrating against me. "I don't want to think about what I smelled like before." Her arms slide around me and I lift my chin until our noses touch.

"Still lavender, but dusty lavender."

She bursts out laughing and pushes me away, but I grab her hand and press my mouth to hers. Her laughter fades as I deepen the kiss, and there really is something to be said for kissing on a soft mattress instead of the hard canyon floor.

"Ahem," Jess says from the other bed.

We jump apart, scrambling so we're sitting on opposite ends of the bed.

Jess sighs. "You're allowed to touch each other in front of

me. Just maybe chill the full-on make-out sessions when I'm in the room."

"Sorry," we both mumble.

Jess sits up and rubs a hand against the side of her head. "Now quit stalling and show us the video." A smile spreads over her face, softening the panic in my gut. We can do this. Steph and I can date and the three of us can still be the Bestie Brigade. It may not always be perfect, but Jess is too important to let slip away.

"You sure?" I ask.

"Omigod, gimme my phone!" Steph grabs her phone from my hand and slides into bed next to Jess.

They watch silently, the words I recorded a few minutes ago sounding clear and strong. My impulse to grab the phone from her and rerecord the audio makes my fingers twitch, but I force myself to stay quiet and watch their reactions. Posting videos online means validation from thousands of strangers, and while some of them have become real friends, the most important opinions are the two right here.

Steph's hand flutters to her mouth as it ends, and Jess whispers, "Play it again." As my intro repeats, Steph catches my eye and smiles.

"Is that okay?" I ask. "To use that picture?"

She nods, tears shining in her eyes. "I'm good if you are."

I slide off the bed and kneel on the floor so my elbows are on the bed next to her. I clasp her hands. "I am."

Jess sighs, but it's followed by a laugh. "You two are adorable and that picture at the end is perfect."

"And it's the perfect response to He Who Shall Not Be Named." Steph presses her fingers to her lips and does a chef's kiss.

"Even though I don't care about him anymore."

"Yes," Jess says.

I appreciate that she doesn't feel the need to placate me. It's enough. Period.

"So," Steph says. "What are you waiting for?" She hands me her phone and I cradle it in my palm.

Jess raises her brows and purses her lips to one side. "As the OG Melties, we love you and support you. And we're not leaving until you post it. Even though I'm so hungry I could eat my foot."

My heart feels like it might burst. "I love you both, too." I avoid Steph's eyes and try not to overthink my words. I switch to the app, log into my account, and fall onto the other bed. "There are so many comments." I rarely go a full day without logging in, mainly so the comments don't get out of hand. "There's thousands."

Jess shakes her head. "You can reply to those after dinner." She points at me and raises her brows. "No more stalling."

I nod as I upload the file, then add a couple animations that I use a lot in my videos and tap out the caption *Life is Grand*. "Too cheesy?"

"It's perfect," Steph says while Jess nods. "It goes with the video and also says you don't fricking care what anyone thinks."

And I don't. I feel like I left a part of myself in the canyon— the part that let the trolling trolls get to me. From here on out, I do things on my terms.

My thumb hovers over the Post button. This hesitancy isn't new, I'm always a little nervous before sharing a video, but I'm announcing to the world that I'm not only proud of who I am, I know who I am. And nothing anyone can say will change that.

I take a deep breath and tap Post.

22
STEPHANIE

An alarm goes off from the middle the room. And keeps going off. There's a thump and the beeping gets softer, but it doesn't stop.

"What the blazes are you doing over there?" Jess asks with a scratchy voice next to me. Even though things seem to be good with us, Mel didn't protest when I climbed into bed with Jess, and I turned the light off before she could see my disappointment. It would have been really nice to wake up in her arms.

"Sorry!" Mel says. "Steph's phone fell under the bed." She groans as she slides onto the floor.

"Ew, there's no telling what you'll find under there!" I say.

"Can you turn on a light for me?"

I fumble for Jess's phone, careful not to cut my finger on the broken screen, drop to the carpet, and aim the phone's flashlight across the floor. Mel's eyes shine back at me in the darkness. Random bits of who-knows-what dot the floor under the bed, surrounding my phone. She stretches her arm under the bed and holds it above her head in victory, with the alarm still going off.

"Pleeeeeeeease," Jess says. "I need a few more minutes."

The alarm goes silent. Mel climbs back into bed and holds her hand out to me in the semi-darkness. I turn off the light and slip under the covers without a second thought. We scoot toward each other until her arm wraps around my waist and her forehead presses against mine.

"How do you feel?" I whisper.

"Everything hurts," she whispers back. Our bare knees bump as I rest my hand on her hip. "But I need a snuggle before we get up."

I inhale deeply. The scent of her strawberry shampoo still lingers in her hair and the feel of her skin on mine makes my head spin. Sleep tugs at my mind, but I don't want to miss a second of this. The minutes crawl by as we lie together, then my eyes snap open.

"You hit snooze, right?"

She shakes her head, knocking her forehead against my chin. "Promise not to think I'm silly?"

"Your silliness is what I like about you," I say, my voice catching a little. "Among a lot of other things."

"I set an early alarm because I hoped we could have time together before the real alarm goes off."

My heart swells. "You set a snuggle alarm?"

She nods and lifts her face so we're nose to nose. "I want to hang onto vacation for as long as I can."

And just like that, my heart clenches. I pull back and try to look into her eyes, but it's too dark. "Are you thinking this is just a vacation thing?"

Please don't say yes. I don't think I could go back to being friends after knowing what it's like to be more.

Mel inhales sharply. "What? No! This isn't even just a high school thing." My body relaxes against hers and she pulls me closer.

"I guess I still can't believe this is real." I brush a kiss across her cheek and slide my hand so I'm cradling her head against mine. "I'm dreading going home and dealing with my parents, but the thought of having you by my side while I figure it out makes facing them less scary." Her lips brush my throat and my eyes close. "Not saying you wouldn't be there if we weren't together, but—"

"I know what you mean. Now shush." Mel tilts her head until our lips connect. Her hands move to my face and slide through my hair, and our mouths move together.

My hand trails up her ribcage, and I brush my lips over hers. "Is this okay?" She nods, and my mouth moves to her neck. "How about this?"

"Mm-hmm."

Her hand glides over my waist until her arm's wrapped around me, pulling me against her. We lose ourselves in the soft bed in a tangle of arms and giggles and then her mouth is on mine and it's everything I've ever wanted.

Until the real alarm goes off half an hour later.

Mel brings my phone under the sheets. "I haven't checked the video."

"Not at all?"

"Uh-uh. Not since I posted it."

I grab the phone from her and tap the app myself. "My phone, my rules," I whisper, and she laughs. She's still logged into her account, and we both gasp when the notifications appear at the bottom. There are thousands. Like tens of thousands.

Mel buries her face in the pillow. "What if they hate it?"

"Impossible." I tap the notifications and scroll through the first couple pages. It's filled with hearts and clapping hands and exclamation points. "There's a kind of mean duet from a random girl named Cammie, but she looks like she's just desperate for followers. The rest all seem to be positive." That's a complete understatement, but she should experience this firsthand. "Here." I grab her hand from my hip and rest my phone against her palm.

She starts reading, the phone tucked between us. The light from the phone is like a spotlight on her smile, and I openly stare. I never imagined happiness was right in front of me the whole time, and yet here we are.

"I could do this all day, but we should probably get up," Mel says.

With a final kiss, we roll out of bed, wake up Jess, and get dressed.

Our energy level is non-existent when we get to breakfast, but when we enter the room, everyone starts clapping. We freeze, and they keep clapping.

"What's going on?" Mel asks while Jess and I exchange confused looks.

"Your video!" Theo waves his hands straight up in the air and wiggles in his seat. "You crushed it."

Mel's cheeks go red. Her smile widens as she looks from one happy face to the next. "You all watched it?"

"How could we not?" Naomi asks. "We're all very invested in your success."

Hunter wraps an arm around Naomi's shoulders and beams at his sister. "You really nailed it, Mel." Naomi cuddles closer to him, like she's trying to soak up as much of him as she can until they go home.

"Thanks, everyone," Mel says. "For putting up with me, for letting me use your phones, and for generally being awesome and supportive. I've been thinking a lot since my brush with death yesterday."

Margo gasps and covers her face.

Mel bites her lip, then continues. "My mission with my account is important to me, but it's not the only thing that matters. All of you have a special place in my heart. I don't know what I'd do without you, and I'm sorry if I haven't always shown that."

"We love you, Mel," Theo says. "Your self-centeredness is part of your charm."

Mel's mouth falls open and Naomi yells, "Theo!"

He blocks his face with his arm like he expects Naomi to throw something at him. "I'm kidding!"

"We do love you," Naomi says. The others murmur in agreement, and the three of us grab seats at the end of the table. Mel presses her knee against mine. We haven't fully outed ourselves in front of the parents, but now that vacation is over, hiding it seems childish.

I reach for her hand and pull it into my lap, not caring who's watching. She laces her fingers through mine and smiles.

Margo taps her fork against her water glass. "Normally I'd ask you all to recap your goals for the trip and share how you feel like you've changed, but I think we might be too tired for that." Everyone nods, followed by a loud groan from Theo. "Instead, I simply want to thank all of you for being here, on this trip, and making it so special. This has been a life-changing experience, and you will forever be a part of that for me." She locks eyes with Bryan, who grabs her hand and lifts it to his lips.

Sage holds her left hand out in front of her and smiles at her ring. "I could say the same thing. Obviously I'm never going to forget this trip, and I'm really glad all of you were able to share this moment with us."

Neb leans toward her and kisses her cheek, and Mel sighs next to me. "Agreed," Neb says. "And Mel, I can't wait to see what you put together from the eclipse. Maybe we can make another video in the future."

Mel yanks her hand from mine and claps. "Omigod, I would love that! Do you know when the next eclipse is? And where? Would we have to camp or can we stay in more civilized quarters?"

Theo raises a brow at her last question while Neb laughs.

"The next Great American Eclipse is next year in October." Neb glances at Naomi and Sage. "And the path of totality will pass just south of Portland."

Naomi claps her hands. "Repeat trip!"

"That would be epic," Sage says.

Mel reaches for her phone but comes up empty. "Can someone please text that to me?"

Sage runs her hand down Neb's arm. "You might have to start an account so she can tag you."

Theo holds up his phone. "Hot lumberjacky scientist is available!"

"How can you already know that?" Mel asks.

"I have a niche," he says, and we laugh.

Hunter clears his throat. "We, uh, have news-ish too."

Naomi turns bright red as Hunter grabs her hand.

"Did everyone get together on this trip?" Jess whispers. "I like Theo and all, but he's too old for me."

I laugh, filled with a happiness I haven't felt in a really long time. Even knowing what I'm going home to and how my life is about to be torn apart, it feels like it's on pause for a little while longer.

"Hunter and I decided to try to, to uh…" Naomi says.

"Yes, dear sister, we all know you're back together." Theo's voice is sarcastic but the softness in his eyes is real. He's happy for his sister. She throws a piece of bacon at him, which he catches and pops in his mouth.

Hunter rubs a hand over his face and he and Naomi share a smile. "Yeah, our lives are a lot different than they were when we first dated. I'm excited to see what happens with this amazing woman."

Naomi snorts and Mel bursts out laughing before pumping her arms in the air. "Operation Amazing is officially complete!"

"Operation what?" Nancy says.

Naomi points at the three of us. "They get some credit."

Nancy smiles at Naomi, then looks down at her plate. "I admit this trip has been a little more difficult for me, but being around all this happiness, it's impossible not to feel hopeful for my own future."

Margo reaches for her hand and they smile at each other. "You know what I'm going to say."

"Others' happiness does not define my own," they say together.

"I know," Nancy says. "And I think I'm finally starting to believe it."

"I like that," Jess says. "Like, you can be happy for other people, even if your life is a complete mess."

Nancy wipes the corner of her eye and laughs. "Yes, exactly like that."

Mel presses her leg tighter against mine and gives me a serious look. If I know her at all, and I think I do, she's saying that Jess is our next Operation Amazing.

"I already told you all how much I love you," Mel says. "I realize I can be a bit much with the videos and all that, and

I really appreciate you not only tolerating me, but playing along." Mel looks at Margo and Bryan. "I'm so happy for the two of you. You clearly make each other happy, and some days that feels like the most important thing you can do for someone." She reaches for my hand on top of the table and our fingers twine together. Margo and Bryan's eyes jump to our hands and I swear I can see them calculating how much time we've spent alone in a tent or hotel room under their watch.

Or maybe that's me projecting.

Mel shakes her head. "And the fact that I get to go to Oregon is incredible. This means more to me than I can express, so hopefully thanking you in front of everyone shows how much I mean it."

Theo smiles from the other end of the table. "Even though it is the ultimate flattery that you want to be near me, this decision needs to be for you and your future."

Mel's mouth falls open. "I totally forgot you live there!" Her lips twitch as she fights a smile.

Theo presses a hand to his chest. "I'm hurt." Then he glances at my hand holding Mel's and I swear his eyes twinkle.

Mel squeezes my hand and looks at me expectantly.

"Oh, my turn?" Everyone smiles, and there's no judgment on their faces. If they have an opinion about me, or me and Mel, it hasn't changed the fact that they're treating me like I'm part of the group. "I haven't shared because I have a mess waiting for me when I get home. Thank you to those of you who've listened and given advice, and for distracting me when I didn't want to think about my parents. I'm not really sure how things are gonna go, but I've got enough good in my life that I'm hopeful things will balance out." My words come out on a long exhale and I take a slow, shaky breath.

"Three good things!" Naomi shouts from next to Hunter. Theo holds his hand out over the table and they high-five.

"What?" I ask.

"Her podcast," Mel says. "Well, her OG podcast. It's about finding three good things in each day."

I lock eyes with her, not sure if she means for me to tell everyone about our unofficial status or just my general happiness about the good things in my life.

"Only if you want to," Naomi says.

"Three good things?" I count off on my fingers. "Well, meeting and getting to know all of you. Graduating soon and leaving for college. And, um." I glance at Mel and decide to go for it. "Finding out that the most amazing girl I know likes me."

Several people "aww" and the women clasp their hands to their chests.

"I was really happy to learn that, too," Mel says. Then before I realize what's happening, she's leaning closer and our lips are touching and nothing else matters. Not my parents or the divorce or all the big questions about my future.

All that matters is that we've found each other.

Two Months Later

"I need another piece of cake," Steph says, reaching past me to the rows of paper plates on the table beneath the tent in my front yard. It's a week after graduation and Jess, Steph, and I are hosting a joint graduation party with our friends and families. Steph's free hand trails over my arm and she brushes a kiss on my bare shoulder.

"How are they doing?" I ask. Her parents started out on opposite ends of the tent, but slowly migrated toward each other. Steph assured me not to get excited about them getting back together, but seems happy they can be in the same space without fighting.

"Oddly good," she says. "It's like once they removed the whole marriage thing from their relationship, they get along." She holds up the piece of cake. "This is for them. To split." She shakes her head, her purple curls bouncing against her cheek, and my heart does a double take.

Things between us since the Grand Canyon have gone really well. Like, alarmingly well. It's not that I didn't expect them to, but in those early weeks, I kept waiting for something to explode in our faces. Another fight like in the Grand Canyon. But it never did. Steph is loving and supportive and calls me on my BS when I get too wrapped up in my own head.

I kiss her cheek and she weaves through the tables of aunts and uncles and our classmates' parents.

"You should be hanging out with your friends, not manning the cake table," Hunter says as he grabs two pieces. "Enjoy your day."

My elbow nudges his side. "Where's your girlfriend?" I sing-song.

His cheeks color and his gaze flicks to the house. I love how happy he is with Naomi and that he's finally stopped trying to fight how he feels about her. "In the bathroom."

I look past the faces under the tent and beyond to the yard. Kids I've known my entire life will soon scatter across the state and the country, and as excited as I am to head to Oregon, I'm a little sad this part of my life is ending.

"It's surreal that I'm done with high school," I say. "And that I'm going to college. And I have a girlfriend."

He sets the cake down, wraps an arm around my shoulders, and pulls me to his side. "I'm really proud of you."

"Ooh, is that for me?" Naomi asks, taking one of the pieces. "Sage texted. She and Neb send their love."

It would have been cool to see them, but they're all the way in Seattle and a high school graduation party is totally not worth that many hours in a car.

Naomi smiles at me. "Neb got more fan mail this week. Another marriage proposal."

"That video is the gift that keeps on giving," Hunter says.

When we got home from the Grand Canyon, I was able to salvage my SIM card and, combined with the footage from the other phones, made a series of videos that I shared over the next few weeks.

The video I posted the last day of the trip went semi-viral and earned me a ton of new followers, which Jess dubbed the Melty Brigade. People loved that I didn't lower myself to JFB's level— I've stopped saying his full name to prevent a rage attack—and I feel like I'm actually making a difference in Science Tok. When I shared the final version of the eclipse video, it was like I set SciTok on fire. Within a week, national news outlets picked it up and more teachers than I can keep track of reached out for permission to share it in their classes.

My dream to help teach kids about science has already come true, all before I finished high school.

Neb had his own brush with fame when the eclipse video went viral. People nearly lost their minds over the hot scientist dude and my legitimacy in SciTok grew even stronger. I also posted their proposal—with their permission, of course—and that landed us on the national evening news.

"Have you thought any more about adding public speaking as a minor?" Hunter asks.

Naomi taps him on the nose. "Give her time." Then she boops me on my nose. "Despite what your over-achieving brother seems to think, you do not have to have your life planned out before you set foot on campus."

Hunter smirks, the corner of his mouth lifting in the smile that looks so much like mine. "I'm just saying, you've given yourself a lot of options and you could make a real difference."

I swipe a piece of his cake and pop it in my mouth. "I'll think about it." I wander off to find Steph and Jess and my eyes connect with Mom's on the far side of the yard. She and Bryan are standing with a handful of other parents, and the pride on Mom's face nearly undoes me.

"Mel, over here!" Jess shouts. A group of our friends stand in a tight circle, their hands clasped in the middle like Steph and Jess did for the centrifugal force video. "Grab your phone, this is gonna be epic!"

ACKNOWLEDGEMENTS

Writing a book is always challenging. Setting it in a place you've never been is even more difficult. Beginning the first draft the day after you bring home a new puppy is nearly impossible.

Countless people deserve my thanks for helping me finish this book and the Campfire series:

Roberta King and Travis Erwin for sharing their personal stories of hiking to the bottom of the Grand Canyon and camping overnight. Your experiences are reflected in this story and I hope you know how much I appreciate your help.

Andrea Riddle and Nancy Matuszak for sharing your observations from closer to the surface, and the kind gentleman from the Grand Canyon who spent far too long on the phone with me and confirmed, among other details, that those camping at Bright Angel Campground do not have access to power outlets in the Phantom Ranch lodge.

My early readers: Stephanie, Cheyenne, Carolyn, Sarah, and my master proofreader, Judy Hooyenga. Your insight, while not always what I wanted to hear, made this story stronger.

The Twitter and Instagram writing community for both encouraging and distracting me along the way.

Sara and Nancy, thank you for being my endless cheerleaders, my voices of reason, and the most amazing friends ever. This wouldn't be nearly as much fun without you.

And Jeremy, for never complaining when I'm lost in my laptop with my imaginary friends.

Multi-award winning young adult author Melanie Hooyenga writes books about strong girls who learn to navigate life despite its challenges. She first started writing as a teenager and finds she still relates best to that age group.

Her award-winning YA sports romance series, *The Rules Series*, is about girls from Colorado falling in love and learning to stand up on their own. Her YA time travel trilogy, *The Flicker Effect*, is about a teen who uses sunlight to travel back to yesterday.

When not writing books, you can find her wrangling her Miniature Schnauzer Gus and playing every sport imaginable with her husband Jeremy.

www.ingramcontent.com/pod-product-compliance
Lightning Source LLC
Chambersburg PA
CBHW021649110726
47902CB00007B/1891